The Fall of America

Book 5 – Fallout

WR Benton

LOOSE CANNON ENTERPRISES
Paradise, CA

Ingram Edition
ISBN 978-1-944476-59-5

© Copyright 2016 W.R. Benton
All Rights Reserved

www.loose-cannon.com

"Loyalty to country ALWAYS. Loyalty to government, when it deserves it."
— Mark Twain

"I am an American; free born and free bred, where I acknowledge no man as my superior, except for his own worth, or as my inferior, except for his own demerit."
— Theodore Roosevelt

"I predict future happiness for Americans if they can prevent the government from wasting the labors of the people under the pretense of taking care of them."
—Thomas Jefferson

"My reading of history convinces me that most bad government results from too much government."
—Thomas Jefferson

"The soldier is the Army. No army is better than its soldiers. The soldier is also a citizen. In fact, the highest obligation and privilege of citizenship is that of bearing arms for one's country"
— George S. Patton Jr.

Books in this series by W.R. Benton

The Fall of America, Book 5, Fallout

The Fall of America, Book 4, Winter Ops

The Fall of America, Book 3, Enemy Within

— *Also available in Audio Edition*

The Fall of America, Book 2, Fatal Encounters

— *Also available in Audio Edition*

The Fall of America: Book 1, Premonition of Death

— *Also available in Audio Edition*

Visit http://www.amazon.com/author/wrbenton/

for more WR Benton titles.

DEDICATIONS

To all veterans, past, present, and future, who have served, died, or been wounded while doing their duty protecting our great county. As a fellow vet, I salute your total dedication to your chosen profession, your personal sacrifices, and your strong belief in keeping our nation safe. Not many Americans have sworn to protect the Constitution from all enemies — both foreign and domestic. The last count I read was about 3% of the eligible population actually serves our nation by donning a uniform. Since my retirement from 26 years of active duty, I am proud of the men and women who have continued to serve our great county. Y'all make me proud.

To the memory of Betty Benton, a good woman who died much too young.

What is the series "The Fall of America" about?

It started with the biggest stock market crash in history. Banks closed down under the weight of their bogus investments, and the financial sector failed. People looked to the government to make it all better. However, they couldn't. Hyper-inflation, mass unemployment and infrastructure started to breakdown. The food trucks didn't show up at the stores, and the shelves went empty.

Things turned ugly fast when there was no power for long parts of the day—then forever. Cops, doctors, and trash collectors just stopped showing up for work when the paychecks were delayed too often, or never came. Things started falling apart quickly after that. Whole regions declared a "State of Emergency" in an effort to maintain order and civility, but it wasn't always enough. Starvation, looting and murder became the norm. Then, our American civilization collapsed completely.

The Fall of America, Book 1: Premonition of Death is the beginning of a new series, about an average man whose life goes downhill fast once society breaks down. Set in the rural south, a scorched-earth showdown with some local thugs leaves John and his wife homeless and on the run. He encounters a member of a survivalist group, made up of former military personnel, and joining them may be his only hope. Just basic survival becomes vicious and resistance is at any cost, as the devastated country comes under a new siege—invading Russian troops.

The Fall of America, Book 2: Fatal Encounters is the continuing saga of the fall. John and his friends come face to face with Russian troops, but unlike the first book, this time they're ready and able to offer much more resistance. Russian invaders try to pacify the areas of the South under their control. The American resistance groups divide their forces into small cells to better operate effectively behind enemy lines. But as their efforts begin to gain ground, the Russians respond with harsh reprisals; mass executions become the norm and prison camps soon spring up in remote small towns. "Fear brings compliance," is their motto. The battle for control of Mississippi gets hot, and a violent world gets even more ugly.

The Fall of America, Book 3: Enemy Within. Things are turning more organized by the partisans and with this organization comes larger attacks on Russian targets, which results in more Americans killed in reprisals. As the partisans become better organized, the Russians become more sadistic. The Americans are now attacking gulags and air bases when the opportunity arises and Russian casualties mount, but there is at least one traitor or more within the partisans. Can the Americans discover the enemy within?

The Fall of America, Book 4: Winter Operations. The partisans turn mean after ambushing a Russian convoy and discovering cases of the 9K32 Strela-2M missiles, or as the Russians call them, arrows. The missiles soon change how the partisans operate; they are a portable, shoulder-fired, low-altitude surface-to-air missile system with a highly explosive warhead. They have an infrared guidance system. Soon the partisans are attacking Air Bases and shooting down random helicopters using the missiles and Moscow is not pleased. However, it is the discovery of two nuclear weapons, called suitcase bombs, by the Russians, that is about to change this war in ways that have never been considered. Which side will use the nuclear weapons first?

A Word from the Author

Writing this series is both interesting and depressing work, because I try to imagine how America will be once it falls, and, sadly, I'm positive it *will* one day fall. A nation cannot survive at the rate our government is currently spending money, and we need to stop being the world's police force. Sooner or later, we'll run out of money. There will come a time in our future when others will see us as a serious credit risk due to our uncontrolled spending, and we'll be unable to borrow funds. America's credit rating has already dropped. Spending aside, we must step back and view our nation with unbiased eyes. We cannot afford to let millions of illegal aliens stay here, nor can we allow great numbers of refugees into our country, and cost aside, how many of those two groups may be criminals or terrorists? Think about that, and give it serious thought, too.

We have become a nation that produces very little in the way of products and most jobs these days provide a service. I can remember as a child picking up almost anything in a store and seeing 'made in America' or 'USA' stamped on it. Today it's likely to be made in Korea, Japan, China, or Thailand. I recently looked over a Vietnam veteran's hat and it was made in Vietnam. I found it ironic his prior enemies were now selling him hats. Even the flag I fly on my front porch was manufactured in Hong Kong. I think an important reason America produces little these days is we have priced ourselves out of business. No one will buy an American product if it's priced three or four times what other similar products cost, with the only serious difference being it's made in another country. Other countries are simply able to supply cheaper products because their standard of living is considerably lower than ours, thus the workers are paid much less. Additionally, third world nations often have sweatshops where kids, women, the sick and lame work, for much less than they'd pay a man. I think unions and other organizations are good, but only to a point. All workers need protecting, but it's the benefits and high wages of the American worker combined with our poor economy that forces the average American to buy foreign made products. If you live on a limited income, you are forced financially to always buy the cheapest products made.

I have yet to fully understand why we are sending billions of dollars to nations that hate us and want us all dead. It makes no sense, unless we are paying them not to attack us. Even a child knows you can't buy friends. We are sending billions of dollars that would be better used right here at home. The money we spend in aid to those nations could be used to pay off the trillions of dollars we owe and take care of our nation's poor, and let me go on record as saying, "all poor Americans are not of the black race." One political figure hinted recently that white people have no poor and only black folks know poverty, which is *so* untrue. Poverty knows no racial lines and it hits many Americans hard. I know, because I was raised poor and at one point, our house had a dirt floor, and for the longest time we did without a wooden floor. We had a wood-stove, no electricity, and no running water, but this was in the early 1960's, and there was no public assistance then. Mom raised five kids without public assistance, and it was never easy. Poverty has not disappeared, and only a fool would think black Americans are our nations only poor folks. Sometimes I'm surprised by statements that come from our elected politicians and wonder how they've survived to reach the age they are.

We could better use the money saved by caring for our veterans or our elderly. For those of you who have never served, you have no idea of the sacrifices made by these brave men and women. You may not know what it takes to even qualify to be a member of the best military in the world. It takes hard work and dedication to even make it through basic training, and then on to other schools. Now, every service is a bit different but each has an oath of enlistment that is the same and it reads, "I, ________________, do solemnly swear (or affirm) that *I will support and defend the Constitution of the United States against all enemies, foreign and domestic;* that I will bear true faith and allegiance to the same; and that I will obey the orders of the President of the United States and the orders of the officers appointed over me, according to regulations and the Uniform Code of Military Justice. So help me God." (Title 10, US Code; Act of 5 May 1960 replacing the wording first adopted in 1789, with amendment effective 5 October 1962). How many of our elderly lack the money from their Social Security checks to pay for their medications. My momma, a couple of years before she died, told me, "I know people that have to choose between their medication or paying their utility bills. Some take a pill every other day." I don't think any American should be doing that, not a single American. Not if billions of dollars are lining the pockets of leaders in other countries, not to mention those of our own politicians, who all seem to retire as millionaires.

The key sentence in the short enlistment oath, in my opinion, is, "I will support and defend the Constitution of the United States against all enemies, *foreign and domestic.*" If invaded by another nation I know millions of veterans, even old men like me, will rise up and fight. Just stick us on a stump on a hill, give us a loaded M-16, and we'll knock down our fair share. If someone attempts to take over our country from within, the active military, as well as all veterans, have sworn to prevent that from happening, too. Again, millions of veterans will answer the call to serve once more. The system our forefathers put together is pretty awesome with all the right checks and balances. And over the last almost eight years, I have thanked God many times for the exact wording of our Constitution.

Let's get our nation back on track and adhere to the Constitution as we should. Stop adding to it, stop ignoring it, and by all means, stop trying to get rid of that valuable paper. At all costs we must protect it, and by doing so we'll keep our God given rights. If we don't, one day we may wake up and find ourselves in a totally different America. In an America where we're no longer free, no

longer able to speak out, and no longer able to legally buy a gun.
Can you imagine living in an America where we no longer want to
live? An America without our rights? I think those who would
try to take over our nation would soon awaken the largest unorganized and best trained military unit in the known world —our veterans.

This is what the *Fall of America* Series is about. Veterans and normal day to day Americans of all races and both genders coming
together and uniting in a bloody fight against a common enemy, in
this case, Russia. So, sit back, get your favorite drink, and read,
Fall of America; Fallout, Book 5, and enjoy.

WR Benton
Jackson, Mississippi
15 April 2016

BOOK 5

FALLOUT

CHAPTER 1

I was moving with my old squad when I noticed a blinding light south of the Russian Base at Edwards, and it was a little after midnight. Immediately I knew it wasn't anything other than a nuclear device of some sort. The light was so bright I had to turn my head away from the source. I hoped if it was a nuke, it was accidentally discharged on the Russian base, even though hundreds of Americans at the nearby Gulag would die; it would be a much more merciful death than the mass executions carried out daily, or by starvation. As I stood, I absentmindedly scratched Dolly's ears. The big German shepherd loved her ears played with, and she was all I had left of my past life.

One of the troops said, "My God, I pray that wasn't what I fear it was."

Then there sounded a number of whispers and low talking.

"Quiet as we move; you all know better." Mary said just above a whisper, and the low voices and whispers stopped instantly.

I suggested to Mary that we stop and discuss what we'd just seen. If the Russians had gone nuclear, it must mean we were making our presence felt, and they were starting to run scared. She soon had all our troops in a defensive position, so I sat on a log and asked, "Did you see that light?"

"Oh, I saw it, and think the Russians just upped the ante in this game."

"I can't see them detonating a nuclear device that close to their own facilities, so it must have been an accident. As soon as we arrive at a safe house, I want to know the weather forecast and the wind directions every 30 minutes. The only safety from fallout is distance and shielding. Depending on the direction of the winds, we may have to leave the state."

"We have some cells moving in that part of the country, very close to the Russian Air Base at Edwards. They were assigned to kill stragglers when they could, disrupt the Russian transportation system, and basically, just raise hell."

"Well, I hate to say this, but I think those not killed by the blast will soon die from radiation sickness. So, I want to double our rate of march and we will not stop until we reach the safe house. I know some will complain, but when they do, tell them lives depend on the information we have about the bright light."

Ten minutes later we were moving.

All went well until about two hours before daylight when the point man walked to Mary and said, "Big ass tank right in the middle of the road we're to cross."

"Did you see any of the crew outside the tank or other troops?"

"Two privates were looking in the engine compartment with a flashlight and talking in low tones. I suspect the rest of the crew are asleep in the tank."

"We have orders to destroy any armor we can within reason. If we can, we'll knock this big beast out."

Mary thought for a minute and then said, "Smith, you and Bunch circle the tank and use your NVG's. I can't believe the Russians would leave a broken tank in the middle of a macadam road, deep in partisan country, without a couple of squads or so to provide security."

"How do you intend to attack this thing?" I asked.

"We can take the two men outside the tank out with a sniper using a silencer. Then, since the weather is warm, it's very likely the crew has the hatches all open. We move to the tank, drop a couple of eggs, and one Russian tank kaput."

I laughed internally, because things never go as planned. I just hoped things wouldn't get so bad we'd lose a bunch of experienced troops. People we had, but experienced folks were hard to come by.

Ten minutes later Smith and Bunch returned. Bunch said, "A squad of infantry on each side of the tank. They're dug in pretty good, or so it seems to me, with a machine-gun with each group. I saw no guards and no one appeared awake in the foxholes either. If they're all sleeping, attacking quickly will work. The tank looked like all the hatches were open, probably for fresh air."

"How many flamethrowers do we have?" I asked, knowing even the Russians were afraid of fire.

"Just one, why?"

I'm going to use the flamethrower and I think my plan will work, because of the element of surprise, I thought, but said, "Have your sniper take out the two mechanics silently, then have two people on the tank ready to drop the grenades, and when I spray the squad on the left with flames, they each drop their surprises. Each person on the tank should drop a single grenade. Have them run toward me, and once behind me, I'll spray the right side and the tank. Then, I'll run like hell to put some distance between me and the expected explosion, which will be big. Now, stress to them to move toward me instantly, because if I start taking fire from the right side, I'll start squirting flames." I didn't care for what I was about to do; it wasn't a good way to die, but I'd not have someone else do the job that I'd dreamed up. As the Commander, I often gave orders, only this was different, and I was here in place.

Mary called James and Morgan to her, explained my plan and then said, "You two will drop the grenades down the open hatches. I want one dropped down the driver's hatch and other thrown in the main hatch on top. Then, beat feet out of there. The Colonel will be spraying the Russians troops with flames. If you hang back too long, or he starts taking fire, he'll start shooting flames."

Both men nodded and then Morgan asked, "What's the odds of mines in the area?"

"Maybe fair, I'd guess. Most units would put mines out where they spend the night, so approach the tank from the rear, on the blacktop and all should go well. I can't see them mining the road, it's too hard, but use some common sense, because they may have a line stretched across the road. You trip it and a Russian claymore, called a NON-50, might just ruin your day. The mine has about 540 steel balls or close to 385 short metal rods inside, and I've seen the damage they can do. Take your time getting to the tank, this is not a race. But, once you drop the grenades, you'd better start hauling ass away from that steel beast."

Both men nodded. It was then I looked the two over closely.

James, like all of us, was thin, close to six feet tall, brown hair and beard, and in his late twenties was my guess. He was dressed in a mix of civilian and Russian clothing, wore a white armband on his left arm and I'd not heard him talk much since I'd joined the group. I remembered his eyes as being brown, but right now I was unable to see them clearly due to the darkness.

Morgan I'd worked with before, and he was a real professional. He was short, too short to have joined the military in the old days, which was their loss. While he was small, he was one hell of a tough man. His auburn hair and beard were always trimmed neatly and it was obvious he tried his best to remain clean. He had green eyes and they usually looked serious, especially when in the field.

"Get your sniper in place and let's get this over with. I want to do this before first light, so we can hopefully do the job with minimal or no casualties."

Mary said, "Alford, I have a job for you."

Twenty minutes later, I neared the front of the Russian T-90 battle tank. It was a big beast too, at 46 tons, and a crew of three. Looking behind the beast, I saw both Morgan and James moving toward the tank. One of the mechanics had fallen to the side after being shot and I could clearly see his dark body in the dim moonlight. I watched one man, maybe Morgan, climb on top of the tank, while the other stood ready to drop his grenade down the driver's hatch.

I moved in closer, squeezed the trigger on the flamethrower and started sending Russians to hell on the left side. I gave them a good half-dozen squirts, then saw both partisans running toward me, so I squirted the Russians on the right side of the tank.

I heard a loud scream of warning from inside the tank and then things started happening quickly.

The early morning air was suddenly filled with screaming of the injured and dying, but I felt absolutely nothing. They'd invaded my home and, just by them being here, justified my killing. One man, fully engulfed in flames, moved from his foxhole stumbling around in a rough circle. I heard a few shots and one bullet zipped by my head close enough I heard it pass. I raised the barrel of the flamethrower so my spurting flames would hopefully hit the furthest foxholes. I gave them a couple of long squirts and then took off running as quickly as I could. All of this happened in a few short seconds.

I'd not gotten far when I heard the first grenade go off and a split second later, the second detonated, which made me run faster. To me, there seemed to be a pause before the tank blew because I expected to be blown off my feet any second, but it didn't happen. I glanced over my shoulder to look back just as the monster exploded, sending the turret spinning high into the air. Flames, a dark red, mixed with burning oil and fuel, rolled inside of themselves as they moved for the overcast sky. The infantry men were screaming and shrieking now, the sticky flames I sent doing the job it was supposed to do. Then, the ammunition exploded, followed by pressurized bottles inside the tank. The noise, as far as I was concerned, was loud enough to wake the whole state of Mississippi.

Glancing to my left and then right, I spotted Morgan and James running beside me. After about 100 meters, we slowed to a walk. We circled around and moved to Mary and the rest.

When we neared, from the darkness Alfred said, "Roast."

"Beef," I replied, knowing that was the correct counter password.

"Enter." the man replied.

Mary was anxious and I didn't blame her. The resulting explosion, plus the flamethrower, had lighted the area as bright as day.

"The flamethrower messed the infantry up and I think you killed well over half of them, but it's hard to tell with it being as dark as it is now. We need to get moving, before —"

"Chopper!" someone yelled.

I watched as ponchos were pulled and I pulled mine as well. While not the best protection in the world, it did offer some limited protection if the bird was equipped with Infrared gear. I covered my prone body with my poncho, praying we weren't spotted. The poncho worked well for a couple of minutes, but then body heat would start releasing on the ends and sides. It normally was enough protection, unless the chopper stayed in position and scanned the area. I heard the distinctive sound of a Kamov Ka-50, "Black Shark," chopper nearing.

Suddenly, a line of dirt was thrown six feet in the air as a 30 mm cannon on the aircraft began to walk across an area just slightly north of us. I watched as one of our troops, Marsha Wied, raised a Russian 9K32 Strela-2 missile launcher, a portable, low-altitude surface-to-air missile that is shoulder-fired. I watched her squeeze the trigger and even saw the fins unfurl as it left the launch container. A second later I heard an explosion and the chopper's engine had a severe change in pitch. Looking up through the trees, I saw parts of the aircraft falling and a second later it was spinning horizontally as it lost altitude.

For a second, just before the explosion of the aircraft hitting the ground, I was hoping the pilot would bring it under control. That was not to be, and the fireball was huge when compared to the tank, or maybe I just had a better view of it all.

I heard Mary order, "Let's move out at a slow trot. I want some distance between us and here, and I want it quickly. Betty, you pull drag, while Beverly, you're my point. Let's move, and do the job now."

Beverly was a short woman, closer to five feet than six, wore her blond hair cut short, and her blue eyes were bottomless. She was attractive and knew it, but wasn't the type to tease or lead men on. I always found her totally professional, but under different circumstances, I'd have been drawn to her. Today she was walking in front of us, looking for ambushes, traps, mines or other danger.

Mary is doing the proper thing, getting all of us moving. In less than ten minutes this area around the downed chopper and destroyed tank will be filled with Russians, I thought as I held a limb out of my way so I could follow the person in front of me. I tried to walk in the other person's footprints, but that didn't always work. Some of the women had much smaller feet than my size 12 boots and it always made me a bit nervous, because a fraction of an inch could mean the difference in life or death, especially with mines or traps.

The morning was uneventful as we moved at a fast walk overland and avoided trails. At one point, a Russian squad was sighted off our left a good 1,000 meters, so we remained still until they were well out of sight. I made a mental note to double our guards for the night.

We soon came to an open spot, most likely a fire break from the days before the fall, and we stopped. Mary sent Beverly across alone and she searched the trees for an ambush, but found the area clean. She signaled us it was all clear.

Then, one at a time, she sent our troops over the clearing. I was the next to last to cross. I listened closely, listening for aircraft engines or vehicles, but heard nothing. I made it across the clearing safely and turned to watch Betty, our person on drag, cross. She was halfway across the clearing when I heard the *whop-whop-whop* of helicopter blades, but couldn't tell where it was at.

As I watched, a long line of machine-gun bullets ripped the soil apart, sending ricocheting bullets and stones in all directions, and then they struck Betty.

I was looking in her eyes as the bullets struck her and she seemed surprised at being killed. The bullets struck her with such power an arm and leg were sent flying just before she was struck in the head. Her head simply vanished, leaving a fine mist of red floating in the air, and her screams stopped instantly. Her body fell unnaturally, and immediately a puddle of blood started forming.

"Move, and *now!*" Mary yelled, knowing the chopper crew could not hear her over the aircraft engines.

I ran as hard as a middle-aged man can run with about fifty pounds or more of gear loaded on his back. A minute later, still running, I heard a jet aircraft overhead. I heard rockets striking where we'd been just a few seconds ago. I expected napalm to be dropped next and I was right.

All that saved us was the direction Mary ran was 90 degrees from the path of the sticky flames of the napalm. I knew we'd come close to dying when the air grew thin, sucked into the massive fireball behind us, but on I ran until I actually worried about passing out from the lack of air. It was then I felt a slight breeze.

Dropping back beside me, Mary said, "You know that Russian pilot will notify his base of 20 or so partisans burned to death back there, right?"

"Probably, but I hated losing Betty. She'd been a partisan for a lot of years."

"Death doesn't scare me as it once did." Mary said and then added, "But she went fast, very fast, and that's about all a person can ask for these days. I've seen folks killed in many different ways and while none are good, some are faster than others. We should be at the safe house near dusk. Okay, people, form on me. Sara, you pull drag and Thomas, you take the point."

All was quiet as we walked, with nothing heard except an occasional stone kicked or a small twig snapping. I knew the only reason we made any noise at all was because we were tired. Packing a heavy pack plus a weapon was hard on all of us. While we rested ten minutes every hour, it was never enough. By the end of the day, most of us were completely exhausted. As a Colonel and the Commander, I didn't need to pack my gear, but I did. I would never ask my people to do something I could not or would not do. I was a strong believer in leadership by example but in this case, the weight was killing me.

From the darkness, I heard, "Roast."

"Beef." Mary replied.

"I hope you have the Colonel with you, because the brown stuff has hit the fan. Looks like the Russians set off a small tactical nuke to kill a bunch of partisans." the unknown voice said.

"He's with me; just give us time to get inside your perimeter and remove some gear. This stuff gets heavy after a few miles."

"I hear you. When the Colonel can, have him move into the house."

"Will do," I replied as I moved past the man.

Inside the house sat six other Commanders from around the state and all were Colonels. When I walked in, a young Captain said, "I will start now that we are all here."

"My name is Captain John H. Quinn and I'm the Commander of the intelligence section. This briefing is classified top secret. If you do not have a top secret clearance, please leave the room now."

Silence, and no one left the room.

"Okay, gentlemen we have a problem, and a big one. At close to midnight last night the Russians detonated a small tactical nuke, instantly killing over 3000 Americans, of which we estimate half were civilians that lived in the area. I mean they were vaporized, and we have no trace of any units in the area, of which we guessed should have been between 150 and 200 partisans. Of course, since some of our units operate independently of us, the real number of deaths may never be known."

"What directions are the winds blowing right now? Is there a chance of rain?" I asked, hoping we were due a hard rain which might knock many of the radioactive particles from the air, and keep it from traveling far.

"Winds are out of the west, at around ten miles an hour with gusts to fifteen at times. The weather guessers tell us no rain for at least a week, maybe ten days."

"Any idea what made the Russians use a nuke?" Colonel James Ellis asked.

"We knew the base had approval to use a nuclear weapon, sir, but never seriously thought they'd do the job. To be honest, I have absolutely no idea, unless our partisan activities have them antsy or frustrated."

"Well," Ellis said, "detonating a nuke is damned serious business. Do y'all have any estimates of how many will get radiation poisoning from this?"

"Uh, yes we do, and the numbers are high. We fully expect to lose well over half of the civilian population in Jackson and cities downwind of the fallout. We know the Russians won't treat our sick and few partisans know much about radiation at all. It's our guess most folks will die, many that might be saved, by not getting any treatment at all. We lack the manpower to assist civilians that become ill."

"Lawdy, what a mess." I said aloud without realizing it.

"You have that correct, Colonel." Ellis said and then continued, "We don't even have a way to warn or evacuate those in danger, do we?"

"Right now we have flyers being printed that volunteers will post in most of the towns we feel that are downwind or in danger. And, no, we have no way to evacuate folks, so they're on their own through all of this."

"Sonofabitch!" Ellis almost screamed and then he added, "I think we need to use a suitcase nuke on these bastards."

"There has been talk of having a volunteer sneak a nuke on the base and having it explode within ten minutes. Since it's dry, the idea was to drop it in a manhole, because there is no water running under the base except for sewage. By the way, water, drainage, and sewage, all run independently of each other."

"Ten minutes? Good God, the volunteer would be killed too." I said.

"Uh, that's the reason we've not found a volunteer yet."

"Hell, if you can time it for 30 minutes I'll get it on the base myself." Ellis said.

"Sorry sir, but no volunteers over the rank of Captain."

"Get the word out on any safety measures folks can take to protect themselves, what the symptoms of radiation poisoning are, and any treatments they can try."

"We're working on that. I would like to say a volunteer that is an attractive female would have a better chance of going on the base, with the misconception of seeking employment, then retrieving the hidden nuke and placing it. She could then arm it and be gone, safely I might add, if hidden in a good spot with a long enough timer. Of course, the person chosen can set the timer as needed to insure it does go off as planned. We do not view this mission as a suicide effort but it could turn into one."

I said, "I have just the woman for you, but let me speak with her first."

CHAPTER 2

"Colonel, this is General Bronislav Faddey in Moscow, and I want to know what in the hell is going on at your station! Our satellites just picked up a nuclear detonation almost on your base! Are things so poorly run there that you have partisans breeching your wire? I want to know, in your own words, what justified the use of a tactical nuke. I am warning you, the reason had better be damned good, or a gulag in Siberia will soon have a new prisoner."

Vasiliev grew nervous, knowing not only his career, but his very life was hanging on his response. "Sir, we had word the Americans were transporting one of our stolen suitcase bombs in the area south of the base. Our informer had very reliable information, but they would not be in the area long, less than an hour. Since it would be like searching for a needle in a haystack, I used the bomb. I was assured by my staff the other nuclear weapon would not explode, and it did not."

"Is that not like using a cannon on an ant? Why did your stool pigeon not carry a small locator to speed up the process?"

"Uh, well, he was killed, sir. Right after he reported to me, he was assassinated in town square as he walked back to his apartment."

Faddey gave an insane laugh and then said, "So, you have no idea if the nuclear bomb you detonated destroyed the other, do you? If they killed your spy, it is likely they changed the date and time of the movement, you damned fool. I want you to listen to my orders closely. I want you on the next aircraft back to Moscow, where you will brief the General Staff personally on your actions. You had better hope I and the rest of the Generals believe you, or Siberia will be your next assignment. Do you understand me? I have a Colonel Matveev that is coming to assume command of your base. You, Colonel, are relieved of command effective immediately."

Gulping, Vasiliev said, "Yes, sir. Will that be all?"

"No, it will *not* be all. When you come, I want your chief of Intelligence, uh, Lieutenant Colonel Borisovich, to return home with you. Perhaps the idiot can shed some light on why nuclear weapons were required against a bunch of cowboys and rednecks. If he cannot explain the use, then he will join you in your journey."

"Yes sir. I will inform the Colonel." Vasiliev said and felt himself shiver. *They will kill us*, he thought.

"Now, I am finished. Your travel has the highest priority. Your foolish use of a nuclear weapon against the partisans has shown the world Mother Russia cannot defeat a bunch of peasants by conventional means! Get your ass and that fool you call your chief of intelligence here, and do it now!"

"Yes, sir."

The phone line suddenly went dead.

The Colonel was shaking violently when he hung up the phone. A minute later he dialed a number and said, "This is Colonel Vasiliev and I want to speak to Colonel Borisovich now."

"Uh, he is in a meeting, sir." the Sergeant said.

"Pull him from the damned thing, and do it now. If I have to come over there, everyone working in your intelligence section will be shot."

"Yes, sir. I will have him for you quickly."

Three minutes later, "This is Lieutenant Colonel Borisovich. What can I do for you, Colonel?"

After explaining his call from General Faddey, Borisovich didn't say a word.

"Are you still there, Sambor?"

"Yes, of course, sir, but overwhelmed that the General wants our heads. I am sure they are not calling us back home to present us with medals. Damn, this is not good at all."

"I want you in my office in less than 30 minutes. We need to discuss this in detail to see if we can logically justify the use of the weapon."

"I think we are both dead men, sir."

"If we must die, we will do it as Russian soldiers, with our heads held high. Now get over here and do it now."

"Yes sir, on my way now." He hung up the phone, turned and yelled, "Driver."

Standing and snapping to attention, the young man saluted and said, "Yes, sir."

Walking toward the door, the Lieutenant Colonel said, "Hurry, I need to get to the Base Commander's office and *now*."

"Of course, sir."

Lieutenant Colonel Borisovich sat in his quarters later, drinking vodka. The discussion with Vasiliev had been a waste of time. He was drunk, depressed, and knew once they landed in Moscow they'd be marched in front of a wall and executed. The more he thought about detonating the small nuclear device the more worried he became. According to the Colonel, they both had passage straight to Moscow in less than four hours, and he knew nothing shy of his death would be a good enough reason to miss the flight.

He stood, drained his glass, and then refilled it. He moved to his desk and began writing a short letter to his wife. He wrote a few short paragraphs, signed with love, and then licked the envelope closed. He continued to sit as his desk as he thought of his career up to this point. As he thought of the resistance movement against them, he knew the Russians could never win. The biggest weapons the Americans had was stubbornness, unity, and pride in country. He'd heard more than one American go to their death singing their National Anthem or the pledge of allegiance to a flag of a country that no longer existed. Russia would never break the American spirit.

Whispering a short prayer, begging for forgiveness, Lieutenant Colonel Borisovich pulled his pistol, slipped the safety off, and placing the barrel against his ear, he pulled the trigger. His shot was loud in the small room, and a few minutes later his enlisted aide opened the door to find his boss dead and the wall behind him splattered with blood, brains, and shards of skull.

Growing sick to his stomach, the Sergeant puked, wiped the vomit from his mouth and called the base Commander.

"Colonel Vasiliev's quarters." an enlisted aide said.

"Ian, Sergei; Colonel Borisovich just killed himself. I think I need to speak to the Commander, and now."

"Damn, he has had a lot to drink this evening. Let me get him to the phone."

Many long minutes later, Sergei heard, "Colonel Vasiliev here and what is this about Lieutenant Colonel Borisovich killing himself?" His voice was tired and his words slurred.

"It is true, sir, because I am standing beside his body right now. I have called no one else but you, sir."

"Are you sure he is dead?"

"Very sure, sir half his brain is on the wall behind him."

"Contact the medics and have them collect his body. This way the coward can go home a hero, but in a metal box."

"Yes, sir, I will do that. Is that all, sir?"

"For right now. I want you to go through his things, pack them for shipment home, and see the new Commander gets him a medal. No, forget the last part of that about the medal; I will do that before I leave this morning."

"Good night, sir, and have a pleasant journey home."

"Right." the Colonel said and then hung up the phone. He moved to his desk and began writing out a recommendation for a medal for his dead intelligence officer. *Maybe he had the right idea with suicide, but I do not think I can kill myself over something like this. I will take my chances in Moscow,* he thought as he started filling out forms.

At 0400 hours, Colonel Vasiliev had his suitcases placed in his car, and climbed in the back seat for his ride to the Jackson Air Base to catch a 0600 hours flight to Moscow. They drove out the front gate and he never looked back. The drive from Edwards was short, but halfway there the motorcycle in front of his car suddenly went down and the rider rolled into a ditch. Gun fire opened up a whole line of bullet holes that worked their way across the side of the car. With it's driver now dead, the car slammed into a ditch and instantly came to a complete stop. Reaching over the seat, Vasiliev grabbed a Bison sub machine gun, four magazines, and two grenades from his dead driver. He then opened the door on the opposite side of incoming fire and exited.

He had a small hand-held radio, and pushed the transmission button, "Base Ops, this is Commander Vasiliev and I'm under heavy ground fire. I need fire support about half way to Jackson."

"Uh, copy, sir. Wait one, while I see what I have in the air near you."

The motorcycle riding behind him went down and the rider rolled and rolled to almost the back bumper of the staff car. The Private came to a stop and then quickly crawled behind the car. He glanced at the Colonel and said, "We are in big trouble, huh, sir?"

"Maybe not. I am arranging for some aircraft to come to our aid. If you see anything that gives you a clear shot, take it, but go easy on your ammo."

"Sir, I have three helicopters; two are Kamov Ka-50, "*Black Sharks*," and the other is a Navy Kamov Ka-27 helicopter. As the Black Sharks attack the ground forces, the rescue aircraft will land on the highway. Do not approach the aircraft until a crewmember comes to you. Do you understand, sir?"

"Copy, what kind of wait do I have? I can see them moving toward me now."

"Three minutes at the most."

The motorcyclist raised and then threw one of his grenades, smiling when it exploded in the middle of a group of people. Once again the incoming small arms fire grew strong.

Overhead a Black Shark pilot said, "Get your head down, sir, I am rolling in hot from east to west."

The Colonel pulled the Private down and yelled to be heard. "Helicopters are coming to our rescue, so get down and stay down."

The Private was scared but not as scared as he thought he'd be under fire. He'd often wondered if he'd fight or run. He knew now he had no place to run, so fighting back was his only option.

There came a sound like a gigantic zipper being pulled down quickly and the Colonel knew a 30 MM cannon had opened up, sending dirt, rocks and pieces of bodies high into the air. Screams were heard as the helicopter banked for an even lower run this time.

It looked like a thousand guns firing at the Black Shark, but he knew there were only a hundred or less. It was still an hour before dawn and he was growing worried, because he could not miss this flight. After the second run on the partisans, the second helicopter arrived, and with it came the rescue aircraft. While both Black Sharks worked on the partisans on the ground the rescue pilot didn't flinch and landed in the middle of the highway. A crewmember ran to them, then all three moved for the rescue bird. About half way there the Colonel and the crewmember went down, both by small arms fire. The motorcyclist pulled the two men to the chopper and threw them inside. He climbed in and when the copilot looked at him, he gave a thumb up.

Just as power was applied to the aircraft and the tail came up as the nose went down, the motorcyclist heard one of the pilots yell, "Missile!"

The man reached for a knob between the seats, but before he could touch it, the chopper exploded into flames. Still not buckled in, the motorcyclist was knocked out of the aircraft by the blast and landed in the grass of the median as the helicopter continued to move forward for another 200 feet. It then rolled on it's left side and fell to earth, creating a huge reddish-black oily fireball when it struck. As the fuel went up, oxygen cylinders and ammunition started cooking off, too. Suspecting all the Russians had been killed on the burning helicopter, the Black Sharks began shooting at anything moving or seen. Thirty minutes later, they radioed the base and were told to return to base to refuel and rearm. As they moved toward the base, they passed over a rescue convoy moving toward the Colonel's car.

"Black Shark one, this is Base Actual." the convoy Commander said.

"Go, Actual."

"I am in the convoy, so I want both of you back overhead as quickly as you can be."

"Copy Actual, and you can depend on us."

"Good." Colonel Gleb said. As the acting Base Commander, here was his chance to show Moscow what he could do as a Commander. He picked the radio up, changed the frequency and said, "I want the tank, when we arrive, to pull up beside Colonel Vasiliev's car. The rest of you quickly get your troops out of the trucks and in defensive positions. This is our chance, men, to shine for Moscow."

He didn't hear the laughter and catcalls his last sentence brought.

When he spotted the oily fire from the helicopter, Gleb pulled his flask and took a long pull. He knew the bodies would be charred and positive identification would be done using DNA and dental records. He usually got sick easily after a battle if dealing with bodies. Now, due to his rank, he could avoid much because it made little sense for him, as the acting Commander, to be looking at dead people.

They pulled up beside the rear of the wrecked staff car and troops began jumping from the deuce and a half trucks.

Knowing most of his troops were green, Colonel Gleb called out, "Watch out for mines or trip wires. Do not touch any —"

A loud explosion was heard, followed by screams. When the Colonel glanced in the direction of the sound, he had half a dozen men down and all were shrieking. Three medics ran toward them, but one stepped on a toe-popper and took most of the load from a12 gauge shell in the lower stomach. As he fell, his screams joined the rest.

"I want Explosive Ordance Disposal (EOD) to sweep this area before we go another foot toward the crash site. I suspect everything, the gear and even our dead comrades, is mined." Gleb yelled as his EOD members moved forward slowly.

They began to disarm and place the mines on the road. They found a stack of cheap but effective mines around the area. Toe poppers were found in all calibers of ammunition, and they were the most common. All was going well, until the motorcyclist that was knocked from the helicopter by the blast sat up and yelled for help. He was in pain from burns, two bullet holes, and severe bruises. Two medical technicians moved for the man at a run and just before they reached him, one technician disappeared in a flash of bright red flame and white light. He'd stepped on a Russian anti-personnel mine and was dead before he had time to worry. The other technician froze in place.

"EOD, clear a walkway for that medic!" the Colonel ordered and then added, "And place what is left of the other medic in a body bag."

"I want my medical personnel to remove the bodies from the helicopter, now! Move and let's get them in body bags, and return to base."

"Colonel, you need to stop giving orders and being so animated when you talk. If the partisans have a sniper around, he will know you are the boss, sir." Captain Valery Polzin said in an attempt to get the Colonel under control. Snipers often waited to shoot so their first shot takes out the senior person, because it creates chaos.

Getting right in the Captain's face, Gleb shouted, "I am in charge here, Captain, not you! Now come to attention and salute me. Now!"

"Sir, I think this is dangerous." the Captain replied, and then snapped to attention and saluted his Colonel.

"I'll teach you to respect a senior —"

Captain Polzin was looking right in the Colonel's eyes when he heard a bullet zing past his ear and he saw it strike the Commander in the middle of his chest. The shot had been made behind the Captain and the round punched a hole through the Colonel's chest, throwing blood, bone and gore out his back. The bullet hit the concrete on the roadway, ricocheted, and struck a Private in the groin. Both men fell.

A doctor who was supervising the removal of the remains of Colonel Pasha Vasiliev, ran to the Commander and started treating him. Before the Captain could say a word, there was the sound of another shot and the doctor fell forward, dead before he ever saw the Colonel's injury. He'd taken a round in the neck, right where his throat met his torso. The bullet blew most of his spine away.

A Senior Sergeant yelled, "Place the Commander and the doctor in the ambulance, you fools, as the attacking aircraft force the partisans to hunt a hole! Load them both now!"

"Base Actual, this is Black Shark 1, and I have returned. Do you need any assistance at this time?" the attack helicopter pilot asked.

"Yes, be advised Base Actual is wounded. I am Base 2. South of us from the highway is a grove of wood; we have a sniper about half the distance down the tree line."

"I hear you, and I have some fast movers around too, so let me make a pass and then I will send them to work over the same area." Just as the chopper banked the pilot said, "I have the trees in sight and starting my run now."

Empty brass fell from the belly of the helicopter as he used his Gatling guns on the tree line. As he pulled up and gained altitude, he radioed, "Now come the fast movers with some napalm for our partisan friends."

The jets came over the trees low and as they moved, what looked like fuel tanks separated and tumbled into the trees. A huge splash of fire was suddenly moving like a wave from the momentum of the storage containers. The flames stretched out a good 50 meters or more and then fell on the forest below. While the jet pilot didn't hear the screams of the partisans, the folks on the ground did.

"Black Shark 1, Badger 2, we took some ground fire down there, almost dead center of the trees. I am making another pass."

"Go, and good hunting."

With it's siren blaring the ambulance took off at a great speed to reach the hospital.

While the ambulance was leaving and more napalm was being dropped on the partisans, a Master Sergeant walked to Captain Polzin and said, "We need to leave here, sir, and immediately. The winds have shifted to our direction and I am showing a radioactive reading on my dosimeter."

"Oh, God, no! Not with all the men that are here." the Captain said, and wondered what to do next.

CHAPTER 3

I glanced around the meeting room meeting the eyes of each man there, knowing nuking the Russians was all they'd understand. As Willy once told me, the Russians were vicious; all they respected was when they met an adversary more barbarous than them. I think it was time for a payback and with aces, too.

"Captain, we don't need to get a tactical nuke on the base to destroy Edwards Air Base. The town is close enough. As every man in this room knows, the nuke will flatten everything for miles around, including the military complex. But, if the General is determined to place the bomb on the base, I have an attractive woman that might do the job." I said.

"Well that is a valid point, and it may be our best option, because I think it can be camouflaged near the base or in town easier than getting it through base security. Let me speak with the General about this. Now, we'd prefer to have the suitcase delivered by a unit that knows Edwards well, so that means it's down to two Colonels. While we don't want to use a Colonel, I see no other choice. Anyone want to volunteer?" he asked, looking at me and Colonel Wilcox. I knew Wilcox would never volunteer for a mission like this, but he'd go if ordered.

"The 'Aces' will do it and with pride. The only problem I see is how do we warn the civilians of the coming explosion?" I asked.

"They cannot be informed, and that's a direct order from the General. No one but you and your troops are to know when, or where, the suitcase is left."

"Good God, you don't expect me to blow all those innocent people to hell and back without warning them, do you?" I was shocked, and started to stand.

"Sir, we can't afford to let the Russians know what we are planning to do. At first we started to nuke the airport and base at Jackson, but since most of the Russians important supplies come in there by air, we need it working. It's much the same with Vicksburg, but it's mostly clothing and food coming down the Mississippi. Much of our needed gear is stolen from the Russians as it leaves one of those two facilities. But all of this may change."

Wilcox said, "I don't see any way to tell our civilians to leave without compromising our tactical nuclear weapon. If the Russians even suspect what we're doing, the bastards will bring even more people from the gulags to force us to kill them, too. I hate to say it, John, but the General is right on this one."

"Now I know how the pilot that bombed Hiroshima, Japan, felt, except at least he was killing civilians in an enemy nation. We'll be killing our own people."

The Chaplain, said, "We'll pray for you, and I feel what you are doing will help free our nation some day. God truly knows you are no murderer in your heart, John. I know you and have for years, so let this concern over the civilians go, and complete your mission. He will understand."

"Uh, okay, I guess. When and where do I pick this suitcase up?" I was still not comfortable with this mission, only because of the civilians.

"I will give you a map with a spot marked on it. You will meet there in two days. Once you have the bomb, do not hesitate, and move immediately to Edwards. I will say this much as a warning to you, once you insert the key and enter the code, we have no way of turning it off. It will detonate at the time you have set. So, give yourselves enough time to clear maybe 10 miles, and keep moving. Where you hide the bomb is up to you. From what I was told, our bomb has a blast radius of 8 miles."

I nodded, not real pleased that I'd soon murder a couple hundred thousand people. The population was less now than before the war, but what right did I have to kill these people in order to avenge our nation? I was confused, angry, and more than a little scared. No, not scared of dying, but of being caught before I could set the timer. If I had to kill innocents, I damned sure wanted to smoke all the Russians I could.

"Any questions?" the Captain asked.

Silence.

"Remember gentlemen, this briefing is classified Top Secret. That concludes my presentation and sir, I need to speak with you privately, if I may." he said as he approached me.

"What can I do for you now, Captain?" I asked, suddenly not liking this man, but I knew he was only speaking for the old man. This was what the General wanted, not this young officer.

"Sir, the General said when you moved into town with your bomb, only you and two others are to go. He wants no screw-ups, and too large of a group will draw attention and maybe compromise your mission. This mission *must* happen, sir."

I gave a loud sigh, shook my head and said, "Okay, I'll do the best I can to set this thing off. Where will I get the code to arm the beast, and the key?"

Opening his briefcase, he handed both to me and said, "Guard those with your life. We have no others and it took a long time to make these."

Then it dawned on me, "We don't even know if these will work, do we?"

"Uh, well, no we don't. But, according to the nuclear scientists working on the other bomb, this *should* work fine."

"*Should?* Shit, *should?* The General is willing to sacrifice the lives of my men and women with a piece of equipment that should work? *I'm not real pleased with this.* Nonetheless, I can see where the old man is coming from. Let him know the Aces will not let him down, Captain." I could fully understand the General's situation, but I didn't like being the group that had to do the job. What if I lost a bunch of folks, only to have the bomb malfunction later? As an old military man, I knew the order was legal, so I had no choice but to do what I was told.

"If it makes you feel better, there is a 99% chance the key and code will work. But, remember, once the timer is set, you need to move your ass, and fast, too."

"Anything else?"

"Yes, when you return to your people you'll find a woman named Captain Carol Logan with you. She has been trained on this bomb and will do the key programming. Now, have her teach you, if time allows, how to do the job, in case she is wounded or killed. It's not difficult, but she's also been trained to use alternate ways to explode the weapon, and a couple of those methods will take her life. No, she is not on a suicide mission, but she can make the thing work in most cases."

"Any more surprises?" I asked and decided right then, I'd take good care of Carol Logan.

"No, I think we've pretty well covered all the bases." the Captain said. Extending his hand, we shook as he said, "Good luck, and God bless you, sir."

When I returned to my people, I discovered Carol Logan sitting on a stump, just inside a forest of pine, oak and hickory. When I neared, she stood and started to salute.

"As you were, Captain; we don't come to attention, salute, or usually call folks by rank, especially in the field. Either of the three can get the senior person killed."

"Uh, then what do I call you, sir?"

"John is good enough. Do you have much field experience?"

Lowering her head, she replied, "No, not at all, and this will be my first mission."

I liked what I saw of her. I guessed she was about about five feet and maybe eight inches tall. She wore her blonde hair short, was as thin as the rest of us, her green eyes reflected intelligence, and overall I was impressed. She was wearing a Russian field uniform and wore white cloth wrapped around her left arm to identify her as a partisan. Like most women in the field, she wore no makeup or perfumes.

"Do you have what you need for about a week? I mean in food and ammo for your weapon?"

"Yes, I'm carrying a Russian Bison and I know how to use it. I have a mix of American MRE's and Russian rations."

"Medical supplies? First aid kit?"

"I have all I'll need, and I have some bottles of morphine to give your medic. These bottles are in case we have to leave any-one behind, including me."

So, now they want no one left behind alive, I thought and realized our mission was an important one. "Okay, my medic is Marsha Wied, and she was a Nurse Practitioner prior to the fall. What'd you do prior to the fall? Any military service experience? Come with me now and I'll introduce you to my people."

"I spent a tour in the Marines, got out and went to school us-ing my G.I. Bill." she said as we neared the group.

"Alright, everyone gather around. We've been assigned a spe-cial mission. And, to help us complete our mission, we're taking Captain Logan along. Captain Logan is a prior Marine, so she's well qualified. You can all meet and chat with her after this. Wied, you need to see her because she has some medication for you. Two days from now we're to meet at a farm house south of here, where we will get the tools we need to do a job and be told exactly where our job is located. That's all I know, and when I get more information, if you need to be told, I'll pass it along. We leave two hours before dawn, so I suggest all of you get some hot food in you and then some sleep."

I was beat and twice the age of some of my troops. I was very lucky because most of them got along well with each other. I'd seen some units in the past where one or two people were always causing trouble. I missed my old life with my wife and the home we had. I'd had it all then, but really didn't appreciate anything. When I returned from my last tour in the sandbox, I got out and started losing interest in politics completely. Some of our politi-cians were dumber than a box of mud, and I wondered how they kept being reelected. A few of the old fools had been in public office for over fifty years, and I wouldn't have voted for them as a dogcatcher, much less a Congressman or Senator. I think in retrospect, I should have followed politics much closer than I did. I later heard of corruption from many small city councilmen all the way up to the President. Hardly a man or woman in office at the time that didn't have a price, so all could be bought.

I walked out the back door of the house and sat on the top step. I then opened an MRE and fed Dolly some of the hamburger patty, parts of my cookie, and all the crackers. Then I opened a full ration and fed it all to her. She served a valuable service to us, having saved our bacon a number of times when we'd almost walked into ambushes. She was even promoted to the rank of Sergeant and had two rations a day issued to her, just like the troops did.

The next morning at 0400 hours we walked from the safe house moving south by west. Mary was carrying the map, while Stevens counted our paces. Stevens was a likable man, who claimed before the fall he'd been obese weighing over 350 pounds, but now he'd be lucky to weigh 135. He was a tall man, close to seven feet tall and black. His kinky hair was worn short, his mind was active, and he had an excellent eye for spotting booby-traps and mines. Like most of us from the South, he had a great sense of humor, loved fresh beef when we could get it, and killed every cannibal he could find. I liked the man, but as the Commander of the Aces I couldn't get too close to any of my troops.

The winds were light, blowing to the northeast so radiation would not fall around us. I carried a dosimeter, which was Russian, and it read zero. We set a good pace and were moving well. The sky was partly cloudy and I prayed for rain.

After a couple of hours I glanced at Logan to see how well she was doing. She knew I was seeing how well she was holding out. She gave a me a quick wink and a big smile.

For some reason that bothered me. Oh, I'd had women come on to me since I'd been with the partisans, but my wife had only been dead a few short months. Besides, I was old enough to be her father. I nodded at her and she gave me a thumbs up.

It was when we stopped for our noon break that Logan sat down beside me and asked, "Is it true your wife died fighting the Russians?"

"Yes, she did; her name was Sandra and she was a nurse."

"I'm sorry to hear that. I've never married, can't have kids, so I've never had any, but I did adopt a boy before the fall. I was a re-gional manager for a large restaurant chain and making good money at the time." She pulled a Russian ration from her pocket and began opening the containers.

"Uh, what happened to your son?"

"Oh, one night, maybe a month after the fall I had two men and a woman break into my home. They all three boasted of how they'd use me and kill me when they were finished. I was still in bed, because they'd climbed in the open window in the kitchen. One held a knife to my son's throat and I knew then, no matter what I gave them, we were both going to die."

Wrapped up in her story I asked, "What happened then?"

"I pulled a 9 mm pistol I kept under my pillow and shot all three of them, only not before the man holding my son cut his throat. When I got out of bed, I shot two in the head, but saved the one that killed my son. He'd taken a round low and in his gut, so the odds were good he'd survive long enough. I moved to my boy, Steve, and I held his hand as he bled out. By then there were no hospitals or 911 any longer. The week before, I'd been invited to join a partisan group, but turned the offer down to care for my son."

"What happened to the man that was wounded?"

"I doused him and the walls of my home with gasoline. Then, I tossed in a burning rag and burned the place down, but the wounded man must have died or was unconscious, because I heard no screaming. I listened for a long time but heard nothing. I felt cheated in my quest for revenge. I then buried my son and you know the rest of my story."

Her story and others like it were all too common. "I don't know which is worst, fighting the Russians or the scum on the streets. I knew when the fall happened that bad folks would soon come out of the walls like cockroaches at night to rape, plunder, and kill. I just never realized how many there would be. I lost my first wife when she was raped and killed by some thugs, while I was out trading for what we needed, and for years I blamed myself. I've finally come to realize it wasn't my fault, because even if I'd been there, I might have just been killed and she'd have died anyways. I found evidence it was a large group.

"Were you married?" I asked.

"For a while and I was happy. He was much older than me, by 25 years, and when the fall came along he could no longer get his blood pressure pills at any price. He lasted almost a year without his meds and then he had a heart attack one afternoon and I lost him."

"Why an older man? I mean it's none of my business, but you must still be in your twenties."

"Older men treat women better than younger men. I had many dates with younger men before the war and they spent most of their time on our date texting on some social media site. They weren't interested in me, or they would have given me a little of their time. Then along came my husband and it was different."

"That explains it well enough that even I can understand it. Thank you for sharing your personal information. I try to know a little about all my troops."

Giving me a warm smile, she said, "I'd like to know you better."

"That's not likely because I am your Commander. I've discovered that business and pleasure do not mix."

She laughed, gave me another wink and replied, "You're only my Commander for this mission; then I go back to Headquarters and work manpower issues."

"Why the interest in me? I own nothing, have nothing except what I can carry in my pack, and I know it's not my looks."

"I see you as a man's man. I want you, and I usually get what I want."

I laughed and said, "Oh? Don't I get a say in this?"

She smiled, lowered her head and said, "Maybe."

"If you are still interested in me after this mission, then you and I will talk about it, okay?"

"Deal."

Five minutes later we were back on the trail. Carol had a lot to offer the right man and I knew Sandra wouldn't want me to spend the rest of my life grieving for her, because we'd talked about death before. I decided to put all of this out of my mind for now because I had a difficult mission to complete, and this mission could very well cost all of us our lives.

It was mid-afternoon when a chopper flew overhead and then the engine pitch changed and we watched as it descended and landed in a small field and troops were seen leaving the aircraft. *A squad of men, Spetsnaz I suspected. This is either a real strange coincidence or the Russians have found out about my mission. I must find a way to kill every man on that team, if I can*, I thought as the chopper pilot was heard to apply power, the nose lowered, and the aircraft began to raise in the air. The team was lost from view.

Mary quickly set up an ambush alongside the trail and we rushed to position Claymore mines and other command detonated explosives. We had no idea where the Russian troops had gone, but usually they were placed in front of a unit to setup an ambush, or they moved down the trail to engage the partisans. If this group were setting up an ambush, they'll have one hell of a long wait, because I'd change direction on them if need be. My biggest concern was how they knew where we were.

I had Alford, my sniper, high in a tree and he sent me indicators the Russians were nearing. He held out five fingers twice, meaning 10 men and then used his index and middle finger to indicate they were walking. He then pointed straight down. So that meant 10 men were walking here.

We were in an area near a swamp and there was a lot of under-brush, vines, and growth. I saw their point man, who Alford had been instructed to kill, along with the man on drag. Then came the main body of 8 men, of which none wore rank, or any badges or patches.

When the group was right in front of us, Mary squeezed a clacker, a Claymore mine exploded, and in a matter of seconds the group was on the ground screaming or dead. A mist of blood floated above the bodies. I heard two shots from Alford, then a shot from where the Russian drag man should have been, and then my sniper screamed.

I sent Sgt. Morgan and Corporal Hall after the Russian survivor and I suspected he was seriously injured. I let them know that a wounded Spetsnaz should be treated like a wounded bear. I told them to take no chances and shoot the man before they touched him.

After about 30 minutes, I had Stevens and Walker check the downed Russians. I also had them shoot each man in the head. Once they knew they were dead, they stripped them of all gear and ammo we could use.

I then had James climb the tree and lower the wounded Alford to the ground using a rope. He was in sad shape, a hole punched through his shoulder, but it had missed his collar bone and the flat bone in his back. It was a clean shot through the meaty part of his shoulder, near his neck, and the pain was severe. Marsha Wied gave him a shot of morphine, just enough to kill his pain, dressed his wound, and we prepared to leave. Just then I heard a series of gunshots, followed by a loud explosion.

Minutes later, Hall returned with Morgan over his shoulder. Morgan was shrieking from pain.

When Morgan was placed on his back on the ground, the whole front of his shirt was soaked in blood. When the medic cut his shirt off, I saw a good two dozen holes in his stomach and all were oozing blood.

Wied looked James over and then said, "Grenade fragments in his stomach, and not a thing I can do for him in the field, Colonel."

"Use a full dose of morphine on him then. Nothing can be allowed to slow our mission down." Carol said.

"Do you mean you want me to kill him?"

"That's exactly what I want you to do. I expect it to be done to any of us, should we be seriously wounded."

I said, "We can't take him with us, Marsha, and I'll not leave him alive so the Russians can torture him for days; the risk is too high he'll talk. Put him down."

She injected the drug into the man's arm, met my eyes and said, "I hate this job at times."

"He'll feel no pain when he goes." Carol said.

A minute or so later, Morgan shivered, gave a loud sigh and died.

"I hope you can walk, Alford," I asked.

"After seeing that done to a man who can't walk, I can run, need be."

"Stevens on point and Walker, you take drag. Let's move, folks, so we can make up for lost time."

We walked until dusk, seeing no one and hearing nothing. I knew Russians would soon be on our trail because they'd want to avenge the deaths of their elite men. I had my people surround our night spot with mines, toe-poppers, and three Claymores positioned, too.

"Okay," I whispered, "cold camp and we sit back to back all night. I want every other person awake at all times. If you want to eat, eat it cold." I said, and then sat in the grass and Dolly moved to me and laid by my side. After a few minutes her head was in my lap.

It's rough sleeping sitting up, but this way we had every point on the compass covered with a set of eyes, each wearing Russian NVGs.

It was an hour before sunrise, when Thompson whispered, "I have movement coming down the trail."

CHAPTER 4

aster Sergeant Vlad Sokoloff moved to the dead Russian bodies lining the hallway of the hospital. White sheets, soaked in blood, covered the men in groups of two. He said a short prayer, turned to Senior Sergeant Pajari and said, "I hope your men took their radiation pills, or more bodies will be littering this floor."

"We took them, but I do not have much faith in the damned things. I wish you would have seen Colonel Gleb out there. He actually ordered a Captain to salute him. A second later he was shot, and he is lucky it did not kill him. These officers need more field time to learn how we operate these days. Any word on him or his injury?"

"The last I heard was they are taking him to Jackson Air Base and he will be returned to Moscow. The shot struck his lung and messed up his spine when it exited. I think he will be retired because of his injury. Tell me, Albert, just between us, what in the hell are we doing here?" The Master Sergeant stood with his hands on his hips.

Giving a low chuckle, Pajari said, "Getting our asses kicked. I do not think the Generals would know what to do with America if they had it, which they never will have. These people are stubborn, and I have never seen so many guns in my life. On my last tour here, I was in a field unit, and I saw soldiers shot with bows and arrows, shotguns, crossbows, hunting rifles, and one old man killed a Colonel with an old black powder muzzle loaded pistol. I have seen many die singing 'God Bless America.'"

At that moment a side door opened and a Full Colonel walked in. The two Senior NCO's snapped to attention, and Colonel

Yegor, the Gulag Commander said, "These are two of our best Sergeants, sir. Master Sergeant Vlad Sokoloff and Senior Sergeant Albert Pajari."

"I am Colonel Matveev, and I am the new Base Commander. I want to see both of you in my office, first thing in the morning. I want to get a feel for my enlisted personnel."

"Yes, sir." the Master Sergeant replied.

The Colonel ignored the bodies and continued walking down the hall.

"He has pissed off somebody and will never make General, not as a Base Commander. He should be in charge of a much larger fighting unit." Vlad said as the two men made their way outside and put their forage hats on.

Albert replied, "I am just wanting to make Master Sergeant before I retire, because of the increase in my retirement pay. I am not the least bit worried about the political careers of our officers."

A Private ran to the two men and said, "The Senior Sergeant running communications asked me to tell you, Master Sergeant, that all ten of the special forces that were deployed this morning are dead. He also gave me this paper to give you."

He handed the note to Vlad and then stood waiting. Not wanting to read it in front of the young man, he said, "What are you waiting for, boy? I hope you do not expect a tip! Get your ass back to work, unless the Sergeant sent something else."

"No, Master Sergeant. That is all." The man then turned and ran for his unit.

Unfolding the note, he read with assistance from the flood light that lit the huge red cross on the side of the hospital. He finished reading and said, "The new Colonel is in for rough first day. The Spetsnaz men were wiped out to the man in an ambush. And, in the Southern part of the state a couple of guards were killed and a warehouse broken into. They did not just take a little, they emptied the place. The thieves made off with radiation pills, cases of food, and clothing. Of course any weapons were taken. Then some minor clashes with the partisans that add another dozen to the total killed this day."

"Oh, not good. Welcome to Edwards Air Base, Colonel." Albert said, and then gave a dry chuckle.

"Running this base is like running after a greased pig. Just when you think you have it under control, it gets out of hand."

"Let's go by the club for a couple of drinks."

"Not me, because tomorrow will be a lot of yelling at the 0600 hours staff meeting. If you want a few drinks, come by my tent. I want to be alert and ready for the meeting."

At exactly 0600 hours, Master Sergeant Sokoloff said from the very pit of his stomach, "Ten-hoooaaa!"

Twenty or so Russian officers stood at attention. Colonel Matveev entered the room wearing his full dress uniform. As he moved to his chair he said, "Please be seated, gentlemen."

It was then a Major opened the door and as he entered, the Colonel said, "Major, you can leave this briefing. It starts at 0600, not 0602 and I expect you in your chair ready to brief me on time. Now, call your boss and I want to speak to both of you in my office as soon as this meeting is finished."

"Yes, sir. I will call him as I wait, sir."

Men around the table looked at others and each knew the new Commander wasn't a vodka drinking fool like many of the previous ones.

"Weather, I need a briefing from your shop twice a day. I need to know the winds because of the nuclear bomb we detonated. I want all men under the age of 40 taking the radiation pill. I have been told by Moscow the pill will not work for older adults. Additionally, I want a comprehensive briefing from the disaster preparedness people on what steps we have taken to keep our people safe and from the hospital, on how we intend to treat our ill men and women. I want the briefing in my office before the close of business today."

"Sir," the Master Sergeant said, "should we keep this briefing as is, or are there certain aspects that you consider high priority?"

"Aircraft Maintenance, how many helicopters do we have right this moment that are mission ready?"

"Uh," the young Captain said, "I have no idea, sir."

"And if you don't know, who *does* know?"

"I don't know, sir."

"Obviously, Captain, you do not know much. I want every aircraft we can get in the air safely out looking for partisans. I want a company of men and women always on standby, to insert into the field to fight our enemy. I cannot do this, Captain, unless I have numbers from you. At 1300 hours today, I want you and your boss in my office, and you had better have some answers. Now, weather, let's hope you can do a better job than Aircraft Maintenance."

The weather briefing was excellent and at the end the Colonel asked, "So, do you really think most of the winds will be to the east for the next 20 days?"

"Oh, yes, sir. Well, at least that is what my computer model shows, and it is 99% correct."

"Damn. That means most of the fallout will be sent over Jackson. Colonel Vasiliev must have been a fool to order the bomb. Did he discuss the future weather conditions with your people before the bomb was sent out?"

"Yes sir, and I personally told him what the conditions would be, and my forecast was perfect."

"Okay, no more about Colonel Vasiliev, because it has already been done. I want this base cleaned up, I want haircuts, and I want sharp troops. I want us to look like what we are, the best damned troops Mother Russia can produce. I want the partisans harassed 24/7 and by using all means at our disposal. Gentlemen, know your jobs, know the numbers I need from you. I am a patient man, but for those of you who do not know me, I will fire you in a minute and send you back home in disgrace. You are officers in the mightiest army in the world, so act, look, talk, and think like you are. Dismissed!" The Colonel stood and left the room, plainly upset.

"Ten-hoooaaa!"

The officers snapped to attention.

The Master Sergeant heard not a word about the Colonel as folks filed from the room, but he knew they'd talk later over a glass of vodka.

Strange he did not bring up the deaths or injured from yesterday. He was clearly disgusted that most were not prepared for his briefing. I will bet in a day or two the Commanders will start showing up, and not some Lieutenant or Captain, Master Sergeant Sokoloff thought as he turned off the lights and closed the door.

He walked to the dining facility and had a quick lunch of stew and bread. Then, back to his office to prepare his initial briefing for the new Commander. By the time for lights out, he had accounted for every man on base, regardless if they were working or in the hospital. He also had ideas to help the sagging morale of his troops, but didn't know enough about the Colonel to suggest anything yet. *He will want a full accounting of the troops, then a breakdown of where they are assigned.*

He'd just undressed and turned off his light when he heard helicopters starting their engines and the sound of men running as orders were being shouted. Opening his door, still in his boxer shorts, he saw combat troops loading into the aircraft.

He quickly dressed and made his way to the command post.

The room was full of cigarette smoke as he made his way to a Senior Sergeant calling out orders. He waited beside the man for things to slow down and then asked, "What is going on?"

"A couple of Black Sharks caught a company of partisans on the ground and in the open. From the initial reports, at least 40 partisans were killed and we have infrared equipped helicopters out now hunting. Colonel Matveev ordered a company to be dropped in the area by helicopter."

"Are they all gone yet?" Sokoloff asked, hoping he could go out with them.

"The Colonel is personally going out in about twenty minutes, as soon as they have secured the area. He seems —"

"Shark Two reports two transport helicopters down and in flames. He says the partisans have rockets or missiles."

"Tell him to clear the area where the Colonel will be going and then return to refuel, rearm, and escort the man's helicopter out to his troops. Tell him to do the job now, too." a Major the Master Sergeant didn't know ordered.

"Yes, sir."

"Put me on the manifest, because I want to go out with the old man. I'll be on the flight line near the helicopters."

The Senior Sergeant shrugged his shoulders and said, "Okay, but it is your ass on the line, not mine." and he went back to shouting orders.

Sokoloff ran to his quarters for his field gear and weapon.

Twenty-five minutes later the helicopter was moving toward the ground troops and Sokoloff enjoyed the cool air in his face. The aircraft had a crew member sitting behind a machine-gun where each door used to be, ready to fire if need be. The removal of the doors allowed the cool night air to blow into the passenger compartment and the passengers enjoyed the ride. The Master Sergeant saw the Colonel and a Lieutenant Colonel were the only passengers. The Commander had a headset to speak with the crew.

When they began to lose altitude there were a number of *twing* and *ping* sounds as small arms fire punched holes through the aircraft. The machine-guns on both doors opened up, but the Master Sergeant knew they were firing at muzzle flashes, and saw no one in the darkness. The noise was deafening and it was then a line of holes appeared, as by magic, in the floor. The Lieutenant Colonel sitting by him fell forward, limp in his seat-belt.

"This is Big Rooster." the pilot said, "We have heavy ground fire and are taking hits. This landing zone is hot, repeat, the landing zone is hot."

Sokoloff felt the man's neck, found no pulse and watched as a puddle of fresh blood formed by his boots. He saw the exit wound was close to his Adams apple, so he suspected the bullet had traveled from his rear to his throat. The red canvas seat under the man was soaked in blood. The aircraft banked sharply, shuddered and then the flight machine gunner looked at him and raised one finger. He knew they'd be landing in one minute. He lowered his Night Vision goggles, tightened his seat belt, and prepared mentally to exit the aircraft under fire.

As they lowered to the ground, tracers of all colors were seen criss-crossing in front and at the sides of the helicopter. If not so deadly, they would have been considered beautiful. Thuds were heard and the *pings* and *zings* returned. The man up front and sitting on the right suddenly jerked and twitched violently in his seat. Seconds later blood splattered on the right side of the windscreen and the man fell limply to the left, with only his harness holding him upright. The Master Sergeant noticed a stream of blood dripping from his chin, to land on the instrument panel between him and the pilot.

When the aircraft touched the ground, everyone but the dead Lieutenant Colonel ran from the helicopter. The door-gunners were still shooting at targets they couldn't see, but then one on the right fell to the floor and started bucking and jerking. It was then the aircraft started to lift back into the air once more. The Master Sergeant saw what he thought was a rocket zoom past the helicopter, missing it by mere inches. No one noticed a row of bullet holes run along the engine panel and then smoke began to pour from the bird. Slowly the pilot raised the aircraft and started limping home, smoking badly, with at least two dead and one injured.

Even with his NVGs on, the Master Sergeant saw no one but dug-in Russians. Four helicopters lay burning in the surrounding field, the light showing bodies near each aircraft. He followed the base Commander to the company Commander and listened as they talked.

"It is estimated we have run into at least one company of partisans, but more likely two." Captain Alexey Alexeev said from the darkness.

"I find this hard to believe. I was told partisans always work in small groups." Colonel Matveev said and then asked, "Are your men in a good defensive position?"

"Fairly good, sir, and I think the partisans will start to withdraw now, because they hung around to shoot at our aircraft."

Suddenly, the *popping* sound of gunfire intensified. Then grenades exploding added to the noise level. The radioman, squatted by the Commander, suddenly had a third eye and the back of his head exploded. He dropped to the ground unmoving and was dead before he'd felt any pain. The radio was removed from the dead man's back by the Commander, and he picked up the handset. Pushing his helmet back slightly to allow the speaker to be against his ear he said, "Base, this is Big Rooster Actual, and I need artillery assistance."

The Colonel read off the coordinates from the map, had the person on the other end read them back to him, and said, "I will correct you as you fire. I want the first round to be white phosphorous as a mark and I will correct you from there. Understand, first shot on the way."

With all the bullets flying around the Colonel didn't have to tell anyone to lower their heads. Seconds later, a shell struck about 500 meters from them and then mushroomed into what looked like an inverted white Christmas tree. The shell produced a stunning white image, but Sokoloff knew white phosphorous produced painful wounds that burned until the air source as removed.

"Drop the next one. I want it 100 meters lower."

By the time the second shell landed, all incoming small arms fire was gone. The second shell was as beautiful as the first, but the partisans had run the second they heard the first shell screaming toward earth. As a result the two shells had only killed one man.

"Cease fire, cease fire!" the company Commander yelled, as the base Commander ended the artillery support.

A Lieutenant stood, a distant shot was heard, and the man fell screaming as blood spurted from a wound to the inside of his left thigh. The medic ran to him and as he opened his pouch of supplies, he was shot in the head, his helmet punctured like a can of soup. His bloody body fell over the Lieutenant, who was screaming hysterically. Then an unknown Private crawled to the officer and pulled him behind cover. Minutes later his screaming ceased as morphine flowed through his veins.

"Looks like they have stolen a Russian sniper rifle with a night vision scope from us." the Company Commander said.

"Yes, have your snipers look too, Captain. I have yet to see a partisan body."

"I want us on a fifty-fifty alert, and my snipers looking for targets. If you scope a partisan, fire at will." the Captain ordered, which meant half of the men could sleep as the rest pulled guard. The snipers had just been given approval to shoot when they found a target.

Like most soldiers, Sokoloff hated snipers. He knew they had a mission too, but they were cowards in his mind. Some sitting back a mile or so to kill unsuspecting soldiers, wasn't an honorable thing to do, at least not in his mind. And a sniper didn't usually kill the first person shot, but waited for folks to try and rescue the injured one. If his first victim was a high ranking officer, it might be possible to kill a half-dozen soldiers as they tried to get the man to safety. Then, after bagging his limit, the sniper would usually kill the first one shot, because the game was over.

The remainder of the night was quiet, but at the odd times a loud cough of a sniper's rifle with a silencer was heard. At sunup, the Company Commander gave his marching orders and then allowed the men time to eat.

Colonel Matveev was a smart man, and like most of the line troops wore no rank. He also made it known that saluting or doing anything for him in the field was a no-no. He wanted no unnecessary attention drawn to him, so he'd pack his own pack, prepare his own meals, and live the life of a private soldier, except he'd not walk point or guard at night. Snipers loved officers and senior NCO's as targets.

"Sir, I think the partisans have broken into small cells by now. One of our helicopter reports seeing where they moved through a large field. The dew was wiped from the grasses by their trousers and they are moving south by west."

"Get on the radio and have some paratroopers dropped in front of the partisans suspected line of travel. I think it might be smart to drop the airborne troops in squad sizes and spread them out a bit. If they tell you they do not have the authority to do as I asked, give the headset to me."

The morning dawned nice, with a clear sky, cool but not cold, and it was a good day to track partisans. Two medics were counting the dead and wounded as they waited for helicopters to return to take the injured and dead back to the base.

"Sir, will you be returning to base with the helicopters this morning?" Captain Alexeev asked. He prayed the man would leave, because it was difficult to run a company with his boss watching his every move.

"You seem to have it all well controlled, so yes, I think I will return. Master Sergeant Sokoloff, will you return or stay with the men?"

"I would like to stay, unless you need me, sir."

"Stay; at some point they may have need of your many years of experience. Radioman, have the first helicopter seen to fly a slow 360 degree course around us and count bodies."

"I will inform them, sir." The radioman was wiping blood from the radio gear, blood left by the prior user.

Abruptly there sounded four gunshots, screams of pain, followed by a loud explosion. Every man there went to ground, as someone yelled for a medic in Russian.

CHAPTER 5

I heard our safeties all click to the off position and we were ready to 'Rock and Roll' if needed. Dolly gave a low warning growl. That confirmed to me it was the enemy. One of the last things done before we'd settled in for the night was planting a Russian mine, an OZM-72, which worked like a Bouncing Betty mine. It would bounce up and explode at about 3 or 4 feet, usually with excellent kill potential. The trip wire ran across the trail and it was about 6 inches high. Around the mine were a couple of toe-poppers, and an anti-personnel mine, courtesy of the Russian army, in the event they spotted the trip wire and got nosy.

I then, with the help of my NVGs, spotted the main body of men, and they were not walking on the trail but about three feet from it. The leader of this group of Russians was smarter than most leaders, and on this day he kept them all alive. As long as they didn't bother us, we'd not bother them, because what I carried was much more important than a fight with the Russians. I saw they were wearing NVGs too, but unless we moved, it was unlikely we'd be seen. They continued walking and were soon out of view.

I felt an elbow in my side from Carol and saw the Russian drag man walk right by us.

We were lucky on this trip because we had a modified Russian radio. Of course the frequencies were changed to allow us to speak to Headquarters or any other partisan units with radios. Near dawn, I could hear a big battle taking place north of us on the radio and it sounded like a real ball buster of a fight. Then just minutes later, as the sun started up, the partisans involved in the fight broke down into squad size units and then vanished.

I knew the Russians had dogs usually, and they'd soon get on the trail of a unit and stay on it, unless the partisans pulled an ambush, which was hard to do against a dog. Eventually, the dog would have to be killed. I could kill an enemy in a second and give it no further thought, but the hardest thing I've ever had to do in my life was to shoot a dog, which I had to do in my old barn.[1]

As the sun broke over the distant hills, we began to eat and move to the trees to take care of business. Less than 30 minutes later, our mines and traps recovered, we were back on the trail. I could hear aircraft flying high overhead, but they posed no direct threat to us.

Then a Russian transport plane flew over considerably lower than other flights, and I watched 10 men exit the aircraft. From what I could tell, they would land about 90 degrees from us in a field that I knew was there. *Surely they can't know I have the key or code, so why all the attention now? While it may be a coincidence, I'm beginning to wonder. How would they know where I am?* I thought as I met Mary's eyes.

"If we can get to the safe house," I whispered to her, "we can check everyone for a locator device and if found, they'll be shot."

"That's if we live long enough to get to the house. I'm beginning to feel a bit trapped."

I pulled my troops in close and said, "I suspect one of us is carrying a bug. Now, if you have it, I want it now. If you give it to me, you'll be able to leave alive. If I have to search you and find one, you'll face a firing squad. So, which will it be?"

After a few minutes, Private John Stevens said, "It's me. The Russians have my family and the last time we were in Edwards, I spoke with one of their Captains. I was told if I did not cooperate, he'd return and kill both of them. Don't you see, I had to do this to save my parents."

"Drop all your weapons and gear, all of it. And, hand me the bug."

He handed the thing to me, and it was no bigger than a dime. I placed it on a rock and struck it hard with another rock. It broke

---

1 See *The Fall of America #1*

into small pieces as I struck it again and again. I then scooped the pieces up and threw them into the wind.

"You know by rights I should kill you, right?"

"Colonel, I was just trying to keep my family alive."

"Sure you were, but what would our cost be in partisan lives to keep two people alive? How do you know your parents are still above ground? The Russians will use whatever they can to get others to do what they wish, including lying."

"I want your pistol, too." Mary said bluntly, and held her hand out.

"What? You mean I'm to leave unarmed, dressed as a partisan, and with no place to go?"

I pulled my big knife and said, "Give your pistol to her and then leave. We've lost our trust in you, Stevens. Maybe you'll do better as a civilian than a partisan. Now scat."

"This is so wrong. How long do you think I'll live dressed like this?" He handed his pistol over.

"I can kill you, if that's what you want, and not miss a second of sleep tonight. I suggest you move north-east and try to avoid the paratroopers we just saw. I don't think they'll consider you a friend now." I intentionally let the sun sparkle off the sharp cutting edge.

When he turned and walked away, totally unarmed, I realized I was probably sending him to his death, but I could not feel sorry for the man. Everyone knew the rules and our laws. Just because the Russians had his family was not an okay to compromise our security. He was actually the only person I'd ever let go for being a traitor. I let him go mainly because of the paratroopers I saw and the fact I think the Russians will kill him for us. I couldn't afford a gunshot, so I felt this was best. Besides, he knew little as a Private and didn't even know where we were headed.

We hurried down the trail and we'd covered about a quarter of a mile, when I heard three or four sub-machine-guns open up. I suspected then Stevens was no longer a problem. It's very likely the only Russian who knew he was a plant was the Captain who gave him the device. I thought, *I hope Satan has a special place in hell for traitors.*

We moved quickly, because I knew we were being followed. At different distances, I'd have mines placed and toe-poppers, but so far I'd not heard a single explosion. Aircraft were now in the air and I think destroying the bug alerted them. They'd move to our last known position and then work out from there. It worked well in search and rescue in the civilian world, but partisans were experts with camouflage, and today we'd really put it to the test. I spotted a trail that I knew led to a swamp from my map, and we changed course. The Russians didn't like swamps much, and more than one squad had to be rescued after a few days wandering around in the wet and gator infested waters.

Mary neared and asked, "Why the direction change?"

"I don't want to get any closer to the safe house with the possibility of having two groups of Russians on my butt. So, I figure to take these boys muddin' a spell."

Mary took the radio and using code, since my mission was top secret, informed the General what was going on. He in turn, alerted some partisans and ordered them to come to our assistance. Some, from what I gathered, were close. In the meantime, we were to enter the swamp.

We moved through the water toward a trail Mary knew about that was almost 100 meters from our entry point. As we moved, gators raised their eyes to watch us, leaving their bodies underwater while water moccasins swam on the top of the water attempting to avoid us. I noticed the swimming snakes left small ripples in the water.

Once on the trail, I ordered mines placed at unusual locations and in one spot, when the trail forked, I had a large number of toe-poppers planted. Knowing we'd now have advanced warning if being followed, I had our speed increased. I glanced at the sun and knew it would be dark in a couple of hours.

"W . . .what kind . . . kind of snakes are there?" Carol asked and by her tone, she was terrified.

"Well, I've seen water moccasins and copperheads, but there aren't as many here now as there once was."

"Why's that?"

"Gators ate most of 'em." I said, and then smiled.

I heard a couple of low snickers, but Carol said, "I'm scared to death, and here you are joking about nasty snakes. Just the thought makes me shiver, and you joke like an ass."

Mary said, "Let's hope we don't have to spend the night here or you'll go insane. This place really comes alive at night."

"She's serious and so am I when I say this, but the bugs start making noises, the frogs, and mating calls of different animals are heard. A swamp or jungle comes alive with darkness, and that's when most of the critters come alive."

"Just great, but we're heading to a house?"

"Not a house as you know one, but an old structure built way back close to the Civil War, and it ain't much. Seems as the war was ending, a family of black folks fled their old master and ran in the swamp to avoid capture. Over the years, even after they knew they were free, they put up a home and lived there.

Oh, then one by one, malaria and other mosquito-borne diseases killed them. The last time I was here was over three years ago. It has a roof and that's all I can say about it. I want the roof in case they fly over with infrared systems looking for us tonight." Mary replied.

Carol grew quiet, but since I was behind her, I saw her head turning with each little splash of water or the slightest noise, and I suspected tonight would be a living hell for her. Most people have no idea of what a swamp sounds like after dark.

Less than a mile from dry land, we saw the remains of an old house, and it was on poles driven into the mud. It stood a good six feet above the water level and with a boost I sent Mary up to check the place out. Then, one at a time I lifted my troops until most were in the shack.

Finally, Brewer said, "Let me boost you up, sir. Then you can help us by pulling the rest of us in."

The place consisted of a living room, kitchen and one bedroom. I saw old beer cans, discarded papers, and other junk from happier times on the floor. We'd left Corporal Hall on the ground to guard for a couple of hours. Blankets were spread, meals were eaten, and folks moved in close to talk in low voices.

Carol moved closer to me and said, "Oh, this is *so* frightening to me! All the snakes, bugs and gators."

I tossed her a plastic bottle of Russian military issue insect repellent and said, "Rub this on all exposed flesh. The bugs aren't out yet, but they soon will be."

She was all eyes as she scanned the inside of the shack and applied the repellent. I almost laughed, except I knew she was scared.

Finally, she asked, "Can I sit closer to you?"

"Sure, and I can put my arm around you, if you want."

"I'm just scared is all." She scooted over the floor to me.

I put my arm around her and felt her relax. Before long, we were both asleep.

I have no idea how long I'd been asleep, but I woke to distant gunfire. I raised and then lowered Carol's head to the floor. Standing and moving to the door, I listened and heard it again. I'd guess the shots were less than a mile away.

I woke my people, all of them, and said, "Alford and I will move down the trail and see if we can see what's going on. We have NVGs, so we'll be safe enough in the darkness. Just need a quick look, see who came out on top, and then return here. While we're gone, see if you can reach anyone on the radio to see if this was one of the teams trying to link with us."

"I'll have Sara try to get Headquarters. No matter who it was, they either won or lost the fight, because it's grown quiet now."

I dropped my pack to Alford, lowered myself by hanging onto the edge of the floor and dropped to the ground. I landed standing and quickly donned my pack. I took point and pulled a sawed off 12 gauge shotgun from a pouch on my pack. I chambered a round and kept moving. In the distance I saw gators eating, walking on banks, and floating like logs. Snakes were much closer, and some were actually on the bank near the trail. We were almost to the clearing when I spotted movement and dropped to one knee. I saw a group of men moving toward me slowly.

I felt Alford tap me on the shoulder and when I looked back, he pointed down by my side. A water moccasin was laying beside my leg, almost touching it. I reached down with my right hand slowly, grabbed its tail and with a flip of my wrist threw him away from me. As the snake hit the water, I felt a shiver go through my spine, but quickly turned my attention back to the men approaching us.

I was unable to see who they were but they kept walking toward me as if they couldn't see me. I knew with my camouflage clothing and face paint, they saw nothing. I then saw a man with a dog and that was all the identification I needed. I leaned back and whispered, "Take the dog out and then the handler."

His rifle came up, I heard him take a deep breath, and then a second later heard the thunk of his silencer. Twice the rifle sounded and twice a target dropped. I then mined the path we were on and moved back toward the house, laying mines and toe-poppers off and on.

When we got there, Mary said, "Headquarters doesn't think they have a unit near us, but it's possible it's a group without a radio."

"Let Headquarters know it was a dog team. We put the animal and the handler down. They still may come after us, but if so, we'll hear them coming."

Right then I heard a 12 gauge shotgun shell go off and knew at least one man was down for the day. Five or so seconds later, I heard two more explosions. Now, at the least the men had a hole through a foot; at the most, they could have been killed by the shell. Most are seriously wounded, so I knew they would bring in a medical chopper in the morning to airlift the wounded out.

The remainder of the night was quiet and an hour before dawn I moved down the trail with my people. I carried a Russian made Strela 2, which are shoulder-launched surface-to-air missiles, easily capable of downing a chopper or even a jet. I was hoping to down a chopper. We arrived while it was still dark and moved in close to the Russians. Minutes later a false dawn arrived and I suspected my troops were getting antsy waiting.

The normal morning haze was missing on the water and in less than 30 minutes, I heard the familiar *whop-whop* of chopper blades. If I could shoot this baby down, it'd sure make my day complete.

I watched as the chopper grew nearer. I brought the tail section into the cross hairs on the viewfinder and waited for the loading of the wounded, so I'd kill more than a just helicopter crew. I watched as three stretchers were loaded and then a body bag. The chopper was right on the trail, with the right skid actually touching when I squeezed the trigger.

CHAPTER 6

When the Russian unit began to move, the Company Commander relocated them to a spot that would be easier to defend, established it as a staging point, and then sent them out in squad sizes to look for partisans. Each was equipped with a radio and plenty of ammo. He then had another company sized unit flown out to provide security for the supplies and gear that would eventually start arriving.

It was was mid-morning before Colonel Matveev received a report from his special parachute unit, that responded to infrared images picked up by a helicopter that day. The team had accounted for one dead American, and he was unarmed. Understandably the Special Unit Commander and Matveev were angry, but for the report by another unit that had ambushed a squad of Americans killing all of them; while it read great, it went on to say they'd come under sniper fire and lost the dog and the handler. Then, as they attempted to follow some footprints in the dirt, they exploded some booby traps, resulting in the injury of three others, with one critical. Over all, Matveev was pleased to have lost only one man and was able to claim a body count of 11.

Miles away, waiting for a helicopter, Senior Sergeant Pajari tightened the tourniquet on the Lieutenant's right arm and gave him a shot of morphine. He and two others were wounded from a toe-popper and mine. The young officer had been standing beside Junior Sergeant Georgiy when a toe-popper when off, striking both of them. Most of the blast had struck the Sergeant, but while moving during the blast, the Lieutenant detonated another toe-popper. The officer had sustained injury to his right arm and right foot. For Junior Lieutenant Mantorov Yanovich, his war was over.

Junior Sergeant Rykvov Georgiy, had taken the blast of a 12 gauge shell to his groin, which completely destroyed one testicle and tore up the other. He retained his penis, but there were a few holes in it as well. The buckshot then traveled into his lower stomach. From his belly button down to mid-thigh, he was wrapped in gauze. His right foot was mangled by the mine, and the Senior Sergeant didn't think the doctors could save it, so he'd walk with a limp the rest of his life, if he lived. Pajari placed the Junior Sergeant's head on his pack to keep him from the dirt, and fed him a little water, even though he knew not to give water to a stomach injury.

Then he moved to Private First Class Traktirnikov Ilyich and found him unconscious, but breathing easier than he had been earlier. He had been struck with ricocheting buckshot and took three to the lungs. The injury had been sealed, using plastic from a pack of cigarettes, front and back, and he was breathing better now.

Private Shmakov Antonovich, the radioman, said, "Helicopter will arrive in about five minutes. The pilot has requested smoke so he can see the winds."

The Senior Sergeant said, "Private Isaak, when I tell you, pull the pin on a smoke grenade and then drop it to the ground."

The Private moved away from the others and pulled a smoke grenade from a pouch on his belt. He then removed the tape holding the spoon down, placed a finger in the ring, and stood ready.

Thank God the normal fog and haze are missing from the swamp today or it would be hours before we would get these men to a hospital, Pajari thought as he looked to the skies for the aircraft.

"The pilot has us in sight and wants smoke now!" the radioman said.

"Isaak, ignite the smoke grenade, now."

The pin was pulled and the grenade tossed to the ground. Orange smoke began to spew from the metal container.

The Senior Sergeant guided the helicopter in by using his arms, and soon it was hovering near the trail, with one skid actually touching the soil. The three wounded were placed inside and finally the body bag. It was then they began taking small arms fire. A rocket or missile, the Senior Sergeant was unsure which, swooshed by narrowly missing the tail but exploding close enough to cause some damage.

The pilot's fairly calm voice was heard, "This is Medic One. I am taking ground fire! Taking fire, loaded, and departing. I have recovered three wounded and one dead."

The windscreen in front of the copilot shattered, the copilot's body stiffened, and then he went limp, as blood began to run down the front of his helmet.

The crew, machine-gunners at both doors, were now returning fire and seemed to be holding their own.

As the helicopter began to gain altitude, a Strela 2 missile fired, struck near the engine compartment, and while panels were blown away, the helicopter continued to gain altitude. Smoke began to pour from the engine of the aircraft.

"Base, this is Medic One, and I am enroute to the base hospital. Be advised I have taken battle damage and not sure if I can make the return trip. All of my master caution lights are on and my copilot appears dead."

"Copy, Medic One, we have a couple of Black Sharks that are near your position to give you a hand and watch over you on your return flight. If you must sit the aircraft down, let us know and we'll send someone to pick you up."

"Medic One, this is Badger One and I have you visual. I am approaching off your right side and from behind you. I will fly over and around you to check for damage."

"I have some damage to the tail rotor and engine compartment."

"Copy and you are smoking badly too, from your engine. Uh, I see no flames."

Giving a dry chuckle the helicopter pilot replied, "That is the only light that is not on right now, my fire lights. If I have to put this thing down, I do not think I will have much notice, so I may be too busy to talk when it happens. Already the stick is vibrating, so I think it is just a matter of time."

CHAPTER 7

I cursed as my first shot with the Strela 2 just caused some minor damage to the chopper's tail, but we carried one more. I lined up my sights on my last missile and when I squeezed the trigger, the aircraft dispensed chaff and while my aim was true, it exploded near the aircraft, but did not strike it as I wanted. I did have the satisfaction of seeing panels fly off and the bird began to smoke heavily.

I suspected it would go down before it reached Edwards Air Base.

The Russians, now under the leadership of a Senior Sergeant, broke contact with us and moved into the trees to lick their wounds. Normally I would have followed them, but I had a bomb to explode, so I walked from the swamp and started moving toward the safe house. I put Walker on point; she was a proven soldier, and had Brewer bringing up the rear. Dolly, walking at my side always made me feel safe because she could smell, hear and see better than any of us.

I had enough experience to know the Russians were still following us. The Senior Sergeant pulled back into the woods to give his young troops some time to breathe, eat, and unwind. After a short break, they'd come after us again.

Lea neared me and said, "Headquarters just notified me that the Russians are out in force and the units that attempted to reach us earlier are all being followed or have been fighting. Looks like no help any time soon. So, we're more or less on our own right now."

Mary looked at me and said, "We need to change directions and attempt to lose the team behind us. I see no reason to walk straight to the safe house and lead them there, too. I'm going to move to Walker and have her turn west a bit."

"We can try to lose them, but if that doesn't work, we'll ambush them, if we can. Brewer has a few mines to place, so he'll keep them honest."

"Let me climb a tree around here and I'll take out a bunch." Alford, the sniper, said.

"Do that, but take no chances. You know well how the sniper game is played, so do your job and then get back to us. Take no crazy chances."

Giving a dry chuckle, Alford replied, "Sir, I'm a sniper, and not a hero. I'll warn them off with a few well placed shots and then leave."

He then separated from us and moved into the trees. I said a silent prayer for him, knowing his task was difficult and dangerous. The difficult part was getting away, not killing Russians. Like most folks, the Russians hate snipers and if captured, Alford could expect a painful death. They'd probably torture him for days.

Less than twenty minutes later, I heard four evenly spaced shots, then the rapid reply of a Bison sub-machine-gun. I counted Alford as dead, but he showed up later with no injuries. He knew he'd killed one with a head shot, and dropped two more, one man with two bullets in him.

Most of the morning was quiet, but we did have to stop and hide from a couple of choppers that I suspected were working with the Russian team behind us. As far as I know they never spotted us because if they had, they'd have fired on us or called in some fixed wing aircraft. To the men behind us, it must have looked like we'd disappeared. We were experts at leaving few tracks, but no one can move and not leave some. Brewer's job, when he could, was to remove any tracks of us he spotted. At times he'd leave a clear track and then place a couple of booby-traps.

Near dark, we came to an old junk yard full of rusting cars and trucks. There must have been 200 cars and trucks spread over a few acres, and while I saw a building, I wouldn't stay there. That would be the first place the Russians would search. Mary had the troops move through the junk yard, leaving hand grenades with the pins pulled, but the spoon held down by parts of a car body. We then ran some nylon fishing line to another vehicle and secured it. The idea was once the line was pulled far enough, and it'd not take much, the grenade would slide out, the spoon would fly off, and an explosion would result.

We moved to the opposite side of the junk yard and made a night camp. It would be a cold camp since we were being followed. I then took Thompson with me and we walked to the house. I placed a couple of mines out front and then entered and booby-trapped the door with a grenade. I found two empty propane tanks, the kind used on barbecue grills, and placed them on each side of the grenade, and opened the valves. Since the building had two stories, I also booby-trapped the stairs about half way up.

Once we were done, we quickly returned to camp, hoping to eat before it turned dark. Once the meal was complete, we spread out and waited. The air was cool, with a bit of a bite, but not really cold. I had felt fine as long as we were moving, but now I was slightly chilled. I took a hard candy from my pocket and sucked on it for energy and heat. Our wait was a short one, right after the moon came out, and while I heard no grenades explode in the junk yard, I did spot movement.

When I glanced at Mary, she pointed at the house. I saw almost a squad of Russians moving for the place. I then lost them to darkness. I donned my NVGs and could see better, but at the distance much detail was missing.

As I watched, one man kicked the front door in, and seconds later as the Russians rushed in shooting, the grenade between the propane tanks exploded. The resulting explosion was huge with a gigantic fireball.

Must have still been a lot of propane gas in those cylinders, I thought, feeling nothing for my enemy. I was all out of compassion, having used the last of it a few years back.

The house was now in flames and I spotted four Russians outside. I heard the low *thunk* of our sniper rifle twice and two of our enemies dropped.

I moved to Mary and said, "I suggest we leave now. This place will be crawling with Russians, and it won't be long either. I'm sure they'll call this situation in to Headquarters."

Mary stood and said, "Saddle up and lets move. Brewer on point and Wied bringing up our rear. Keep your ears open for choppers."

We had a quiet night, and put some miles behind us. But near daybreak, we ran into a roadblock with a machine-gun nest. It was manned by five Russians, and they were up and cooking breakfast. I wanted to go around it, but trees were sparse here and I didn't want to take the time to walk miles out of my way. I wanted to get the bomb into Edwards and complete my mission. I had Hall crawl forward, with the intent of tossing a grenade in the sandbags. Three of the Russians were sitting on the bags as they ate. The other two were eating as they stood near the bags, making small talk. No one was alert or expecting danger.

I instructed Alford to take out any men the grenade missed.

I watched Hall moving slowly in the darkness and he was about half the distance to the machine-gun. Not once did a Russian soldier stop eating and scan the country-side. These men had been in the field too long, becoming bored and complacent. While I knew it was easy duty, away from Sergeants and officers, failure to stay alert would get them killed this morning.

Hall stopped, pulled two grenades from his web belt, removed the tape around the spoons, and I watched him in the dim moonlight straighten the cotter pins. He left one grenade on the ground, while he pulled the pin on the one in his hand. He let the spoon fly and tossed it right into the sandbags. The second grenade followed the first. The resulting explosions were loud in the cool morning air and the three men eating on the sandbags were no longer seen. Alford's sniper rifle accounted for the other two.

"Everyone stay where you are until sunrise; it's just a few minutes away." Mary ordered.

I was already tired, having carried my pack all night, and what I really needed was a full 8 hours of sleep, without interruption. *I need some serious rest*, I thought as I yawned. A few minutes later it was daylight.

"Let's check them out and if they move, put a bullet in them." Mary said as she stood.

We were well spread out when all of us, except Alford, moved to the gun. He remained behind to take out any trouble that might pop up. While our grenade assault looked effective, people often survive what looks to be a totally devastating attack for the on-looker. I would not be surprised to find two or three men alive.

We found the men dead, except for one. The wounded man had shrapnel in his belly and legs. He was laying on the pavement of the road in a pool of bright red blood. His eyes were large in fear and he was moaning constantly. I knew he was in severe pain, so I told Wied to give him just enough morphine to ease his pain. I warned her not to kill him.

I'd started a new program where we left the wounded alone, except we'd kill their pain and dress their wounds. I hoped it would bring about the same treatment for our wounded when cap-tured. So far, with the new Commander, I had no idea how he'd react. He'd been in place for less than a week.

"Take anything of use. Walker, check the machine-gun and see if it's still in good condition. If so, bring it and all the ammo."

When Walker neared with the weapon in her hand, I saw it was an old, 7.62×54mm, PKM Machine Gun. Lawdy, they'd been around since 1961 or so, but I knew it was an old dependable weapon. We had five boxes of ammunition, but that's a lot of weight to carry. It was then I saw a bicycle laying in the grass; I walked to it and looked it over. We'd do like the Vietnamese did during the Vietnam War and use the bicycle to carry our gear and supplies. I cut a long green limb from an oak tree, trimmed it of branches, and then attached it to the handlebars using the shoe laces of the dead men. With one person holding the limb, we could balance a heavy load easily.

I heard Carol speaking to the wounded Russian in his tongue, and found it strange she knew the language.

"He wants to know if we will kill him." she said, meeting my eyes.

"Tell him if the Russian Commander will stop killing our men, I will no longer kill injured Russian soldiers. This one is to live so he can carry my message."

"Marsha," Mary said to Wied, "Treat the Russian, but Susan, you cover her."

"Dolly, come." I said, and when she walked to my side, I said, "Sit."

"Tell him if he tries to hurt our medic, the dog will eat him alive," I said.

"I told him, and he's scared of Dolly, but wants to know if he'll be a prisoner of war."

"No, we'll leave him for his people to find. We're taking their radio, so when they don't call in a report or two, someone will come looking for them."

"I told him about half, but he's passed out."

"Excellent. Pull him away from the others and plant some mines and toe-poppers. I want grenades under each body. I think the Russians won't expect us to provide medical care to a man and then booby-trap his dead friends."

In their supplies, besides the machine-gun, ammunition, individual weapons, and some boots, we found two cases of rations, two dozen grenades, two bottles of vodka, and some long rolls of freshly baked bread. I placed my pack, all the gear we now had, along with the drink and food on the bike. I found balancing it was easy.

When we called in what happened with the machine-gun nest, we were ordered to move west about five miles and wait to link with another squad that would take us to the suitcase bomb. The safe house had been attacked, with heavy losses on both sides, but the suitcase was still in our possession.

Instead of thinking about my mission, I found myself looking at Carol as she moved around. It's important to remember relationships came up, even with partisans. No matter how badly life treated us, we were still human, and being loved is a basic need. She was a very beautiful woman in my eyes. I found her blonde hair and green eyes had captured my heart, but she was intelligent too, spoke fluent Russian, and her only weakness was she didn't like spending the night in a swamp. She'd impressed me, and that's not easily done. *Not once has she complained about being in the field, and I know it must be hard on her, because she works in intelligence*, I thought. *She's not a quitter, and that is a trait I demand in my women and friends.*

"Alright, let's move. We need to get to the spot so we can meet the other team. Same two on point and drag." Mary said.

Lea said, "Our password has been changed to 'water bill' and the team has been advised as well. Challenge with water and the reply should be bill. Expect rain tonight and part of tomorrow."

We began to move, taking our time. The bike, which I'd handed over to Thompson, was easy to move, and he even had his flamethrower on it. In a little more than an hour we were at the meeting spot and we began to dig in.

Carol neared and asked if she could dig in close to me.

"Sure, but dig deep." I teased, because we rarely dug foxholes.

"What will you do once the Russians leave?" she asked.

"Help put this country back together, if it's possible. See, one of the biggest mistakes we made in the old America was giving so much power to the Federal Government. Toward the end, 90% of the power was in Washington and about 10% with the states. That's exactly backward of what our founding fathers wanted. Thomas Jefferson warned us to avoid a big Federal government because it takes power away from the states, and he didn't trust big government at all. Our politicians were all corrupt, they lied and sold their votes to the highest bidder."

"Oh, I can't believe they were taking money for how they voted."

"You can't? Then explain to me how most of them left politics as millionaires, which was impossible to do honestly using their base pay. Lobbies, in my opinion, were the ones buying the votes and each party was guilty of being bought. The only real difference between the Democrats and Republicans was the sponsors. Some Senators and Congressmen had paying positions with companies that paid them millions a year, but they'd never stepped inside their office. Corruption breeds corruption, which is why some pretty stupid decisions were passed in the last four years of our nation. Folks took the money and voted to pass things they knew would hurt or destroy our country."

"Like what?"

"Well, like granting citizenship to millions of illegal aliens, because it put a tremendous drain on our available assets due to almost all needing some sort of public assistance. These illegals weren't professionals, or at least most weren't; some were criminals, and others were uneducated and worked in minimum wage positions. While we were taking care of illegals, we had veterans dying as they waited for care, and all our efforts seemed to be geared toward helping non-Americans first. I feel our priorities were wrong and our veterans should have been helped first. We should have sent the illegals home, billed their home country for the cost of transportation, and listed each illegal in the computer system as a criminal."

"I remember it happening, but I had no idea how bad off our country was at the time."

"What really showed our intelligence, or lack thereof, was taking almost 2 million Syrian refugees into our nation while they were expecting us to conform to their society. First, we were not in a good enough financial condition to bring others into our nation, and I feel if you come here to live, you become an American or return to your native land. If you think back you'll remember the increase in crime some of these folk caused once relocated here, they were always pushing their laws and religion on us, and some were guilty of terrorist activities. Just think, we brought the terrorists here, gave them a home, money, car, gave them full medical and dental coverage, and then found them a job. In turn, they blew us up to show how grateful they were.

You will remember the turmoil our President caused by siding with this group or that group, clearly against the wishes of the majority of the American people. Soon, it got so bad it seemed like a cop a day was being killed, some by the same organizations the President endorsed. Then, when folks were going to speak to Congress or the Senate about an investigation being conducted, they often had deadly accidents. No, I didn't see it then, but America was destroyed from the inside, not from without."

"So, what kind of America do you want?" she asked, and I could see she was honestly interested in my response.

"First, all political correctness bullshit needs to go out the window. We need a strong President who will have the sense, along with the guts, to make the proper decisions at tough times. We need to return the power of our nation to the people and their states. Politicians should not be able to accept funds, period, outside their basic government pay that we the people provide for him or her for the position they fill. There should be term limits for every politician, too. Lobbying should not be legal, because it's just another word for bribery, and those who accept cash should be charged with a felony. The President should not endorse anyone or any organization, not a one. He should only be allowed so many vacations days a year, paid out of his or her own pocket, and their vacations should be taken in the states, so our nation benefits from their money spent."

"Is that all?"

"Well, not really. I think God should be in all Federal buildings and schools, because our nation was founded on the Christian faith, and the freedom for Christians to worship as they wish. Special groups like atheists or other religions can simply ignore the crosses or statues that they dislike. Finally, our voting should be done by the actual number of votes by the people and not delegates. I couldn't believe the last few years of our nation, where anyone could vote, and no one needed identification to do so. Voting is such an honor and it makes sense to allow only our citizens to vote. I also think our judicial system needs a complete overhaul. I can remember a restaurant being sued because their coffee was hot but it had no warning printed on the throwaway cup, so when it spilled, it burned a customer, and what hot coffee is not hot? Millions of dollars were awarded, because the hot coffee was hot. Our judges need to start using a little common sense. I think there were some unjust sentences passed, too. Most crime was black on black crime, which I never understood. But say a white man killed a black during a robbery, the Department of Justice automatically made it into a hate crime. However, if a black man killed a white man during a robbery, it was a robbery gone bad. Our judges were so dumb most shouldn't have been left alone, much less rendering decisions in many cases."

"You've given this a lot of thought, haven't you?"

"Yes, I have, and still can't see exactly at what point common sense left our nation and the bleeding heart Liberals gained control. I can remember one election toward the end, when we had a man with no prior political experience, but he was one whale of a successful rich business man running against a liberal woman who should have not been allowed to run, because she was under investigation for keeping piles of classified information in her home. Then, we had a man, who in my personal opinion, was an open communist, running against the woman in the same party. Well, the woman won, was later convicted of having all the classified information, and sent to prison. The Vice-President at the time was another liberal, who unfortunately had no idea even how to spell President. Suddenly he was in charge and you know what the first thing he did was?"

"No, what?"

"He pardoned her and gave her a job working for him as an adviser."

I stood, yawned and made my way to the trees to pee. It was time for all of us to get some   sleep. When I returned, Carol asked, "Would you hold me in your arms like you did last night?"

I gave a low chuckle and said, "Sure, come over to me."

An hour before dawn, we were all awake and moving around. No fires were started and we began a day with no coffee, which always put me in a bad mood. I had Lea and Thompson go about five miles down our back trail, which they did, but they saw no one. I was apprehensive, because I couldn't figure out why the Russians didn't have another team on us. Maybe they didn't know what I carried or the importance of my group. They may have just written us off as a bunch of rednecks who could shoot well, but were no serious threat to their military.

Brewer, who was our explosives expert, soon had some C-4 burning, and we took turns heating water for tea or coffee. That stuff burned clean, clear, and gave off no smoke at all. As I sipped my coffee, I used an Arkansas stone on my knife blade. I carried an old skinning knife my dad once owned, and it was made of 440C stainless steel. It had a ten inch blade, and I'd had it since he gave it to me on my tenth birthday. I kept a razor sharp edge on all my knives because my dad used to say, 'More folks are injured with a dull knife that doesn't cut cleanly, than were ever hurt with a sharp knife. Never cut making sawing motions; use a saw, because a sharp knife will slide right through any meat. Your knife should be kept sharp enough to shave with at all times.' He was right, and to this day I keep a sharp edge on all of my edged weapons.

It was mid-afternoon when Carol elbowed me and pointed out a line of men moving toward us. I raised the binoculars I took off a Russian General we killed in retaliation for killing a large number of innocent civilians, and focused the glass. I glassed the area and they looked to be partisans, because each wore a white cloth around their left arm, but I didn't recognize a single person in the group. That in itself meant little, because I didn't know everyone. Our mortality rate was high anyway, especially with officers and senior NCO's. It wasn't unusual for a squad to have a completely new crew by the end of the year. Ours was a dangerous profession, but for damned sure worthwhile.

I handed the glasses to Mary who looked them over.

"They look fine, but something is not right." she said, mirroring my thoughts.

"Whats the new password for the day?" I asked.

"Disney . . . Land." Lea said.

"I saw a radio with them, so they should have the new password, too. Now, when they approach, I'll yell out and then listen for the counter word. If they give the wrong one or don't give a reply at all, I may start shooting. Only, no one fires until I do." Mary said.

I moved the machine-gun we'd stolen, along with a couple of cans of ammo, so James could use it, while Thompson was on the other side with his flamethrower. I hoped they were Americans but if not, it would be the first time the Russians had gone this far.

Mary yelled, "Disney!"

Silence filled the air.

CHAPTER 8

S ome armor, three T-90 tanks, were now with the Colonel in the field, which his troops laughingly called 'Tent City', and the single road down the middle of the tents was called 'Main Street.' Since moving to the forward operating base, he'd surrounded it with hundreds of land mines, barbed wire, razor wire, and construction was going on for two towers. Machine guns were manned 24/7 and they were evenly spaced around the perimeter. Sandbags were seen all over the base and there were never enough on hand.

Like some U. S. bases had done in Vietnam, human waste was collected in modified 55 gallon drums and burned once a week. The lucky troop of the day, removed the containers from the toilets, poured gas and diesel on the dung, then, using a long stick, mixed and burned the fecal matter. It was a horrible job with just the smell causing most men to gag. More than one man had been seen puking or with dry heaves as he worked this detail.

Unfortunately the Colonel was developing a false sense of security and felt, when completed, his staging base would be so strong no one could over run it. What he didn't think of was that half of the base population was usually in the field. Five to ten percent of those remaining were sick or unable to work, and the rest were not infantry, but made up of cooks, bakers, and administrative folks. Out of the 100 assigned to the base as security, only about 15 had ever heard a shot fired in anger. He was absolutely sure he was gaining control over the entire area, but that would change this night.

Colonel Matveev sent Senior Sergeant Pajari out with a T-90 tank to see why a machine-gun crew at a roadblock had not responded to any radio calls. Taking a squad of men, none of them combat troops, he loaded them on the tank and rode to the road-block. The men acted like kids on the big heavy tank, laughing and clowning around. The laughter stopped when they approached the dead men, who were easily seen from atop the tank.

Once the tank stopped the men jumped to the ground. One man moved toward the sandbags, but was suddenly covered with a sheet of red flames as he stepped on a Russian anti-personnel mine. The explosion was loud, but his screams of pain were much louder. Both legs were gone, his left arm was missing, and long coils of purple intestine were on the ground near him.

"Give him morphine, and do it now. You know what he needs." Pajari ordered, and nodded to the field medic, who knew to kill the man with an overdose. No doctor in the world could put this man back together or keep him alive.

"I will give him morphine in a few seconds, Senior Sergeant." the medic said as he checked for mines or booby-traps near the downed man. He marked two additional mines with sticks and then squatted beside the screaming man. Pulling a syringe, he gave the wounded man a fatal dose of the strong drug. Within seconds the screams died down to whimpers and then finally nothing was heard.

"Check each body closely for booby-traps."

Two men moved cautiously to a body beside the sand bags, looked around, and saw nothing out of place. One man took his shoulders and the other raised his legs. They lifted him and had moved for the tank, when an explosion from a grenade filled the air. Four men dropped to the ground, of which three were dead and one was seriously injured, with his left leg missing at the knee.

Growing angry that he'd already lost half of his squad recovering the bodies, Senior Sergeant Pajari said, "Stop and move to the other side of the tank. I will use a rope to pull the other three bodies before we touch them. Behind the tank you will be safe from the explosions."

Thirty minutes later, with five explosions, the job was done. The wounded Russian was found and Pajari was surprised the partisans had given the man first aid. While he was unconscious, he was very much alive and he was the first the Senior Sergeant had heard of that wasn't killed following a partisan attack. He loaded the dead machine-gun crew on the tank, as well as his four dead troops and two wounded, and returned to the base.

Once at the base, the now conscious lone survivor of the machine-gun crew told the Commander that the partisans would stop killing the injured, if the Russians stopped. The injured man was begging the Colonel to not kill Americans when he passed out.

Colonel Matveev laughed and said, "We'll kill every damned partisan we find, injured or not."

The Colonel was more upset the machine-gun and radio were missing, along with the gear the men had, than the deaths of his troops. His frustrations of dealing with partisans were just starting.

"We had four killed and one severely injured recovering the bodies of our comrades, sir. Each of the bodies was booby-trapped and none of the men with me were field troops. The injured man will survive, but he'll get a medical discharge, sir."

"Why don't the bastards stand and fight us, toe to toe? I *hate* this type of fighting because it's the way a coward fights. It reminds me of the old American cowboy movies and how the Indians would hit and then run from the white man."

"Sir," Senior Sergeant Pajari said, "they fight like partisans all over the world fight. However, we will lose less men if we agreed with the no kill policy."

"Enlisted troops are expendable, including you, Senior Sergeant. I will not treat partisans that we find. They will be shot immediately and by my orders. You keep your men under control, while I do the thinking here. God has a reason I am a Full Colonel and you are a Senior Sergeant."

"Yes, sir. I was just offering my thoughts, is all."

"When I want your thoughts, I'll ask you for them, Sergeant. Now go take care of your men."

"Yes sir, I'll do that." Pajari replied, and as he walked away thought, *Why you arrogant ass, your hard-headed attitude will see hundreds, if not thousands, of young Russian boys and girls murdered, but why? Why, Colonel? Is it because you see having a little compassion for our enemy as a weakness? Lord, God, save us all.*

The big tank, as well as the dead and wounded on the tank were seen by two partisan troops that were just outside the wire of the base. They would soon return and bring news of the dead and wounded. They also got a rough estimate of the troops on the base, counted the tanks, and noted the location of all machine-guns on crude maps. They noticed the camp had an entry point that was not mined, so vehicles and personnel could move in and out freely. This was also noted on the map. They then melted into the trees to return to their units.

The rest of the day was normal at the base, with the dead and wounded picked up by helicopters that also dropped off rations, ammunition, and more importantly, the mail. Mail call took place and it was the first mail since they had arrived at the base. For some, their first mail would also be their last. Two lowly Privates stood on a hill, burning human waste, which caused more than one man to refuse to eat supper. The overpowering smell of burning human feces had many men retching with the dry heaves.

Vodka, which was brought on the base by many of the men even though it violated army regulations, was opened and drinks were shared. The Senior Sergeant knew the enlisted men had hard drink, but did nothing about it. He felt if the officers were issued vodka in the field, his enlisted men should be allowed to drink as well, as long as they didn't get out of hand. Vodka was the national drink of all Russians and while Pajari had tasted bourbon, whiskey, tequila, cognac, and other hard drinks, nothing beat the taste of Russian vodka to him.

At dusk the generators came on to power the radio tent, the Commanders quarters, and the search lights. Additionally, all three tanks had powerful search lights mounted on the turret. One tank was down due to a thrown track and the crew was happy it happened on base and not out in the boonies. The night was clear, with millions of stars seen sparkling overhead, and a light warm breeze from the west. While many would eat now because the scent of burning human waste was much less, it still lingered faintly and few would eat a full ration.

At 2100 hours, the base grew quiet except for the men working on the tank, and the troops went to their sleeping bags. Guards manned their positions and settled in for another boring night of passing time. At the end of their shift, they'd be replaced by another bored soldier, and they would then try to sleep.

Pajari was a man who didn't require much sleep, and he was likely to be seen moving around among the young guards, making sure they were awake. He knew that most of these young men and women were still in school or living on the farm a year ago, and they weren't really soldiers. To be a real soldier required years of combat experience, not just completing boot camp and other fast classes on how to survive in the field. While the men and women were as qualified as any new soldier in the world, they had yet to actually apply what they'd learned. Pajari knew application would be a real killer for some.

All was quiet until near 0100 hours, when a machine-gun outside the base opened fire. The gunner was good too, spraying short bursts that wouldn't burn the barrel out. Two of the men working on the broken tank fell, killed instantly by the bullets from the machine-gun. Then small arms fire and the dull thump of mortars being fired were heard outside the Russian base camp.

Pajari ran to the communications center and yelled, "Tell base we need air support, now! This is not a probe!"

It was then that a radio call from a machine-gun crew said, "We have hundreds of partisans in the east wire!"

The old Senior Sergeant knew that was grossly overestimated, but it was likely sappers were moving in the wire to disarm mines and to cause hell if they could breach the wire.

The same radio reported, right after the explosions of four motor shells, "The safe access wire is gone, most of it taken out by the mortars. I am moving my gun to defend the open area!"

The radio room was suddenly a confusing place with calls coming in reporting this or that and it was hard to keep it all straight in his mind. He then heard a big boom from one of the tanks, and a second later another tank fired as well.

Then they heard a man shouting over the radio, "We have a flamethrower at the entrance and the machine-gun is no longer working. For the love of God, we need more troops at the entrance—now! Send people immediately or the next time you hear a voice on this radio, it will not be mine."

Explosions were heard all over the base and the Senior Sergeant wondered where the Commander was, or if they'd gotten lucky and he'd been killed. He left the communications tent and made his way to the Commander's quarters. More than once he had to turn and fire at a dark form running toward him. When he arrived at the Commander's tent it was burning, and looked like it had taken a direct hit from either a mortar round or an RPG.

He moved back to the communication center, knowing the Commander would show up there, if alive, but when he returned the Colonel was not to be seen.

A scared voice said, "They've breached the wire on the north side, I repeat, they've breached the wire on —" The radio went dead, but all heard the firefight in the background.

Pajari went out to move some men to the north side and saw partisans all over the base. They were being overrun. Two of the T-90 tanks were in flames, one was sitting with the main gun lowered. The turret began to move and the cannon barrel was raised. The machine-gun on the tank came alive, dropping partisans in the pathway blown through the wire. Then the big 125 mm smoothbore gun fired and screams were heard. Slowly, the tank began moving, and as it moved, it began killing more partisans. An RPG struck the tank in the side, but the steel-composite-reactive blend armor was not pierced. The projectile struck hard, but caused no real damage. A head showed in the hatch on the turret, and the man began firing a machine-gun mounted on the turret.

Out of the blue, a wall of flame struck the front of the tank, and moved up, engulfing the man in the open hatch with flames. The screams of the burning tank Commander were heard above the other sounds of battle and his body shook and jerked. The man burned a minute or so and then slumped over the hatch, dead. A few seconds later his body was pushed out of the hatch and he fell to the ground still in flames. The hatch then lowered.

A partisan ran to the tank with a canvas bag and placed it right above the tracks as they moved. It looked to the Senior Sergeant as if one side of the bag had tar or something applied to make it stick. He fired twice at the partisan, but saw no indication he'd struck the man. Within seconds, the partisan was gone, blending in well with the others. Slowly the Americans were being beaten back, but right then the bag on the tank exploded. The tank stopped moving, as a long link of track rolled off the right wheels to lay flat on the ground. Smoke from the explosives rolled from the tank. The driver could only drive in a circle now, which he did, sending death in many directions.

Sticking his head in the door of the communications tent, the Sergeant yelled, "Get all available aircraft above us, and do it now!"

"Air support was requested over twenty minutes ago." a young Major said.

The Sergeant walked to a radio and pushing the mic said, "Base, this Senior Sergeant Pajari and I want air support and *now*, damn you. I have partisans up to my ass, cannot find the Commander, and he is assumed dead, so you either give me aircraft now or I will kick your collective asses when I return!"

"No, I do not give a damn if you are a Lieutenant . . . sir! I have Russian men and women dying here and I demand you support us as required. Yes, yes, okay, sir. It had better be here damned soon, or you will find the base under new ownership."

"Tent City, this is Black Shark One. Where do you need us? I am leading a group of three attack helicopters." the leader of the three Black Sharks asked.

"Uh, wait one." Pajari said as he picked up the radio and moved outside.

"I need a couple of runs on the north side and bring your munitions into the wire. I request you use your 30 mm gun on the north side. Then from our perimeter to the trees use rockets. We are under heavy attack."

"Any side that needs the rockets more than others?"

"Negative, they are all over us!"

"Get your heads down. I will spray the north side with 30 mm, and Black Shark 2 will spray the east and the last bird, Black Shark 3, will spray the west. I have some fast movers coming and they will drop napalm. Once they work the ground over, I will place missiles where you need them. I am rolling in hot now."

The chopper's 30 mm rounds did unbelievable damage to the partisans, with body parts thrown high in the air as screams filled the night. The next two passes were just as costly to the Americans, so they began to pull back with long blasts from whistles. The temporary fuel dump for the tanks blew, sending rolling flames high into the air. As the fuel burned, the night was suddenly as bright as day, and partisans were seen moving out of the wire and running toward the trees. The Americans knew from experience napalm was coming next.

Black Shark[2] 3 rolled in and lined up on the west side. As he began spraying the ground with 30 mm rounds, a Strela 2 missile fired, striking the aircraft just aft of the pilot's position. The instant the helicopter exploded, the pilot ejected and was seen dropping to the ground in his parachute, but every partisan on the ground was shooting at him. The chopper fell to land in the wire around the base, exploding with a huge fireball, as the fuel and ammunition detonated. The pilot landed inside the base, but suffered from burns and two gunshot wounds, neither of which were considered life threatening.

The remaining two Black Sharks reported seeing what looked to be thousands of partisans on the ground. They both used up their rockets and then called to say they needed to return to Edwards Air Base to refuel and rearm.

As the choppers left to refuel and rearm, the fast moving jets arrived.

"Uh, Tent City, this is Tiger one. I have two other MiG-31's with me. I will drop my napalm first, so where to you wish me to drop the containers?"

Pajari said, "Tiger one, this is Tent City, the partisans have pulled back into the trees. I need you to drop your napalm in the

---

2 The Russian Black Shark Attack Helicopter is equipped with an ejection seat. Before the ejection seat fires, the rotor blades are blown off, and the canopy is removed as well. A two seat, side by side, version of the Black Shark is made and actually called a Kamov Ka-52 "Alligator," but most troops call both versions a Black Shark.

trees to the west, then have the other two aircraft hit the trees to the north and south sides of us."

"Copy, and will do."

The base was still lit up like it was day, and the Senior Sergeant was out in the open with the radio so he could direct the attacks. He felt a heavy blow to the front of his helmet and it was hard enough it knocked him off his feet. For a minute or two he didn't move, and while he felt warm blood on his face, he felt no serious pain. Crawling to a destroyed machine-gun pit circled with sandbags, he climbed in and then checked himself for injury. His helmet had a bullet hole in the front and an exit hole in the rear. His head had a slight burn from a bullet, right where his hairline started and that was it, or all he could find. The shot came from the west side of camp. He donned his helmet and peered over the sandbags. The MiG-31 was approaching the woods at a high rate of speed and he saw two metal containers fall from the aircraft, tumbling end over end as they dropped to the woods.

There came a big splash of flame, and then a wave of fire crested and fell. The Sergeant knew anything near the fire was dead. The second approach to the north went smoothly and screams were heard as the flames covered the trees. It was with the third aircraft that a serious mistake was made.

The Aircraft lined up properly, along the south. Seconds before the pilot was to release his containers of napalm, two Strela 2 missiles fired, with one missing the aircraft but the other hitting a wing. The aircraft suddenly nosed up and the pilot and weapons system operator ejected. The aircraft continued forward, now out of control, and impacted on the southern section of the base, creating a huge explosion that destroyed all the defensive wire and killed many Russian soldiers. The pilot landed safely on the base, but all watched in horror as the weapons system operator's chute drifted or was pulled to the napalm flames. Then, a couple of the nylon panels on the parachute burst into flames. Within seconds, still hundreds of feet in the air, the whole parachute exploded into flames and the man dropped into the burning woods.

The fight was over for now, but it brought a quiet that was so loud it almost hurt the ears of Senior Sergeant Pajari.

Looking around, he saw the base was a mess with injured and dead bodies of Russians and Americans thrown around like so many toy soldiers. Unfortunately, these soldiers bled and screamed as they died, with few dying quietly. Most of the tents were gone, burned, and the two destroyed tanks were throwing dark black smoke from their engines into the air. The third tank was still spitting machine-gun bullets into the woods. At odd times the cannon would fire at some target only the gunner could see with his NVGs.

As men began climbing out of foxholes and moving from behind sandbags, the Sergeant walked toward the burning aircraft wreckage in the southern wire. Medics were already on the job removing the wounded, but unable to recover many of the dead because many were still burning. The sweet smell of burning human flesh joined the smell of burning human crap, to make even the hardest soldier puke. After wiping his mouth clear of vomit, the Senior Sergeant pulled an aluminum flask from his cargo pocket and drank the whole half-pint without stopping.

Pulling the senior medic aside, Pajari said, "The Commander is missing and was last seen in his quarters. I need some of the men to look for him. I know his tent took a direct hit from a mortar."

"There may not be much to recover then, but we will look for his remains."

It will sure be a shame if they find the sonofabitch dead, the Senior Sergeant thought, and then smiled.

CHAPTER 9

When she didn't get a response, she yelled once more, "Disney!"

"Mickey Mouse." came the response.

"Disney, and if you are wrong this time, we'll start shooting."

Silence.

Finally the same voice said, "Goofy."

Our machine-gun opened up, as well as the flamethrower, and seconds later almost the whole group was dead. Most of the bodies were still partially burning when we heard one young man screaming in pain. Hall disarmed the man and searched him, removing all weapons. Then Wied moved to the man to give him enough morphine to kill his pain, so we could speak with him. While he was dressed as a partisan, I suspected he was a Junior Sergeant or young officer, because of his age.

Five minutes later, I asked him, "Do you speak English? Are you still in pain?"

"I speak English, all of us do. My pain is not as deep, like before, so when will you kill me?"

"All of your comrades spoke English? If you answer my questions, you will live." I was surprised at his English and heard no accent. I pulled my skinning knife to get his attention.

"Yes, I will answer your questions. To be able to speak fluent English was required to be selected for these special units. Those who spoke British English were not accepted."

"Where did you learn American English?"

"I was born in Russia and raised in Saint Louis, Missouri. I can speak both Russian and English well. When my father died, my mother and I returned to Moscow."

"How many units are formed like yours and where are you based?"

"There are six such English speaking units in Mississippi, but more are being assembled all the time in Russia. Once they receive more training on American customs they will be sent here. My home base is in Jackson."

We stripped the dead of anything useful and found a radio, which we also took. I pulled the medic, Marsha Wied aside and said, "When you give him his next morphine shot, give him too much. He has special skills that make him valuable. I seriously dislike doing this since I gave him my word he'd live."

"Colonel, I don't think I can do that. This man will live if found soon enough by his army, and you gave your word to him."

"Damn it, he speaks fluent English. How many American lives will he help take later, once healed?"

"I'm sorry, sir, but I can't do it. I was trained to save lives and not take them, unless my patient is going to die; then I'm to give meds to allow them to pass without pain. You want me to murder that man. Sir, with all due respect, do your own damned killing. I'm more than surprised you are breaking your word, too."

I pulled my Russian pistol, walked to the injured Russian Sergeant and fired twice, both shots hitting a different knee cap. He screamed and jerked around on the ground. Wied ran to the man and began working on him, and I'm sure she silently cursed me as she fixed him up.

I thought, *He might speak English, but he'll need a wheelchair to get around in the future, because they'd be forced to remove both of his legs. Damn, I hate this war, but it's all about survival.*

"Now," I said with my voice filled with sarcasm, "as soon as you're done, Florence Nightingale, we have a mission to complete. unless you want to stay with your patient. By law, I could have shot the man as a spy, since he's out of uniform and dressed like a partisan, but I feel generous this day."

"I have a mind to report you, sir, for abusing a prisoner."

"Report to who? I'm your Commander and I work for the General, who has ordered all Russian prisoners executed, especially spies. He'll laugh you out of his office."

We were soon moving again; Wied was pissed, but I figured she'd either get over it or not, and it didn't matter to me what she did. There was no way in hell I was going to let an English speaking member of a special unit recover and then go right back to work. Now he'd lose both legs, but he was alive. I should have killed the bastard.

I heard of the attack on the Russian Forward Operating Base via our radio and was overwhelmed at the number of dead, wounded and missing in action we'd experienced. We had no idea of the real damage we'd caused, but I wondered if our initial estimates of the attack made it well worth the cost in pain and human lives. The attack had cost the Russians a lot of material, manpower, and equipment. Two T-90 tanks were knocked out, the fuel storage area was destroyed, approximately 80% of all shelters were gone, and we couldn't even guess at the number of dead and wounded the Russians had on their hands. They'd also lost two valuable aircraft, a Black Shark and a MiG-31, and at least one pilot or weapons system operator from the MiG had died when the flames from napalm ignited his parachute.

I thought of the attack and cost to the Russians, but they didn't think like we did. This cost meant nothing to them. What hurt the Russians was our refusal to comply with their orders and for us to raise up against them. While the average soldier wasn't aware of it, the Russian people at home were getting tired of receiving their sons and daughters back from the United States in aluminum boxes. The war had been going for over five years now, with still no end in sight. I knew beyond a doubt we'd never stop fighting as long as one healthy American remained alive.

The area we were in now didn't have many trees and I felt like a sitting duck. After we were about five miles from where I'd shot the Russian, I suggested to Mary we try to cover the open areas tonight, not now in the daytime. Many partisans were killed each year when they were caught out in the open by aircraft.

"Makes sense to me." Mary said and then added, "We'll move under the oaks in that small grove off our left. I want two guards on at all times and wake us all if you hear or see anything."

As the Commander, I wasn't expected to pull guard duty, but in the field, I did everything I expected my men and women to do. I took the first shift with Alford, while the others ate or tried to get some sleep. As a partisan, a hot meal, a shower, and a good nights sleep were hard to come by. Usually we washed in a stream, had our meals out of Russian cans, and slept in blankets or sleeping bags furnished by the Russian bear.

As we sat, Alford said, "It bothers me that the Russians are creating special units of English speaking men and women, sir."

"Why? It's been done before." I replied, and then swept the area once more with my binoculars.

"Really? When?"

"During the Battle of the Bulge in December 1944, the Germans sent special English speaking units forward to confuse the Allies, and it almost worked. The men the Germans used were so good they spoke American slang, knew our baseball teams, knew neighborhoods in parts of the larger US cities, and were hard to tell from the real GI. The special units switched road signs, removed signs with the names of towns, cut phone lines, disrupted communications when they could, and generally made a mess of things. Most where killed when American units determined who they were. All in all, they didn't accomplish as much as the Germans thought they would, but they were dressed and used American gear, right down to dog tags. My great grandfather fought in the battle and said they shot every one of the men they found. They considered them a serious threat and spies, as I do English speaking Russians dressed in partisan clothing."

"Wow," Alford said, "ain't that something."

"Stick with me, son, and I'll learn ya."

He gave a low chuckle and then asked, "Do you ever wonder what kind of future America has?"

"Oh, sure, but it'll damned sure not be as a liberal nation, because that caused most of the problems that led to our fall as a country. When we started spending more money than we had coming in, we were in serious trouble. But, instead of cutting our spending, we just borrowed more money. Can you imagine running your home budget like that? Then, they just printed more money with no gold or silver to back it up. You'd end up in jail for writing bad checks. Anytime a country prints more money than it has assets to back it up, that nation is living on borrowed time."

"Yep, seemed to me we were trying to help the world, while our own people did without."

"That was messed up, too. We learned, and hopefully our new nation will be better and stronger, and it can be, if we remember what led to this fall. Now, enough talk and let's spend more time watching and listening."

Two hours later I slipped into my sleeping bag and few minutes after, heard and then felt Carol place her sleeping bag beside mine. I was instantly asleep. I awoke before dusk to find her in my arms and her head on my chest. I carefully raised her head and lowered her to the sleeping bag.

I walked over to Mary and Lea, who were pulling the last guard shift.

"Quiet?"

"All the night sounds are there and no reports of any aircraft all day."

"When do you want them up?" I asked.

"Give them about thirty more minutes, because moving all night is twice as tiring as moving during the day, or so I think."

"What do you think of those English speaking Russians?" I asked.

"I think our medic needs to grow-up a great deal. That man was clearly out of uniform, looking to blend in with us, learn some secrets, and possibly kill some or all of us. There is only one sentence for spying—death. I think you did the man a favor, but he'll never realize it, or so I think."

"I've found medical folks too tenderhearted for our line of work. To be on the line, so to speak, you have to be a total warrior, plain and simple. No, I don't want or need killers, but we do need people who are willing and capable of killing when it's needed. Now, don't misunderstand me, because most medics are brave folk, but they're into healing, not killing."

"Must be something that makes them different from us then." Lea said.

"I think deep inside most medical folk hate violence, when at times, like in a war, the only thing your enemy will understand is brute force, with no quarter given or asked."

"But yet I've seen many of them run into gun-battles to save a downed person, so they're not cowards." Mary replied.

"No, none are cowards, but medical folk see first hand the wasted resources, the loss of lives, the missing limbs, and other serious injuries that come through their hospitals by the hundreds and thousands. That has to sadden them, because it would anyone. Then, the field medics have to treat people with injuries on the spot, so you know after so many times, a man or woman will have developed PTSD. Hell, I think most of us these days would be classified by the old VA as 100% PTSD disabled. I've shot men, knifed men, blew them up, and have burned some alive, all in the name of America. Do I have bad dreams? You bet I do, and I know you two do as well."

"I have them, but John, there is no other way to get our country back than to fight for it. I'm old enough to remember the old America, with sock-hops, drive-in restaurants, and being able to sleep at night with the front door and windows open so fresh air could enter. I can remember my family, all dead now, gathering around the table, and I want my old America back. All was fine until the hippies grew up." Mary said.

"Quiet, I just saw movement from the south." Lea said, and then went to ground.

I moved back into the dark shadows of the trees and woke the squad, one at a time, by touching their ankles. We all moved into defensive positions and I heard safeties being switched to off.

I looked south and now saw three men and point man moving cautiously over the open field. I watched Mary pickup the clacker for a Claymore mine, preparing to detonate the big beast, and it was then I saw the men were dressed as Partisans. They wore a mix of Russian and civilian clothing.

When all were easily within rifle shot, and most within Claymore distance, Mary said, "Disney."

The point man whispered, "Land."

"Come." Mary said.

The squad moved under the shelter of our trees and we quickly explained about running into the special Russian unit made of men fluent in English. They lowered their heavy packs and other gear, and then I saw an old friend.

"Top, how in the hell are ya?" I asked as I moved to shake his hand.

"I've been better and I've been worse. How is the world treating you, Colonel now, isn't it?"

"Yep, but that means little in a partisan unit."

"Not true, sir, because this is a hard place to get promoted. I've been involved for years and I'm still an E-9."

I laughed and said, "You'd just turn a promotion down. It'd be a lost of prestige for you to become an officer, unless they made you a full bull. I think you'll be the only E-9 in history to have 60 years of active duty under your belt when you finally retire."

"I'm worried to hell and back about the use of nuclear weapons. I'm in disagreement with the General on the use of the suitcase nuke, but I was told to shut my mouth, by him. Look, the use of the nuke by the Russians has given them a lot of bad publicity, not that they give a damn, but the Chinese are now suddenly sending us gear and materials we can use. They've even offered to bring in Chinese troops to help us out, along with armor and aircraft."

"What do they want in return?" I asked as I sat on a log.

"Nothing, they claim, but I think they just haven't spoken what they really want, yet. That, or else they truly hate the Russians, which I'm willing to believe. I don't think they care who's fighting the Russians as long as they beat them."

"I know little of the Chinese."

"I don't care about the Chinese, but as long as they can supply us with what we need to take this fight up a few levels, I'll work with them. Now, before I get busy talkin', we'll take you to where the suitcase is hidden over the next few days. Right now, that's all you need to know. Do you have all you need to complete your mission?"

"Yes, I do."

"Well, get your leader, and why don't the three of us talk?" Top said, and his whole face beamed with a big smile.

I called Mary over and she sat on the log beside me. She knew Top, we all did, but I know neither of us were prepared to hear his words.

"I don't want to use the Nuke, but I will follow orders. The location for detonating the suitcase bomb has changed—to close to Jackson. Intelligence says if worked right, we will be able to pass it off as a Russian nuclear mishap. The Russians have not said a word to the press about us stealing the suitcase bombs and it's not likely they will either. So, right after the bomb detonates, we'll release a statement about the cruelty of the Russian Bear."

"My God," Mary said, "does the General know how many people, American people, that will be killed in Jackson?"

"Mary, those people in Jackson, most of them anyway, are doomed. The first bomb they exploded is dropping radioactive dust all over Jackson, because most of the time our winds come out of the west and blow east. During the last few weeks, well, there have already been some folks come down with radiation poisoning, and from all over the middle of the state. This fallout is a real killer and I'm sure, after this second bomb, we'll lose maybe a million people before it's over. Now, I really don't know what the losses will be, but you're to plant the suitcase in Pearl, and you both know where that is."

"Why Pearl?" I asked, because Pearl was a small town.

"The damage done by the bomb will extend for approximately 8 miles, and the goal is to take out the International Airport, along with the runways, and most of the structures in Jackson. Since the main Russian Headquarters for the state is right on the edge of the Pearl River, it will be flattened too. We estimate around 20,000 Russian deaths, or more, and around 100,000 civilians. Now, that does not consider deaths from fallout, but the blast only. The additional benefit of using the bomb on Jackson is the initial blast will kill, maybe, three General officers, most of the department heads of the various services who are important Full Colonels, along with their intelligence experts and anti-partisan units. What the idiots at Edwards didn't figure was the wind shifts, which have already exposed most of their troops to the fallout."

"How do we intend to keep our own people safe?" I asked, not liking the number of civilian folks I'd kill.

"Most partisan units will be relocated to the southeast and southwest corners of the state, away from prevailing winds. The Russians have bases down that way too, so when your bomb goes off, we'll hit those bases hard. We suspect when we hit them, the confusion caused by your bomb will put a big dent in Russian air support. The Jackson Airport and all the assigned aircraft will be flattened and destroyed. While there are other airports in the state, the runways are too short for all the big cargo planes to land." Top said.

"Hell, Top," Mary said, "they can use a low altitude parachute extraction system (LAPES) to drop anything from tanks to rations."

"Oh, we seriously hope they try that, ma'am, because we'll shoot them down with Russian made Strela 2 missiles. Cargo planes are much slower than a fighter jet and we've downed them, as well as choppers, in large numbers. This has been thoroughly thought out, but I don't like killing all the innocent people in Jackson."

"You just said a few minutes ago that most have been exposed to fallout, so this may end up a mercy killing for them. At least in a nuke detonation, they'll feel nothing. Here one minute and dead the next." Carol said.

"I hear you, but it's not an easy call, only I didn't give the Order, General Bill Thomas did and he's a damn fine Christian man. I'm sure much praying went into his decision, but that aside, we need to show the Russians we will retaliate when we can."

"My God, all those deaths, and caused by this unit. Killing Russians means nothing to me, that's why I'm here. I think I need to concentrate on the fact most of the population of Jackson will die anyway, from fallout. It's the only way I can complete this mission and remain sane." Mary said.

"We'll complete our mission, regardless of the cost in lives, Top, but I want the General to know I disapprove of this on moral grounds and I'm not sure it's a legal order." I said.

"It's no different than when Hiroshima or Nagasaki were bombed with nukes during the second world war."

I ran my fingers through my filthy hair, met his eyes, and replied, "May God have mercy on all our souls. Now, do we leave now, or tomorrow for the bomb?"

"We'll leave here within the hour."

CHAPTER 10

Colonel Matveev was alive, but disoriented and filthy as he was pulled from the rubble of his quarters. He had a nasty gash on his forehead, some bruises and his left earlobe was missing. Once his mind cleared of the fog of being rescued, he sat up and looked around his base. Senior Sergeant Pajari was sitting beside him, feeding him a few sips of vodka, because most of the morphine was used up treating the seriously injured.

"How . . . how many casualties do we have?"

"No clear figures yet, sir, but around 80 killed, wounded, or missing. That is out of 106 assigned to the base. If not for the air support we got, we would likely all be dead right now. We lost two of the T-90's, a Black Shark and a MiG-31."

"Contact Base and tell them I want another company sent out here and I want them on station today. Then when they arrive, I want you to put them to work cleaning this place up. How many confirmed partisan kills?"

"Many of the bodies were removed by their comrades, sir, but at last count, there were over 200 dead and injured."

"Were the injured executed like I ordered?"

"Yes, sir. We are still counting bodies, so it will be close to the end of the day before this mess is organized."

"When you call Base, inform them we need tents, medical supplies and other gear."

"I have a list already, and it is a rather long one."

"Did they breach the wire?" Matveev groaned because his head hurt. He took the bottle from the Sergeant and downed about a half-pint of the strong clear drink.

"The wire did not even slow them down, sir. We need more mines and much more wire in place. I have it on my list."

"Call Base now and get them to moving and if need be, tell them I ordered the supplies and expect them delivered, along with the men, today."

Pajari stood and made his way to the communications tent. When he arrived, the area was roped off and he was told a live mortar round was found right beside the tent with the nose buried in the dirt. The Explosive Ordnance Disposal (EOD) folks were working on it. However, two radios were removed from the tent and near the gate.

The Senior Sergeant placed his request for supplies, gear, and infantry troops, and ordered it all using the Colonel's name. He knew within a couple of hours the stuff would start arriving. In the meantime, he had his people cleaning the base and looking for dead and injured. The place was an absolute mess, with charred gear and tents all over the place, not to mention the dead bodies, Russian and American, were starting to stink. The wounded were lined up with the worst wounded at the front, so they'd be placed on a helicopter first. The crashed MiG was still burning, as well as the fuel storage area, and partisan bodies were hanging in the razor wire.

He'd have the new troops remove the bodies from the wire. His people had been up all night and they were too tired to be messing with land mines. He knew as exhausted as they were, they'd kill a few of their troops trying to do the job. He'd have a bulldozer brought in, have some trenches dug and have the aircraft wreckage pushed outside the base and buried. A series of deep trenches, dug on the base, would make movement under fire safer and easier.

We really do not need to be here at all, he thought as he noticed a human hand in the dirt. He kicked it away and then stood watching the MiG burning. *Millions of rubles for aircraft gone up in smoke. I hate to think how much the aircraft cost and the two T-90 tanks. I wonder what we spend a day in this war.*

"Senior Sergeant!"

"What do you need, Private?"

"We have two helicopters about five minutes out, and they have some of the men you have requested. Then, behind them, we have supplies and gear coming. Base assures me all you requested will be here before dark. Also, the Chief of the Anti-Partisan Unit has requested you return to Base, to personally brief him on what happened here. He seems to think the partisans are up to something and the attack last night was done so we will concentrate our forces in this area."

"Tell him I will be on the first helicopter returning to Base."

"I will do that, Senior Sergeant."

Soon the sound of helicopters approaching filled the dirt base as rotor blades beat the air. One aircraft landed in a clearing, ammunition and rations were kicked out the door, and the Senior Sergeant ran to the aircraft and climbed inside. He immediately took a seat in the red nylon bench-like seats and secured his seat-belt. A gunner in the back, one of two, handed him a headset so he could speak with the crew and hear what was going on.

"Base, this is Wagon Train Two and be advised, I am taking small arms fire."

The Senior Sergeant heard nothing to indicate they were being shot at.

The tail of the helicopter went up, with the nose down, and the bird lifted off the dirt and started to gain altitude.

It was then he heard three loud *pings* and saw holes suddenly appear in the floor. Both gunners opened up, sweeping the trees below them. Suddenly there came another *ping*, followed by a loud scream from the right gunner, and he fell to the floor screaming with his groin area bleeding. Unbuckling his seat-belt, the Senior Sergeant moved to the man, and using his knife, cut his flight suit to where he could see the injury. He'd actually taken a ricocheting round to the inner thigh. He was bleeding profusely, so he pushed a button on his cord and said, "Uh, your right gunner has a severed artery and he is losing a lot of blood. Right now I am holding the artery closed."

"Senior Sergeant, I have my hands full, with a fire warning light on, a vibrating aircraft, and a dead pilot. I suggest you move back to your seat and prepare for a rough landing. The base is not far, but I think the landing will be hard."

"If I move, your gunner will die."

"It is your choice, and we should be landing in about 7 minutes."

"I understand, sir."

It was then the Sergeant noticed thick gray smoke passing the doors. The other gunner leaned out, safe with his harness secured to the floor.

A minute later he said, "No flames, but dense gray smoke coming from under the aircraft, sir."

A clear sticky fluid began to leak from some overhead lines and Pajari prayed it wasn't flammable. He sat with his legs out the door, holding the severed artery to keep the gunner alive.

"Base, this is Wagon Train Two and I have my whole console lighted up looking like a Christmas tree. Every red light in the book is on and according to manual, I should not even be in the air. I request permission to set this thing down as soon as I am over the base."

"Uh, wait one, Wagon Train Two."

"I do not have the damned time to wait. Be advised, I am setting my aircraft down now."

The helicopter hit hard, jarring the Senior Sergeant's bad back, injuring the unhurt door gunner, and bringing a loud scream from the wounded man.

The pilot said, "I have to cut power, but exit as soon as possible, and meet me at the nose of the bird." He then began flipping knobs and turning switches.

With his back hurting, the Sergeant picked up the wounded gunner, placed him over his shoulder and moved to the front of the helicopter. He lowered the man to the ground and then went back to help the other gunner. On his way to the gunner, he felt the side of the pilot's neck and felt a pulse. The co-pilot was having trouble getting out of the aircraft. After helping the injured gunner, he returned for the wounded pilot, and finally the co-pilot. While the aircraft was smoking badly, there were no visible flames. From the fence that surrounded the base, Pajari saw they'd just barely made it to the installation. Fire trucks and ambulances were rushing toward them. Of the five, only the Senior Sergeant was able to stand or walk much.

As the firetrucks moved close to the aircraft, the ambulance backed to the injured men and placed each man on a litter. A medic took over pinching the blood artery and soon they were gone. Another ambulance took the Sergeant to the hospital and gave him a good going over. Other than some back pain from the hard landing, he was fine. The doctor handed him some pain pills, but he threw them in the trash on his way out of the hospital. On the way to seeing the Anti-partisan Commander, he stopped at his quarters and refilled his flask. Of course, he took a good swig to help kill the pain in his back, and then went to brief the Commander.

The briefing with the Colonel went well and then the man said, "I think the partisans are drawing our attention from Edwards and Jackson, so they can do a retaliation for our use of the bomb. I cannot see them sitting on their asses and allowing us to detonate a nuclear weapon and not respond in kind. They have two of our small suitcase bombs, which is exactly the same weapon we used. I think Colonels Vasiliev and Borisovich made a terrible decision when they used the bomb. Intelligence is telling us now that China is supplying the partisans some of what they need."

"Their gear is inferior, sir, but let us hope the Chinese do not send ground troops. There are about a billion Chinese and they would simply overrun us."

"I have given a lot of thought to the problems our using the bomb has caused. I and Moscow do not care about public opinion and never have, but we are concerned if other nations support the partisan efforts. These animals, still called Americans by other countries, are fighting us to a standstill now, so can you imagine if they are suddenly well supplied?"

"Sir, with your permission, I would like to return to my base and assist. Colonel Matveev was shook up in the attack when his quarters took a mortar round and destroyed. As a result, he spent hours trapped under the debris."

"By all means return, Sergeant, but I have heard you were a hero at the helicopter crash site, saved the lives of four men, and actually held a bleeding artery for most the trip here. I have asked Moscow to not only promote you to Master Sergeant, but award you the highest medal they can for bravery. Mother Russia needs more men like you."

"This is a pleasant surprise, sir, but all I did was what any soldier would do for another. I am not a hero, just a man doing his job, sir. I do, however, thank you."

Opening his lower drawer, the Colonel pulled out a quart of premium vodka, handed it to the man and said, "Drink this when you are at your forward operating base. You have earned every drop."

When Pajari returned to the base, he was surprised to see his friend Master Sergeant Sokoloff and his troops there. He called the old Master Sergeant to his new tent and pulled out the bottle given to him by the Colonel at Edwards. After a couple of drinks, he asked, "What brings you here, Vlad?"

"I am to start searching for partisans in the morning. Oh, I do not know if you heard the news or not, but Colonel Gleb died on the way home to Moscow. I cannot believe he was dumb enough to demand a salute in the field. A man at his age and experience knew better."

"Some mistakes out here you only make once."

"That is true, very true. How is the old man to work with in the field like this?"

"He is not bad, but he wants results and he listens to his NCOs a great deal. Before I had suggested bunkers on the base, but he was positive we would never be attacked. I saw a few minutes ago that the bulldozer is now making bunkers. He is a fast learner and he will give you what you need to complete your mission."

"Good to hear this. What time do you serve chow?"

Pajari laughed and once sober said, "We have no dining facility, so why do we not go by supply and get some rations?"

"All I like in the rations is the beef and fried squash pureé. The beef with tomato sauce upsets my stomach and tastes like crap. Seems the army would learn a man wants variety in his menu, not the same food over and over."

"Now, you know we have variety with our meals. Every time they change ration manufacturers we get a different, but equally nasty entree."

They both laughed and moved to supply for their supper.

After eating the meal outside, sitting on sandbags, the Master Sergeant excused himself, "I need to get some sleep. I have a crew to take out early in the morning and, for some, it is their first trip."

"Good night, and good luck tomorrow."

"Just another walk in the sun."

"Let us hope so. I need to check my men."

The night was uneventful, but the Senior Sergeant actually expected an assault on the base. They were down to only one tank, and the perimeter was a mess, but the night was quiet. He awoke early and was able to shake Master Sergeant Sokoloff's hand before they walked from the base. Then, like so many other days, he began riding his troops to remove the partisan bodies from the wire, get bunkers made, and fill thousands of sandbags. The bodies were ripe now and the scent was nasty.

He was sitting in the communications tent with a Sergeant he knew when he heard Master Sergeant Sokoloff say, "Tent City, Falcon 1."

Pajari could hear gunfire on the radio.

"Uh, go ahead Falcon 1."

"We have run into more than we can handle here. I need support in the form of artillery or air. I repeat, I need support."

"Uh, wait one and I will call Base."

"Sounds like one hell of a firefight going on." Pajari said.

"Yep. Uh, Falcon 1, I have two Black Sharks on the way. Estimated Time of Arrival (ETA) is five minutes."

"Copy, two Black Sharks in five minutes."

"You can speak to the flight leader, Eagle 91, directly."

"Eagle 91, this is Falcon 1 and my squad has run into approximately a company of partisans. When you approach me, come in hot and spray the trees west of me, copy?"

"Copy, Falcon, I will roll in hot and my Gatling gun will spray the trees to your west."

In the field, the Master Sergeant was surprised the partisans hadn't flanked him yet, but suspected it was just a matter of time. The small arms fire was heavy, and most of his new troops were terrified and useless to him. To set an example, the Sergeant did not take cover, but walked around kicking men in the ass who did not return fire.

"Falcon, this is Eagle 91. Get your heads down because I am starting my Gatling gun run now. Over."

Looking toward sound of the chopper blades, Sokoloff spotted the lone Black Shark lining up on the trees. He then heard a sound like a huge zipper being unzipped as fast as possible and knew that was the gun. When Eagle 91 nosed up and left the area, Eagle 92 radioed, "Falcon, Eagle 92, and I am doing the same, except once my run is complete, I will return to fire missiles into the woods. Over."

"Copy, Eagle 92."

There came the zipper sound again and then the aircraft banked to the left. Eagle 92, lined up once more and released his missiles.

"Uh, Base, Eagle 92, and I just took some ground fire that time, but nothing serious. I am returning to base to refuel and rearm."

As soon as the aircraft left, partisan fire returned and it was as heavy as before.

"Tent City, Falcon 1, and I request artillery support." The Master Sergeant said then read off the map coordinates to Base.

A minute later a screaming round impacted in the trees and he said, "Fire for effect, and I am requesting white phosphorous."

"Uh, copy, wait one."

A minute later shells were landing in the trees and the explosions were as beautiful as they were deadly. The white of the white phosphorous round exploding reminded Sokoloff of peacocks he'd seen once, with long white tails.

"No one can survive that." a confident Private said.

"I think most will survive that. Never assume your enemy is killed unless you see a dead body."

A soldier off the Master Sergeant's left suddenly jerked and then screamed as he fought to stop the flow of blood from what remained of his left hand. The Medic ran to him and as he applied a dressing, he took a bullet to the head, which dropped him instantly.

The Sergeant walked to the two men, pulled them to relative safety behind a log, and finished wrapping up the soldier. He was surprised to find the medic alive, but he had a deep nasty furrow to his scalp where the bullet had traveled before it exited the back of his helmet. He gave both men a shot of morphine and he was well aware not to give the drug to a head injury, but the wounded man was screaming now and in pain. He suspected the head injury hurt like hell.

Picking up the radio headset he said, "Base, Falcon 1, and I need an emergency medivac for my injured. I have two seriously wounded."

"Copy, but I have no helicopters at the moment. Uh, wait one."

A bullet struck a rock near him and ricocheted off in to space.

"Falcon 1. This is Base, over."

"Go Base."

"You have been ordered to return to Tent City and to bring your wounded with you."

"Copy, Base, understand I am to return to Tent City. How am I to return, Base?"

"That is correct, and you will walk back. Out."

Handing his headset back to his radioman, Master Sergeant Sokoloff said, "Rig a litter up, and we are to return to base and pack our wounded out with us. I want two men to a litter and we will rotate and share the work of packing them home. Now, withdraw to the trees, break contact, and let us head home."

The withdrawal and movement toward Tent City was done perfectly by his men, and the Master Sergeant was proud of his inexperienced young troops. He was only about 5 kilometers from the base and had no idea the partisans had mined the trail for his return trip. As an old war horse, he knew better than to use the same trail leaving and entering, but the stretchers were heavy. So he took the shortest route.

About a kilometer from the base, his point man suddenly stopped and said, "Master Sergeant, I am standing on a mine."

"How do you know?"

"My foot felt some resistance and then I felt and heard a click as something was pushed down."

"Remain calm, Private, and let me find a large rock. I will bring the rock to you and then check for a mine."

Picking up the heaviest rock he could find, the Master Sergeant made his way to the Private. He lowered the rock, pulled his bayonet and sticking it into the ground around the Private's foot he confirmed it was a mine.

"I am scared, Master Sergeant."

"Hell, son, you have a right to be scared. I am scared too, but understand, if the mine explodes, I will be right beside you."

"Thank you, Master Sergeant."

"Now, I am going to put the edge of this heavy rock on your foot. Then I want you to unlace your boot and try to remove your foot without moving the rock. Do you think you can do this?"

"I do not have a choice, do I?"

"No, not really. So, let us get this over with." He moved the rock, held the man in place as he unlaced his boot, and was in the process of helping him remove his foot, when he saw the rock fall.

The explosion was loud to the Master Sergeant.

CHAPTER 11

I was silently battling the placement of the bomb as we walked through the wood, moving overland and avoiding all paths. I knew it was a lawful order, so I would do the job. I wasn't so sure the people in Jackson were getting a lot of fallout or not, and I didn't think the General really knew either. I did know placing the bomb in Pearl would blow the international airport to hell and back, and likely destroy all the bridges over the pearl river, too. Just the loss of Russian lives and equipment made Jackson a much more logical target, but I hoped God would forgive me for the innocent lives I'd snuff out in seconds.

"We're in a dense grove of trees now, so we'll spend the night here and move on at daylight. My men have been awake over 24 hours and they need rest." Top said.

"How much further to the suitcase?" Mary asked.

"Not much further."

I laughed and said, "You haven't changed a bit. Still the same old E-9 you were years ago, huh?"

He smiled and replied, "Old habits die hard, you know."

"They're good habits, Top. Okay folks, form a perimeter and prepare for the evening." Mary said.

Soon supper was behind us, folks moved to their sleeping bags, and others moved to stand watch over the rest of us. Each had a poncho beside them, just in case an aircraft equipped with thermal imaging would fly over.

The night was uneventful, but for some reason I did not sleep well, and when I spoke with Carol the next morning she hadn't either. Like me, she didn't enjoy the deaths of thousands of people on her shoulders, though we both understood the need to complete our mission.

We'd just started to move, when the sound of a low level chopper filled our ears.

"Moving from north to south." Top said.

"Down, and now." Mary ordered.

We all fell to the ground and knew we'd be almost impossible to see from a moving platform of any kind. The chopper stopped, then moved to the east and stopped and did that for all four compass headings. He was looking for someone, but was it us, or was he attempting to make a team that he suspected was in these trees run?

Three or four times he moved, then would stop, as his gunners looked for partisans.

After about thirty minutes, the chopper was still looking for someone.

Mary said, "I've had enough of this bullshit." She pull a Strela 2 missile container from the top of her pack, sighted in the chopper and then squeezed the trigger. I actually saw the fins pop out and followed the missile to the aircraft engine. The missile exploded and the pilot tried his damnedest to maintain control, but it was not to be. The aircraft moved forward about a hundred yards and then dropped like a rock to the ground below.

The pilot must have cut the electrical switches when it began to fall because there was no fire on impact. I moved forward with James and Lea, leading Dolly by her leash. The wreckage was smoking and I could smell aircraft fuel, but we quickly took the machine-guns, side arms and ammo. Both pilots were dead and one gunner seemed to have a broken back, while the other was unconscious. As we were leaving, Top tossed a thermite grenade in the chopper. As we moved, I waited for the explosion and it wasn't long in coming. When the fuel went up, a fireball rolled inside of itself, and the flames were dark red, edged with black smoke. I should have felt something for the two dying gunners and two dead pilots, but I didn't. While I heard the screams of one gunner, I felt nothing at all.

As we moved, I was getting back in my old stomping grounds where I used to hunt. To the west was some swampland and that's exactly where Top moved. The trail through the woods also continued into the swamp, which was filled with Spanish moss in the trees, gators in the water, and snakes on the trail sunning. Top had been walking with a switch off a tree limb that was about five feet long, and for over an hour I wondered why. I found out now. Since he was on point leading us to the suitcase, he'd use the switch to flip snakes from the trail to the water. Each time he did it, Carol moaned. I knew from before that snakes, gators and bugs scared her, but like a real trooper, she continued on.

About half way to the suitcase, we heard a flight of choppers passing to the east of us, slightly over the swamp. Instead of all continuing on, two turned and flew toward us.

"Seek cover!" Mary ordered and I grabbed Carol's hand and jumped into the swamp.

When my head broke the surface I heard machine-guns firing and saw a long row of bullets going right down the center of the trail. I saw three of our troops stitched right down the middle and heard them scream as the bullets struck. Blood, gore and bones flew in all directions. The chopper banked and came around again. I wasn't real happy being in the water with the snakes and gators, but right now, it seemed to be the safest of all options.

Mary climbed up on the bank, pulled out another missile but before she could fire, she was struck three or four times in the chest by a door gunner and she died instantly. Top, who'd been laying on the opposite side of the trail, grabbed the missile launcher and sighted in the chopper. He squeezed the trigger as the bird was in a sharp turn and the missile struck it dead center of the engines, which exploded. Flaming wreckage dropped to the swamp and the other chopper broke contact, flying to the east. I watched the burning fuel on the water and wondered how many men and women we'd lost. Dolly was an excellent swimmer and once on the trail again, she was shaking hard to dry off. I pulled Carol to the trail, found she was fine, and then started checking for dead and injured.

I'd lost Mary and our medic, Marsha Wied, while Top had lost five of his people. Out of twenty, we were down to thirteen and I hoped that was our lucky number. We stripped our dead of all useful gear and then moved on.

After about an hour, Top called for a short rest and said, "Don't be surprised if we have a Russian squad on our asses shortly. The chopper that survived likely called in an inflated kill number and the Commanders are sure to send some men after us."

"Body count is everything when you're losing a war, Top." I joked with him.

"I'm going to have our man on drag plant some mines and booby-traps." he said, and then asked, "Should we move on or wait to deal with the Russians?"

"Move, because if push comes to shove, once I have the suit-case, I can go off on my own with Carol, while you deal with the Russians." I replied.

He smiled and said, "Well, be that way then. Peppy, mine be-hind you when you get the chance."

With Peppy on drag and Top on point, we continued moving.

Near dark we heard choppers again and they were all over the swamp, looking for us, I suspected. However, they were east and west of us, unsure which trail we'd taken.

Top moved to my side and said, "Remember the old duck hunters shack up the trail a ways?"

"Sure, but what about it?"

"The suitcase is buried in the very center of the floor, about a foot or two down. I was one of the men who buried it, so I'll be able to dig it up in no time."

"Chopper!" Hall yelled and by the time I heard the blades, a missile was heading right for us. Fortunately he had misjudged us and the missile went over our heads. The explosion was loud and we were all splashed with swamp water. I saw a snake fall with the water, hit the trail and then wiggle off. Our weapons opened up, the chopper turned sideways to let the door-gunner waste us.

Alford raised his sniper rifle, lined up his sights and struck the gunner between the eyes. The dead man fell from the chopper to stop about six feet below the left skid, held in place, fully extended by a nylon strap connected to the aircraft floor. I could clearly see the outline of his body against the dark gray rain clouds.

When the pilot straightened the aircraft, my sniper fired twice and both rounds struck the pilot in the head. His body slumped back, blood splattered on the windshield and side glass, and the copilot took control. They immediately broke to the left and gained altitude as they left us.

"The shack is about a quarter mile further on this trail." Top said.

"Great shooting, Sergeant Alford," I said, as I patted him on the back.

"Uh, I'm a Private, Colonel."

"No, not after saving our collective asses, you're not. You're a Sergeant, effective right now. Thanks for the superior shooting, Robert."

"You're welcome sir, but I missed with each shot by well over an inch."

"I understand the man who dropped the nuclear bomb on Hiroshima was off course by a mile too, but no one noticed. Thanks." I said, and then grinned.

When we neared the old shack, Top and Brewer, my explosives man, entered and checked for booby-traps. They found none. The shack was small, maybe eight feet by ten, and had once been used as a meeting place for men who hunted gators or ducks in the swamp. The floor was dirt, but it had a roof and three sides covered. Only half of the fourth side was covered, creating a primitive door.

Pulling a folded shovel from his pack, Top started digging.

As he dug, I moved to Carol and asked, "How are you taking all of this?"

"Not good, overall. Do you guys always have so many people trying to kill you all the time? It seems like the animals, snakes, and Russians are *all* out to kill us."

"This is unusual and has had much higher contact than most missions. It's almost like the Russians know where we are. I really think they feel we're up to something, so things are turning rougher for us. They've turned up the heat."

"What does that mean, turned up the heat?"

"Normally on a mission like this we'd not see a Russian the whole time. I think they're worried we'll strike back because of their nuclear detonation, so they have more aircraft in the skies."

I heard Top's shovel hit metal. He glanced at me, smiled and said, "Okay, we're in business."

It was then the clouds opened up and a light rain began to fall. I saw a bright blinding light move across the almost black horizon and then with a loud *boom*, it exploded into many smaller fingers of light. Rain began to fall harder. All of us moved into the shelter, but the suitcase was left in the hole.

I sat in a corner with my arm around Carol as we ate a Russian ration and washed it down with tepid river water. I worried about the water, and hoped we weren't drinking radiation particles in our water. I knew of no way to clean water contaminated by fallout, so I let my mind move on to other things. For a second I did considered the odds of getting cancer from bad water and then realized, I'd probably not live long enough to have to worry about cancer. Dolly moved to my side and I fed her a ration all her own, except for the sweets. Soon, my meal was done, I was asleep, and then I heard the rain pounding on the metal roof. Hail began to fall, which made one hell of a noise on the metal roof, and the winds picked up.

Carol was squeezing my right hand and I knew she was frightened. I was worried about a tornado. "Brewer, since you're nearest the door, check the skies around us for a tornado."

He stepped outside, looked around and said, "I don't see anything now, but a lot of these clouds have the makings of a tornado, Colonel."

"Well?" Top asked.

"Well, what?"

"Do we stay or move on?"

"We stay. If we get caught out in a hail storm with hail the size of baseballs, and we've all seen them here before, how far do you think we'd get?"

"Not far."

"Exactly, and that's why we'll wait the storm out in here. I want one person at the door the rest of the night. I want us all up, fed, and ready go by daylight. So, I want the last guard to wake all of us at 0500."

I then stood with Carol, put my sleeping bag on the floor, and we used hers to cover us with. While it wasn't cold, it was cool. Once we were covered and comfortable I whispered, "Comfortable?"

"Ummm, very. I like sleeping like this."

I spent the next hour watching her sleep, but finally my exhaustion claimed me, like soldiers all over the world, and I fell asleep.

I awoke to shouts, but I could not determine the language. Thompson was on guard and heard him whisper, "Russians."

"Do they have a dog?" I asked.

"Fog is too thick to see, sir, but I've heard no barking."

I stuck my head out the door, and it looked like a scene from a Dracula movie, with a thick white veil of fog down to the ground. It was then I heard a big explosion followed by two smaller ones. I knew at that second exactly where the Russians were. They were about 200 meters from us and moving our way.

Everyone got ready to move; I picked up the suitcase as Top booby-trapped the dirt around the hole in the floor. I then put Walker on point and Top on drag. We moved out at a steady pace, heading deeper into the swamp. Of all of us, only Carol knew nothing of the swamp and she didn't like the place a whole hell of a lot, but neither did the Russian troops.

We'd been walking for about 400 meters, when I heard one and then two explosions, but both were small so I knew Top's booby-traps in the shed had paid off for us. Behind us right this second were two injured Russians and if we were lucky, both would die of their injuries.

The fog grew dense the deeper we moved in the swamp. I didn't expect the troops behind us to follow us far, because there were no accurate maps of the area. Most of us knew the swamp from a lifetime of hunting and fishing in the area, not from maps. That gave us a tremendous advantage over the Russians behind us.

The problem was the mud. No matter what we did, stepping in the mud left tracks.

Top said, "We all need to step off the path and get into the water right here. Move toward the bank on the right. Now, about halfway to the other bank, move to your right about 50 feet and then turn left and go straight. There is a hole there and it's deep, too."

When Carol entered the warm water, she shivered with fear and I knew it was taking all she had to keep moving. Most of the way across the water was up to our waists, but at one spot it was deeper and mid-chest for me. Most of the troops didn't like being in the water at all, and the stretch we covered was about half a football field in length. Soon, we were on the opposite trail, much to the relief of most, and we took off at a slow jog. Water dripped from our clothing and gear, but we did move, with the fear of crossing the swamp-water behind us.

Near noon we got a radio call from Headquarters that more of the English speaking Russians, dressed as partisans, had been encountered. In all but one case the Russians were beaten back or killed. The one situation happened when a partisan group allowed the Russians to mingle with them. The Russian leader had simply stated he had no radio or password. Once they were in position and ready, they'd killed the Americans with small arms. There was only one survivor, who happened to be in the woods taking a pee. He reported their English was perfect, along with a strong Southern dialect. My call sign was changed to Quarterback and when my bomb was planted, I was to transmit "Touchdown."

This concerned me, but I knew it'd take more than Russians who were fluent in the Southern dialect or redneck to matter much in the outcome of our war. I didn't like the idea of what I heard next, that we'd be using code on the radio. Code is good and fine, but it takes time to translate it and to send or receive it. No, we'd not been transmitting in the open and used code for important things, but I was unsure how this was to work. Further word on the code would be coming.

Private Walker was on point, and she was good. We'd slowed down to a fast walk now, because the mud was too deep. The sun came out and began burning the fog away, but it remained in some spots. Suddenly, Walker's body was covered in fire, as an antipersonnel mine exploded. I was looking right at her, when a thin wall of red and white fire shot to the sky, and her body literally flew apart. Everyone went to ground and there was no reason to check her; she had to be dead. I halfway expected a Russian squad in front of us and an ambush. After the ripples in the water grew calm again, I sent Brewer to check her. She was dead as they get and a person couldn't ask for an easier or faster death.

It was right then when Lea handed me the radio and mouthed, "Headquarters."

"Quarterback, go Base."

"Be advised the Russians have learned of your mission and we are attempting to discover how it was compromised. We don't know the extent of their knowledge, so call the plays that will bring a touchdown for us. Use your own game plan."

"Uh, copy Base. I will likely switch to a night game then. I will send you a special copy of my game plan tonight. Do you copy? I also have KIA, Kilo India Alpha, by the name of Walker; Whiskey, Alpha, Lima, Kilo, Echo, Romeo. Do you copy, Base?" I said, more or less telling them a coded plan would be sent later this evening.

"Copy, your KIA is Walker and the coach said the ball is in your court."

"I read you loud and clear. This is Quarterback, out." I handed the handset to the radioman and knew I was authorized to do what it took to complete my mission.

All went well the rest of the day and near dusk we were still in the swamp. Now most folks will tell you that snakes are scared of people, and that's often true, depending on the type of snake. I can assure you a water moccasin is an aggressive snake most of the time and nothing much scares a gator. I thought Carol would start crying when she learned we'd spend the night in the swamp and out in the open. I was more worried about aircraft with infrared gear than snakes or gators. If the Russian Bear knew I was out to nuke them, they'd use every resource available to them to stop me. Hell, that just makes horse sense to me, because I'd do the same thing if our roles were reversed. I did suspect the Russians had no idea which group I was traveling with or my intended target.

Of course, now security would be at least doubled at the bases. Which made me feel safer that Pearl was my actual destination to plant the bomb. I grew up there, and I'd been thinking of putting the bomb in the vacant house my parents once owned. I grew up in the house, had millions of great memories there, and I felt it appropriate for the device. I could place it under the crawl space beneath the house. They were both dead now, so they'd not care, but in my mind it would be like them helping me to resist the Bear.

"John?" Carol asked.

"Yes?" I replied, suddenly jarred back to the present.

"I'm utterly terrified of spending a night out here, in the open."

"I'll tell you what, we'll zip our sleeping bags together and I'll be with you the whole night. I'll keep you safe, but it's really nothing to fear."

"Nothing to fear? All I've seen in this place is snakes, gators, millions of bugs and some creatures I don't even know. I have one on me now, which itches, but I'm too embarrassed to check what it is."

"Where is this unknown creature on your body?"

"I have one on my butt, uh, well, the other near my, uh, vagina. Lawdy, this is embarrassing for me."

I turned to my radio operator and asked, "Something is bothering Carol and she needs a woman to check it out. I'll have myself and another man hold up ponchos so you can look her over."

Lea smiled and said, "Sure, I'll help."

I had Corporal Hall hold one poncho as I held the other. The two women started and after a few minutes, Lea said, "Leaches, sir. I see four on her."

"Do you know how to get them off?" Carol asked, with her tone reflecting her fear.

"Use a squirt of insect repellent on them, but for the one near, uh, well, near her private area, make sure the repellent is only applied outside of her. So you may have to apply the repellent with your finger."

"They're falling off now. I suggest you guys drop your drawers and check, too. I suspect we got them when we crossed the swamp water earlier today."

I found one near my balls, squirted some repellent on it, and the chemical made my balls burn for a minute or so. It was sort of like treating a football player for jock itch. Most of the men had at least one leach and some had more. I did notice that once removed the area where they'd been sucking blood continued to itch.

Soon Carol was beside me and said, "I've never been so embarrassed in my life."

I said, "Nothing to be embarrassed about, it's a swamp problem and it happens. Those of us in the field are not overly concerned with nudity, because at times like this, or when treating a wound, body parts are shown. It's not a big deal. Not a man here who hasn't seen a naked woman before or a woman who hasn't seen a naked man. We just keep it professional, is all."

"I'm a Headquarters puke and this is rough on me." Carol whispered.

I put my arms around her and pulled her close as I said, "You see now the sacrifices our men and women make everyday in an effort to gain our freedom. You've seen the injuries and death, so now you can appreciate the easier life with Headquarters. I will say you're a tough woman and have done well for a first mission. This mission is not one of the easier ones, either."

"John, I think I'm starting to get attached to you."

"Good, because I am to you, too. It's okay, so let it go and see what happens. Love is about the only thing we have left from the old America."

"Can we sleep now? I'm beat."

I held the sleeping bag open and said "After you, my dear." with a wink. It was dark and I knew she didn't see it. I was starting to love this woman and I realized right then, love was needed by all of us.

A guard schedule was established by Top and they'd be rotated with a new guard every two hours. It was a little after midnight when Alford, the guard on duty, said, "Choppers."

Top neared me, chuckled, and said, "I think we're fairly safe from IR detection in the swamp. Surely every gator in here must give off as much heat as a human. Can you imagine their screens?"

Always on the prowl to down a chopper, I asked, "Do we have a Strela 2 or LAW?"

"One of each." one of Top's men said.

"If a chopper gets close enough, we'll take it out. I think the gator heat will mess these birds up, and they'll be coming down low and may use search lights. If they do, Alford, take the lights out."

"Spread out some. No shooting unless I shoot first."

Long minutes passed and I heard the choppers growing near. Then finally, one moved overhead and went into a hover. I felt my stomach tighten and suspected we'd been spotted. I aimed my Strela 2 and took a deep breath.

CHAPTER 12

Senior Sergeant Pajari screamed in pain as blood spurted from a number of serious lacerations and punctures from the exploding mine. He was still whole, but he didn't realize it yet, only because the Private had taken most of the blast and he was splattered all around the mine. Smoke, like a lazy cloud was hanging about six feet above the small crater in the ground.

A Private ran to him, a medic, and began looking him over. He cut his shirt open and he had a good half-dozen punctures to his chest, but he wasn't having any problems breathing. His arms and face were bleeding too, peppered from flying shrapnel. Of the Private who took the majority of the blast, they found his head, left hand and part of a boot, with a foot still inside.

The Junior Sergeant took command and asked, "What is his condition?"

"He will live, but we need a chopper, due to possible internal bleeding. I think he is more seriously injured than he looks to be."

Turning to his radioman, the Sergeant said, "Let Base know the Senior Sergeant is down due to a mine, and needs a helicopter. Tell them he is bleeding internally."

As the man talked to base, the Sergeant placed what few men he had in defensive positions.

"Helicopter on the way but the Commander, Matveev, is mad as a hornet. All I got out of the Corporal on the other end was we are getting a helicopter that is needed for another mission."

"Well, we do not have enough people now to carry our wounded and have no choice. The Colonel will just have to get over his anger."

The medic in the field had given the Senior Sergeant a shot of morphine and then next thing he knew, he woke up in the hospital. He was feeling no pain, but was confused about why he was all wired up to a machine and in a bed.

"Lay still, Senior Sergeant, you are safe." a doctor said from beside his bed.

"Why am I here?"

"Do you remember the mine and explosion?"

"No, nothing yet, but I think it will return to me over time."

"The man you tried so hard to save did not survive. What is left of him has been shipped home. Now, we have pulled all the metal out of you, and it was not a lot. However, if not for the helicopter, you would have bled to death internally, even if there was not much metal in you."

Pajari just grunted, and then asked, "What of my men?""The two wounded are still very much alive and stable. The others were airlifted to the Forward Operation Base and are all safe."

"When can I get out of here?"

The doctor laughed and said, "All you Sergeants ask that question, and my answer is in about a week."

"What hospital am I in, Edwards or Jackson?"

"Jackson and it is a good thing too, because we are closer. I do not think you would have survived the flight to Edwards. We used gallons of blood on you."

"Has anyone been in to see me?"

"Just an old Master Sergeant named, uh, Sokoloff, I think his name was. He is preparing to go into the field and wanted to say goodbye. He said he will be back this afternoon to talk with you."

As the doctor walked away, Pajari felt under his pillow and felt a pint of vodka. He pulled the bottle out, took a long chug, and then placed it under his mattress. When the medication and his alcohol mixed, he fell into a deep sleep.

Hours later he heard a familiar voice say, "You going to sleep all day? Some men will do anything to get a few days off. How are you, Albert?"

"I have no idea, but I am still above ground. Thanks for the bottle."

"I brought another bottle, too, but I will put it in your dresser so you can have it after you start moving around. Oh, your medals came through as well as your promotion for your actions at Tent City. Moscow has approved your Cross of St. George and an Order of Kutuzov, with the last one only given to officers. Which means, sir, you are no longer an enlisted swine. Effective a month ago you were promoted to the rank of Captain."

"Huh? I do not understand. I have no urge to be an officer."

"Moscow has made that decision, my friend, not you. I say take the promotion, and retire with much more money."

"Me a Captain? That cannot be."

The doctor was entering the room and said, "It is true, Pajari, your rank is now Captain. So, you have some back pay coming to you. I know the Master Sergeant brought you vodka, because you Senior NCOs are all the same."

"I do not wish to be a Captain. My goal was to be a Master Sergeant."

The Captain laughed and replied, "The Russian army says you are a Captain, so a Captain you will be, my friend. I think your wife will be pleased and proud of you."

"Zhutova does not care about my rank, but I am sure the extra money will have her confused, and when I come home dressed as a Captain it will shock her. She is but a simple farm woman."

"Well, I have come to tell you that tomorrow we will move you to your own room. As an officer you are to be kept separate of your troops. According to Colonel Matveev you will remain in the infantry, but that is all that is known right now." the doctor said, and then left the room.

Sokoloff glanced at his watch and said, "I must leave, Albert, because I must prepare for a mission. I will be gone a few days, but I will be back. You be a good officer and listen to the doctor and his staff."

"Why are the beds mostly full here, and they did not take me directly to a private room?"

"I am to say nothing, but many of our men and women are down with radiation poisoning and in the hospital. We have had many deaths since you went to Tent City."

"Oh, those fools! Before they used the bomb they should have considered the fallout, but Vasiliev was a strange man anyway. What happened to Colonel Gleb? Did he survive his injury?"

"No, he died a week or so back. I must go now, my friend, but I will return as soon as I am able. You rest and heal up, sir." The Master Sergeant came to attention and gave Pajari a crisp salute.

Captain Pajari returned the salute and then laughed.

Master Sergeant Sokoloff left the aircraft at 6096 meters, or 20,000 feet, and would free fall to 213.36 meters, roughly 700 feet, before deploying his parachute. He did not have a reserve parachute, because it was unlikely he'd have time to deploy it before hitting the ground. He was loaded with gear, but less than he normally carried in the field. He was with a special Russian unit that spoke English and while his use of the language was good, he still had problems with American slang. The ten of them left the aircraft at the same time. Supposedly, they were being dropped in front of an American unit that was carrying a nuclear suitcase bomb. His task was to prevent the partisans from getting revenge on the Russian army. As far as he was concerned, the mission was impossible.

As he kept his back arched, his arms and legs fully extended, his fall was controlled. First, no one knew exactly which group of partisans had the bomb and second, what the intended target would be. Without that information it was a difficult, if not impossible, task.

At 213.36 meters, his chute opened and he heard a loud grunt, knowing full well it was his reaction to opening shock. He struck the ground moving forward and did a perfect parachute landing fall. Gaining his feet, he collapsed his chute and stuck it in some brush. Pulling a map from his pocket, he took a hard look and began moving toward the meeting place. He was the third man of ten to reach the others. In less than 30 minutes, they were all gathered together, and each was wearing partisan clothing and would speak English only from this point on. Each knew if the partisans caught them, they'd be executed as spies. What they were to attempt was to blend in with a partisan unit, discover what the target was, determine if only one bomb was being used, and if the other bomb was held as a back up in the event the first one was taken or did not function. As far as Sokoloff was concerned, it was a wasted effort by the Russians. It was highly unlikely the Americans would tell strange new members anything, even if they were able to contact them without getting killed.

They moved toward where the last American group had been spotted and all were nervous. Each knew one mistake and they were dead men. They even had to avoid their own troops, because to those that didn't know of the mission, this squad was a group of partisans.

It was late afternoon when they entered the swamps. Snakes slithered away, usually by entering the water, and gators either backed into warm water slowly or slapped the surface of the water with their tails, to warn other gators before turning and moving away. The mosquitoes were getting bad, so repellent was applied and onward they moved. Near dusk, they contacted Base and reported, using code, that all was well. They were informed, also in code, that the American unit was estimated to be a little over a mile from them, moving north.

They then tuned in the American radio frequency and listened to different communications. Little was said of interest, except one unit was spotted, just after dark by a Russian helicopter with infrared capability, and it was slowly massacring the partisans. The last words spoken was by the team leader who said, "I've been spotted. Tell my wife I —"

The team leader, a Russian Major Yakovich, said, "We need to get some sleep. Frank, I want you on guard first, then Bill."

Frank was really Capt Tima Ivanovich, but on this mission he was a Sergeant and Bill was Senior Sergeant Feliks Ilych, a farm boy with twenty years of army experience. Sokoloff was Lieutenant Willy Johnston for this mission. All had fictitious names and backgrounds.

It was near midnight, when Kola Georiykoff moved to the Master Sergeant and said, "Willy, I hear something out there."

"Did you wake the Major?"

The Major said, "Everyone is awake now, but keep your voices low."

"I have an uneasy feeling." one of the men said.

"It's nothing, except maybe a gator eating a crane or something."

"No, there it is again." Kola said.

"That's a military radio." the Major said.

"I have movement on the trail at my 9 O'clock position." the Master Sergeant said.

Fog, as normal on the swamp, was thick. Finally a man stepped from the white and stood no more than twenty feet from the Russians. His Bison swung up, he smiled, the barrel lowered.

"Apple." the man said.

"Cobbler?" the Major said, thinking pie would have been too easy.

"Captain Wilson, I have some partisans up here."

Each of the Russians gave a silent sigh of relief. The others would have said pie and they knew it, so it was a lucky guess.

Within ten minutes all were gathered around a small fire heating coffee from Russian rations and talking. Listening closely, the Master Sergeant learned the American Captain was named Dave Wilson, from Jackson, Mississippi.

"So, you grew up in Rolla, Missouri too, huh? By the way, I'm Sergeant Tom Black." a partisan Sergeant said to the Captain.

"Nice to meet you, Tom. Oh, yeah, and used to go to the Uptown theater all the time, but once in a while we'd go to the Ritz, because it was cheaper. I would usually hang around Scott's Drug Store and look at the comic books."

"Nice place to raise a family."

"I liked it a great deal, especially trout fishing on the Little Piney River out at Vida. I can't remember the name of the road we took, but it was about a five mile ride from Vida to the river, which had a low water bridge. On Friday nights we'd go there to talk and drink beer. Had a big swimming hole right off the middle of the bridge."

"I don't remember the road, either. It was one of those CC, DD, or something like that county roads. Used to be a trailer park where we turned." the Sergeant said and then met the eyes of his Captain.

"That's the road, for sure."

Then the Major said, "I'm suppose to link up with a unit out here that is on a special mission."

"Oh?" the American Captain said.

"Yes, but I can't state what the mission is."

"Understandable. Can you contact base by radio and see if they reported in tonight?"

"My radio isn't working properly." the Major lied, and then glanced at his men.

Shit, thought Master Sergeant Sokoloff, *if they call in for us, they will know we are Russians. Odds are no one is looking for that squad of men, not Americans anyway.*

"I'd be happy to contact Base for you and see where the unit is." the American Captain said.

"Uh, thanks." The Major knew he was trapped, but he handled it well, and slipped the safety off his Bison.

Picking up the headset the Captain said, "Base, this is Hotel Six Actual."

"Go, Hotel."

"I have Major James with me that is to link up with a special unit out here, can you verify his mission and then give me a position of the partisans?"

"Wait one, Hotel."

"Now!" the Russian Major screamed and guns blasted. The Americans were not caught completely off guard, because the

American Captain had suspected something was wrong with these partisans, because they were too smooth. Hell, they remembered more details about places than the real Americans remembered.

As bodies fell, with most of the men screaming in one language or another, the voice from Base kept calling for Hotel to answer. Men screamed as bullets punched holes through their bodies and both the Russians and Americans fell side-by-side. A few short minutes later, all the Americans were dead, and the only Russian yet alive was the Master Sergeant.

He shot both radios and gathering up rations and gear, he placed it all in a pile. He checked all the men, Russian and American, but all were dead or dying. The Russian Major had taken a bullet to the face and was dead as hell. From that minute on, Master Sergeant Sokoloff was Sergeant Tom Black. He selected the name because one of the dead Americans was Tom Black. His Commander, Captain Dave Wilson, from Jackson, Mississippi, had been killed along with everyone else, and the bodies were even here to prove it.

He searched the dead men from both sides, and found little except the Russian Major and Captain both carried flasks of Vodka. He placed one in a cargo pocket of his trousers, and took a deep drink from the other to calm his nerves. The close battle was hard on him and his hands were shaking violently as he tried to screw the lid back on the flask.

He loaded the gear he needed in a backpack from one of the Americans and donned a set of NVGs. He had plenty of spare batteries. Then he started moving north, toward the partisans he was to link with. He watched snakes move for the water as he neared, saw gators slide into the water, and saw some animals he didn't know. He remembered the password, Apple Cobbler, and made it a point to not forget it. He had no idea how often they changed the word, but every 24 hours was probable. He'd deal with that problem when it came up.

He wasn't sure it was smart for him to be walking on the trail after dark, even with NVGs on, because he could easily step on a landmine or one of the hated American toe-poppers. He'd seen the damage done by those simple and cheap booby-traps, and almost always the man suffered serious stomach wounds, along with mutilation of his manhood or balls. While he was an old man, pushing 45, he still didn't want to lose his privates. But, this mission was important, and he must learn where the bomb was to be placed. He kept moving and near sunup he knew he was lost. He pulled a map out, attempted to triangulate his position, but saw no landmarks, just swamp.

He stopped, sat under a tree and pulled out a Russian ration. He made a small fire, heated his breakfast and then ate slowly. He was tired, had blood stains on him from the gun battle and needed a hot bath and a bed. Instead, he ate, buried his rations tins, and then started moving again.

As tired as he was, he wasn't paying much attention to the ground and he'd just stepped over a log when he felt pain to his left calf. Looking down at movement, he saw a water moccasin moving away. Using a small .22 with a silencer he'd found on the dead American Captain, he killed the snake. His pain was quickly getting severe.

He wasn't sure it was the proper thing to do or not, but he injected a shot of morphine into his leg. He then pulled his knife, cut two "Xs" over each fang mark a quarter inch deep, and let the leg bleed freely. Again, he wasn't sure if that was the proper thing to do either. He'd first been taught to cut the leg, then taught not to cut, so he used what he'd known was reliable information when he first learned to treat snakebite. Besides, the leg was swelling now, and he used his knife to cut the pant leg up to about 6 inches below the crotch on the outside of the trousers.

After the morphine kicked in, the pain went away, but he turned sleepy.

He was laying in the mud, empty syringe beside him, swollen leg and barely conscious when he heard a yell in English. He then lost the battle to stay awake and his world gradually turned from light gray to black and he passed out.

CHAPTER 13

It was Corporal Hall on point that found the wounded partisan, and he'd been snake bit. His left leg was badly swollen, almost three times it's normal size, and he had an empty morphine syringe in the mud beside him. He was unconscious and mumbling. Headquarters had informed us of the attack on a partisan unit the night before and he looked like he might have been a survivor. His clothing was blood stained and while not wounded, he looked like hell, so I suspected he was the only survivor of the bunch.

How long the man has been in the mud I had no idea, but we cleaned him up, placed him on his sleeping bag, and waited. At one point, during the night, he'd come around enough to tell his name, Tom Black, Sergeant. When we checked in with Base, they confirmed a Tom Black had been with Captain Dave Wilson, from Jackson, Mississippi. When he came around, I'd ask him his Commander's name and the daily password.

Three mornings later, he was awake but in pain. Brewer, our assistant medic, gave him two small white pills containing codeine which seemed to kill his pain.

Over coffee with him, I asked about his Commander and he provided the correct answer and then when I said apple, he replied cobbler. As far as I and the rest were concerned the man was one of us. He just seemed a bit rattled, and I think anyone would be a bit out of it after being bitten by a snake.

On the morning of the fourth day, we had to move and while he had pain, Black moved with all of us and kept up. I'm sure he did the job on guts alone, because he had to be hurting. Brewer kept giving him codeine and he kept moving. That night, after walking all day, I saw him pull a flask from his trouser pocket and take a long drink.

"What's in that?" I asked, suspecting alcohol and I felt he needed it, if that's what it was.

"Russian vodka, I've me a wee bit of pain to get shed of. I think the last hour, I was moving by guts alone."

"You're one tough man, Tom. What'd you do before the fall?"

"I ran a body shop in Pearl, Mississippi."

"How come ya ain't got a hard Southern twang like most of us?"

"I grew up in Missouri, down in the Ozark Mountains. I'm Southern enough, just ain't deep rooted Dixie." He laughed and asked, "Can ya return me to base or what am I to do? All my buddies are dead, and I mean it happened so quickly, too. Or maybe I can be assigned to this team."

"I discussed you with Base earlier today and you're to continue on the mission with us. You'll go with Top and the rest when I leave the team. I have a part of the mission that only two of us will complete."

"I don't mean to sound stupid, but what's in that suitcase you or Alford carry all the time? Don't tell me it belongs to one of these women." Tom asked, but he knew what was in the case.

I laughed and replied, "To be honest, you don't have a need to know. So, the suitcase is not a subject open for discussion."

"I understand, sir."

"Good. Hows the pain level from 1 to 10?" I asked when I saw him wince.

"Right now it's about a 6.5 and that's rough." he said as he rubbed his swollen leg.

I reached into my pack and pulled out a quart of vodka and tossed it to him. I said, "I'd rather have you drinking than taking codeine all the time. That's all we have now, so when that's gone, well, you're out of luck."

"How much longer until we split, or is that classified too?"

"Two days, if all goes well. Just outside the old Pearl High School, I'll split from the rest of you."

"Then I can go back to the base, right?"

"Yep, with Top and the rest."

"Good, I need some time to get my head on straight again. It's hard on a man to see his whole team slaughtered and nothing can be done to stop it. I'm pretty sure out of about 20 men, I was the only survivor."

"I suggest you eat, have a few large gulps of vodka and then get some sleep. The rest of your time with us will be about like to-day. Normally we'd not move, not with you hurt, but we have a reason to be moving now. The swelling in your leg has gone down a great deal, too."

Pulling a Russian ration from his pack, Tom nodded, as he thought, *When you leave, I will follow you and put an end to this plan of yours. You must not be allowed to kill my comrades.*

I walked away and returned to Carol and Dolly. Carol was feeding dolly a beef ration and she was hungry. I sat down by her and asked, "She eating well?"

"She's eating like a German shepherd, and you know how they eat."

I laughed, reached over, and scratched her ears. I then ate, taking my time and enjoying the meal, even though it was loaded with grease. What I missed a great deal was bread, plain white bread in a plastic bag from the store or even home made biscuits. We had no flour now, but at rare times we did get cornmeal and we would have some cornbread.

Out of the blue, Carol said, "I don't trust Mister Tom Black. There's something about his eyes that warns me."

"Baby, he passed all the questions I know to ask him and even lived in Pearl. He said he owned a body shop there. It may be you're right, but I don't think so. I think what you see in his eyes is the horror of seeing all his teammates killed."

"I may be wrong, I'll admit that, but I won't trust him, not until he earns my trust."

"That's fair enough."

"You getting sleepy yet?"

"I feel like I was born tired," I said, and then gave a low chuckle.

"The sleeping bags are ready, but I need to clean up before bed. It's harder for a woman to live out here in woods than a man."

By the time she returned, I was asleep.

It was dark when someone touched my left ankle. My eyes opened and I saw Top in the dim moonlight. He cupped his hand behind his ears and it was then I heard the chopper, but it was some distance off.

"It's been covering grids, like it's looking for someone."

"We know part of our mission has been compromised, so they are likely looking for us."

"Well, all we have is one LAW to fight against the thing and I suspect they'll find targets, then call in fast movers or attack helicopters."

"Wake everyone and, since we're still in the swamp, we need to separate and lay partially in the water. There's a chance, they'll read our images as gators."

"By God, you'd better hope they do or the General is about to lose his suitcase."

We all scattered, and I had Carol beside me and Dolly on the other side. There was a fair chance they'd take us as a male and female gator with a baby. Hell, I didn't know if this would work at all, or even if the chopper had infrared gear or not, but I had to do something. I knew in the past some choppers scared partisans to move by just searching. I heard the chopper move another grid closer to us and felt the little animal that lived in my stomach come alive again. He began chewing on my belly.

About ten minutes later, the bird moved over us and hovered as we all remained still, each fighting our fear in our own ways. I suddenly saw Hall move from the water and extend a LAW.

I watched, shocked when a machine-gun on the chopper opened up and he was stitched across the body, from left to right. The impact of the big bullets knocked him back into the water and his scream was short-lived. I started to move forward, but Black was closer and he crawled to the dropped LAW.

It was then I realized the chopper was not infrared equipped, or they'd see Black's movement. I fired my Bison at the bird, as

Black picked up the LAW and fired. Most of the partisans, from what I could see, were shooting too.

The LAW's 66 mm rocket struck the chopper near the engine and almost immediately dense black smoke began to pour from the engine exhaust. The bird wobbled grossly and then climbed to avoid further damage. As it gained altitude, it turned slowly and then moved north, and I saw a piece of aluminum fall from the engine housing.

I stood, moved to Hall, squatted beside his body but found him dead, the big slugs almost cutting him in two. Black stood on the trail, LAW at his feet and looked shocked.

"Let's move, people, that chopper has at least radioed our location and the bulk of the Russian army may soon visit."

As we moved, just below a jog, I turned to Carol and asked, "Still worried about Black?"

"No, I guess I was wrong about him, but he still feels different to me."

"Some personalities feel different to all of us, but I have complete confidence he's a true patriot now."

As they moved, Tom, or Master Sergeant Sokoloff, knew his firing at the Russian helicopter had proven his loyalties beyond a doubt. He realized, when Corporal Hall fell, it was his chance to be totally accepted into the team. He'd tried to down the aircraft, knowing the lives of the crew was a small price to pay to prevent a nuclear weapon from being used against his countrymen.

The rest of the day, we heard choppers moving and noticed the change in engine pitch as they landed, dropping off teams to search for us, or making false insertions. I had no idea how many teams were looking for us, but suspected at least five. Our only advantage was we knew the area and this allowed us to move faster. We had few mines or toe-poppers left, but planted them when we could.

We also rigged grenades to explode by securing them to brush near the trail, and then running thin fishing line across the trail. Most of us carried one or two small circular cans that allowed us to pull the grenade's pin and slip the grenade into a can. The can's shape prevented the spoon from flying off. If the line was anchored securely on one side and then attached to the grenade, just walking into the line would pull the explosive from the can, allowing the spoon to fly off and it would explode.

So far, we'd heard no explosions. Which either meant they've not found our trail yet or they've spotted and avoided our booby-traps. We continued to move just a tad faster than a normal walk, so we were covering some ground. If all worked out properly, we'd leave the swamp the next day, near noon.

We didn't stop like we usually did at noon for a meal. Instead, we ate as we moved and kept the pace fast. Tom was having a difficult time keeping up, even with most of the swelling down in his leg. I knew his pain was bad when I saw him take a few slugs from the vodka bottle. But, he never complained and kept moving with the rest of us. An hour after dark, we established a cold camp and got comfortable for the night.

As I moved around, talking with my team members, I heard our radio operator, Sara Lea, say, "Colonel, they want to speak to you."

This was our normal evening call in to get the next day's password, to give them a status of our team, and to let them know our position.

"Base, Quarterback here."

"We have two other teams in your area that are searching for the Russian Bear. They reported seeing four teams inserted earlier today. One team was taken out in an ambush, but the partisans lost half of their team. At that time we had three teams in your area, but the team with the ambush has been ordered to return to base."

"Any idea how close they may be to my team's position now?"

"Not exactly, but one Russian unit was known to be less than three miles from you and another near five. A great deal depends on if they stop for the night or not."

"And, what are the chances of a partisan unit catching up with us?"

"Both have orders to link with you, if they can, once the Russian threat has been terminated."

"Negative, do not have them link with us. A smaller unit is easier to hide, makes less noise, and takes less gear and supplies. Keep them behind us, so they can keep our back trail clear."

"Copy, negative on the link up. How are your supplies holding up?"

"We're good overall, but have no ground to air defense, nothing."

"The General has a unit in front of you to resupply you. The unit is currently moving to meet you tomorrow. Be prepared to meet near mid-morning."

"Roger that, so anything else?"

"Negative and your new man, Tom Black, has been verified as not among the dead. Now many of the dead were torn up, but no one who knew the man spotted his body. As far as base is concerned, your man Black is cleared and with a top secret clearance, which is what he's had from the start. Your new password and counter password for tomorrow is Black Forest ham."

"Copy on the password, and I'll have it decoded in a few minutes. This is Quarterback, out."

"Base out."

A few minutes later, Lea said, "Black Forest ham decodes to Rapid - Deployment."

"Good." I said and then looking around, I said, "I want the same guards as every night, but Top, I need to speak to you privately if I can for a few minutes."

Top stood, gave me a big grin and said, "I always have time for a Full Bull."

We walked off a bit and I shared what base had told me about Black. We both sat on the log and I was a bit surprised when he said, "I like the man, I really do, and his effort to down the chopper with the LAW showed his dedication to our cause, but there is something about him that's different."

I said, "He's not much of a talker, and Carol is watching the man, too. Headquarters said Tom Black's body was not among the dead when they checked for it, just to confirm the man had survived. They just informed me that he has a top secret clearance and has had for a long time."

"Well, I don't think the man is a spy, I simply said he's different. Even our old friend Willy Williams was different, so write it off as a personality quirk he has. Some men and women are loners and that's what I think our Tom Black is, a loner."

"Tomorrow when we split, I may take another person with me to provide security as I place and arm the bomb. I've learned from this trip that Carol may be the best person to work with me on arming the bomb, but she's not much of a fighter. She's a staff person and not a field grunt."

"Who will you take? And, watch the staff troop comments too, sir, because I'm one." Top smiled.

"Hell, I don't know who I'll take, and it doesn't make much difference to me." I ignored his comment about staff personnel.

"One is as good as the other and while I'd love to go with you, the General has other plans for me when I get back. Did you get the password for the day?"

"The password is Rapid - Deployment."

"Let's get back and prepare for the night. I want everyone up and moving an hour before first light." I said, and then yawned.

We walked back to camp and settled in for the evening. It was near 0200 hours when I got up to pee, when I saw Thompson on guard. I did my business and then moved to his side to talk a few minutes.

"Quiet?"

"Yes, sir, not so much as a gator breaking wind."

"Tomorrow most of you will return to base. I'm sure you'll get a little time off to eat and rest."

"What I really need is a hot shower and then get some hot food in me."

"I think we all need that. I miss the simple things from before the fall."

"Like what?"

"Being able to heat things in a microwave, getting meat pre-cut, sliced bread in plastic bags, and eating cereal from a box and getting milk in containers."

"I've had no milk since the fall and very little meat that required cutting. The first couple of years I did bag some deer, attempting to keep my family alive."

"Were you able to keep them alive?"

"There were five of us to start, my wife and I, and then our kids. We lost the two youngest babies to an unknown fever way before I joined the resistance, but Brad is as strong as an ox. They're back living with the civilians at Base. At least there they have security and food."

"If you're an American, Base is as safe as it gets in this country right now."

"I've heard some strange noises on the radio on my shift. One partisan unit, west, near Vicksburg, attacked a train leaving the city. They found a bunch of pills for nuclear radiation, dosimeters, and other testing gear. Along with some suits that look different than our chemical suits. They think they're some kind of radiation protective suits. They reported the train engine destroyed and almost half a company of Russians killed."

"We can use all that gear and more. I suspect we're getting fallout right now."

"Does it cause cancer?"

"I'm no doctor and really don't know for sure, but I would suspect it could. That's one of the reasons we're here, under trees. The only thing that will keep a person really safe is distance and shielding. Thick concrete or in a cave would work."

"We can't sit on our asses and let the Russians rule the roost, just because a nuke has exploded. It's worth the lives of all partisans to free our country of occupational forces."

I stood, stretched and said, "I agree, but right now I need some sleep."

"Goodnight, Colonel."

"Night, John." I said as I walked back to my sleeping bag. I slid in beside Carol and felt her reaching for me to pull me closer.

Morning was chilly with a light drizzle and gray skies from horizon to horizon. While not really cold, it was excellent hypothermia weather, so I had folks buddy up and watch each other. We were moving up the trail, using our NVGs, as Brewer was on point and Thompson was on drag. Thompson had complained he only had one toe-popper and no mines left. A unit our size was limited and could only carry so much, because our backs paid for every ounce we carried. Our first priorities were ammo and food, then mines, and finally surface-to-air defense. If all worked out well this morning, we'd link up with another team and be resupplied.

We'd come a long way in a few short years. I can remember fighting off my neighbors with Molotov cocktails and homemade napalm. While it worked, we were much better supplied now than at that time. Of course most of our gear is stolen from the Russians, and I've heard from the General that the Chinese will soon be supplying us, too. I'll not trust that rumor until I unpack a box of something they send us. Talk is cheap, while supporting a war is expensive.

Brewer had marked a couple of old mines the rains had uncovered, and I was glad he was on point. Good point people were hard to find, and while some of my folks did better then others, all did the job well.

I looked up, saw Brewer down on one knee with a balled fist in the air. His sign language was for us to stop he'd seen something.

CHAPTER 14

Captain Pajari was released from the hospital with orders to not return to work for at least 10 days, and when he returned to his quarters, it was empty. He finally found the Lieutenant in charge of quarters and he was assured all his belongings were in his new home, on officers row. Angry at the thought of moving, he'd gone to his new place and found it too much for him. He now had a kitchen, bathroom, bedroom, and living room. Before, he'd had one room and it was a tent. He was overwhelmed by the space and didn't need most of it. But, he'd been in the army long enough to realize fighting the system would do him no good, except label him as a problem child, and that he didn't need.

On his second day free from the hospital, the phone in his quarters rang and he was instructed to be at the 1800 meeting the Commander had each day. He would officially be promoted, his medals presented, and he would be welcomed into the officer corps. He disliked going but knocked back a few stiff drinks after 1700 and was feeling no pain when he arrived.

Promptly at 1800, a Master Sergeant yelled, "Teeennn-hooot!"

Everyone in the room stood at attention as the Commander walked in.

Walking to the podium, the Colonel said, "Please, remain standing. Standing beside me on stage is prior Senior Sergeant Albert Pajari. The Sergeant was personally responsible for the defense of our forward operating base, 'Tent City', and when it came under attack by an estimated three thousand partisans, with his Commander unconscious, he and he alone saved the entire base by taking command. Additionally, when being returned to the

Base as ordered, one door-gunner was severely injured and this man held a bleeding artery closed with his fingers to prevent loss of life. The helicopter Commander and crew were all injured in the crash, but our brave Senior Sergeant saved their lives as well. The quick action of Sergeant Pajari has been recognized by Moscow."

Removing a tab with a Captain's rank from a tray held by a Master Sergeant, the Base Commander and another full Colonel placed the rank on Pajari.

"Now if you will all stand, my executive officer will read the citation to award both the Cross of St. George and the Order of Kutuzov."

Ten minutes later, Pajari was standing by the door shaking hands with all the officers as they left, and turning down invitations to have some drinks later. He used the excuse he was on medication to avoid mingling with any officers. However, when the Commander walked near, handed him a glass of vodka, then toasted Mother Russia and to his future as a new Russian officer, he knocked the drink back. He knew the old Master Sergeant who was pouring the drinks well, and at one point he winked at the new Captain.

After he had shared three drinks with the Commander, he was dismissed and he quickly returned to his quarters. He changed into a t-shirt and baggy military running shorts. Since his new quarters had a television with only one channel, a military one, he began watching an old Russian movie. He heard a knock on his door.

He opened the door to see the Master Sergeant who'd been at the staff meeting.

"How is Russia's newest Captain, Albert?"

"Come in, please, Emin. How have you been?" He pointed to a plush chair in the living room.

"I brought you a good bottle of vodka to celebrate your promotion, and have a drink to the memory of Master Sergeant Sokoloff."

Caught off guard by the comment about Sokoloff, he asked, "Has something happened to Vlad?"

"His unit was an all English speaking team, and by listening to the American radio transmissions, we have learned his group was killed, with no survivors."

"Oh, not good. His wife will not take that well, because he was to retire next year. Has his death been confirmed?"

"No body recovered, if that is what you mean. A field unit visited the site, but found no survivors, and some of the bodies were shot to hell. I am sorry, Albert, but I thought you knew."

Sitting down on the sofa, his mind racing, he hoped it was all one big mistake. Then he asked, "Have his belongings been sent home?"

"I boxed them up myself this morning, and by now they are in the air. We sure do not leave much behind when we die, either. I think most of his stuff would have fit in a shoebox."

"I am sorry, Emin, I am just shocked by this is all. Please, pour the drinks, if you will."

After a few drinks things loosened up a little and the conversation moved on to other things, like the foods they missed, the theater, and after retirement plans. Albert was going to retire back on the farm, where he could enjoy his remaining years in peace and quiet. Emin was going to start a second career, so he'd be financially ready to retire in a few more years.

It was close to 2300 hours when a slightly drunk Emin said goodnight and left. For a long time, Albert sat on the sofa thinking of Vlad and what a good man he had been.

In order to draw attention from the moving suitcase bomb, the partisans kept their usual pressure on both Edwards and Jackson, suspecting the Russians would notice if they relaxed anyway. Normally, at least once a month the partisans attacked the bases and then pulled back. They were just reminding the Russians that they were still there and the night belonged to the people of the United States.

It was early evening, and Emin and Albert were sitting outside the Master Sergeants quarters, making small talk, when an explosion sounded. The secondary explosion was even louder and it was coming from the flight line. Knowing the partisans usually struck the base and then pulled out of the area, neither man moved.

"What do you think they struck this time?" Albert asked.

"From the size of the fireball, either a transport aircraft or a fuel truck. Have you screened for radiation sickness?" Emin asked.

"I do not know exactly what all they did to me when I came into the hospital. I was pretty much out of it, and do not know."

"Well, they have found some of us with messed up white blood cell counts, and we are being sent home for more medical evaluations."

"You are one of them?"

"Yes, but I feel fine."

"Not good, because it could be cancer."

"I do not know, and there is nothing I can do about it anyway. You know how the army works as well as the next man. If I am ill they will retire me, leave me to die, and go recruit more men. As individuals, we mean little to the government."

"That is the truth. How many of you are to be returned?"

"Over a hundred of us, so far. That does not even count those in Jackson, either."

"Detonating that bomb was one serious mistake, and there was no need. I personally think the vodka Vasiliev was drinking got to his head. I heard from his aide he was drinking a quart a day. He should have been relieved of command shortly after arriving here." Albert said.

Then, the base sirens went off.

Screaming to be heard, Emin said, "I need to join my men, we are under attack."

Laughing, Albert said, "It is the monthly reminder by the partisans they are still here."

"I will be back later, if it is not too late."

Albert laughed and moved toward his quarters. He had just turned on the television, when two bullets struck his prefab quarters, flew through his living room, and then exited the structure.

The T.V. showed a red screen that stated, 'We are under attack. This is not a drill. Report to your duty section immediately.'

Unsure what to do, he moved toward the perimeter fence. The first foxhole he spotted had a dead man in it, so he took the man's weapons, ammo, grenades and other gear. From what he could see, the bulk of the attack was on the flight line, but that didn't mean it was the primary target. Often an area would come under heavy attack, only to have the attack changed after men were rushed there.

As he squatted and thought, he heard a huge explosion and, looking behind him, he saw the fuel tanks blow and the petroleum, oxygen, and liquids (POL) storage area went up. Secondary explosions were rocking the base. He saw a refueling truck leave the fuel storage area at a high rate of speed, only to explode less than a hundred meters from the gate to the facility.

Then, he heard the sound of a rocket, followed by an explosion, or he thought it was a rocket.

Gradually, over a period of maybe ten minutes, the partisans withdrew, taking most of their dead and wounded with them. He remained where he was, mainly because many of the troops would be trigger happy right now.

Thirty minutes later the all clear siren was heard.

Slinging the weapon over his shoulder, then turning, he made his way back to his quarters.

The next morning, while looking near where he'd seen the rocket explode, Albert found the remains of a Chinese type 98 rocket, a 120mm unguided anti-tank rocket system, called a "Queen Bee." He picked up a few pieces and made his way to the Commander's office. He had to wait for the man, but he was in no hurry.

Two hours later, he walked into the Commander's office, saluted and said, "I think we have a serious problem, sir. The rockets fired on the base last night were of Chinese manufacture, and I think it was a rocket called a Queen Bee, which is an anti-tank rocket mainly."

"So, why is that a problem?"

"Sir, it may be the Chinese are now arming the Americans."

"Oh, I see. Ummm, that *could* be a real problem. Captain, this will be our secret for right now, and share it with no one. I will form a team to determine if most of the rockets fired at us last night were Chinese. If so, I will file an official report to the Chinese, through Moscow. Additionally I will have all partisans killed or captured searched for Chinese products. They very well may have started to aid this band of peasants."

"As you wish, sir. I just thought I should bring it to your attention."

"Thank you, Captain. I do not think these peasants can last another year, even with the help of the Chinese."

Peasants, my ass, and you called them that twice. These men are mostly prior military, experienced hunters, and a great number of older retirees with combat experience. They make up the largest unorganized military in the world, with enough personal guns to most likely arm each of them with two weapons. No, we are not fighting peasants, he thought as he saluted and left the office.

Later, Albert discovered the Colonel had sent the parts of the rockets to Moscow and claimed they were part of a Chinese rocket called a Queen Bee. He'd discovered hand grenades, some did not explode, and a number of magazines, and weapons of Chinese make. All were forwarded to Moscow, and they made a big deal over the Colonel's fine observation. He was notified he was almost assured of being on the next list of Full Colonels being promoted to the General ranks. He decided if he made General, Pajari would be promoted to Major.

It was at his next 0600 meeting when the chief of communications asked to speak for a moment in front of the group. Matveev was frustrated his usual briefing was to be interrupted, but said, "You have five minutes, Colonel."

The Lieutenant Colonel pulled a message from Moscow and read, 'Effective this date and time, Colonel Ivan Matveev, of Edwards Air Base, North America, is hereby promoted to the rank of Major General.[3] Please pass on our congratulations to him. Signed, Vitvinin Zinoviy Anatolievich, Army General.' Sir, my staff and I would like to be the first to congratulate you on your first of many stars."

The Commander was speechless, but after a few seconds, he said, "An officer should always reward those men who have helped him climb the ladder of rank. Captain Albert Pajari, please stand."

Albert stood, feeling out of place in a room full of officers.

"Gentlemen, I considered promoting this man, once again, to the rank of Major, but I will not. Instead, he is now Lieutenant Colonel Pajari, and will be the new head of Partisan Operations. This meeting will close early today, so I can call my wife, and then Moscow." He started for the door, and the room was called to attention.

Master Sergeant Emin Ivanovna approached Albert and said, "My, I have never seen an enlisted man get promoted as often or as high as you have, my friend. Care to share your secret?"

Lieutenant Colonel Pajari said, "I was able to recover parts of a rocket fired on us during the last attack and also found a few weapons used. They were of Chinese make. Which means the partisans are now supplied, at least partially, by China. I think Moscow was so happy to find proof to use as propaganda against the Chinese, they promoted our Colonel. He in turn promoted me. The odd thing is, all I wanted to be was a Master Sergeant and now I am a Lieutenant Colonel."

"The army is the army, and usually is not concerned with our wishes. I do not envy your new job as the Chief of Partisan Operations. It will be a job, I fear, that may bring you many ass-chewings at meetings like this one."

"Let them chew on me. I have already been chewed out many times, so they will not get a virgin. Come, and let us eat breakfast together. Once that is done, I need to get my new rank sewed on my uniforms. My wife will be very pleased with my increase in pay. Being overseas in a combat zone, having access to classified

---

3 The one star rank in the Russian military is called a Major General.

information, and all the other pay incentives will raise my base pay a great deal as a senior officer."

"You will earn every ruble, my friend. The army gives very few free rides."

The same afternoon, as General Matveev was packing things in his office and getting ready to leave for Moscow, Lieutenant Colonel Pajari showed up, as ordered. The General had the Colonel sit, and he moved to his chair. Pulling a bottle out of his lower right desk drawer, he poured into two glasses about three fingers of vodka. He handed one to Albert and then said, "My last act as the Commander here is for you to join our special teams that are creating problems for the Americans. No, you are not to spend a great deal of time with them, since you do not speak English, but perhaps a couple of days and one night will be enough. Since you are their Commander, you should have a working knowledge of their operations."

"I agree, sir." Albert agreed, but didn't really like the idea. He knew any Russian caught dressed as a partisan would be treated as a spy, and shot.

"If you do your job well here, Albert, I will see you make Full Colonel. My new assignment is Chief of Army manpower and promotions."

"I understand, sir." he replied, but didn't care what officer rank he was. He missed his enlisted friends and most, except for a couple of Master Sergeants, no longer spent time with him. The Russian army had strict rules against fraternization of the officer and enlisted grades.

"When am I to be inserted with a team?"

"You will be inserted alone, with a team already in the field, when we resupply them this morning. We have determined the Americans have a suitcase bomb; they are attempting to move it near Jackson, and they plan to detonate it. We have no idea which team of partisans has the bomb, not really, and we are attempting to meet all units moving north or toward Jackson. That task is a difficult one, because the Americans are frequently moving around Edwards and I-20 and I-55, the highways that run around and to Jackson.

Your teams are not to engage any unit, unless they are positive they have the suitcase bomb. I have no desire to scare the Americans away, because this way we may recover one of the two bombs stolen earlier from a train. Later this morning you will be shown the container the bomb comes in, given partisan clothing, and then flown out to meet your team. You are not to speak in the field at all, unless it is important, or an actual emergency. The teams will only speak English, so you may be confused at times."

"Yes, sir. Why aren't Spetsnaz doing this work for us?" Albert asked.

"They are currently tied up in another part of the world. The idea to do this is mine, which I took from the Germans in World War II where they used Operation Grief during the Battle of the Bulge. The original genius who came up with the idea was Waffen-SS commando Otto Skorzeny, of the German army, and while his attempt did not work, ours is having great success. Many of our units have misled the partisans, changed signs, and even issued false orders over the radio. Much confusion has been caused by just a few Russians."

"How many teams are currently in the field that speak English, sir?"

"Six, but that may double over the next year, because in the Motherland, they are searching now for those people who are fluent in English and have lived in this country at some point."

"My only concern is if our people are caught, will they not be executed as spies? It is illegal to fight in the uniform of your enemy, is it not, sir?"

The General laughed and replied, "Of course our troops know they will be executed if caught. It is a risky job, Colonel, but one vital to the Russian Army. A single unit of squad size can cause more problems for the Americans than a battalion of infantry. It is well worth the risk."

"Uh, I see, sir. And, where is this special unit I will join?"

Moving to a large map of central Mississippi on his wall, drink in his left hand, he used his index finger to point at an area just south of Pearl, Mississippi. He took a drink of his vodka and said, "They are currently about five miles south of Pearl."

"Why Pearl, if the target is Jackson?"

"If the partisans can detonate a nuclear bomb at Pearl, Colonel, they will get all of the international airport and all of Jackson, or at least the bulk of the city with the blast alone."

"What of the civilians in the area?" Albert asked, and then took a sip of his drink.

"What about them? I think the Americans are willing to sacrifice the civilian population to show us they will retaliate when and where they wish. They have more or less proven over the last year that they are willing to allow civilian deaths to further their cause, which is to have us leave this country. That, Colonel, will never happen."

"Oh, and why not, General?"

"There are any number of reasons we will stay; many are political, but this country is rich in raw materials that Russia wants and needs. Over the next few decades, we will rape this nation of what we want and need, and then, when the time is proper, we will leave."

"I understand, sir."

Major General Matveev, looked at his watch and then said, "Finish your drink and then get to supply and speak with Master Sergeant Khramov. He is to have your partisan clothing and gear ready for you. If you run into any problems with clothing or weapons, call me."

Yes, sir." Albert threw back his drink, stood, and then saluted. As he left the room, the General said, "Best of luck on your visit with your team."

"Yes, sir."

At 1000 hours, after the helicopter made a number of false insertions, Albert was unloaded with a small mountain of food, ammo, and munitions in a small field. Seeing movement, he squatted and flipped the safety off his Bison. He waited.

"We are friends." a voice said in Russian.

"Captain Kuklov, is that you?

"Yes, Colonel, it is I. We need to move both you and the sup-plies to the trees, and quickly."

"Oh, is there a reason to rush?"

"Yes, sir, we are in position to block an American unit moving this way. They may or may not have what we are looking for."

"Good, I will move to the trees with some boxes."

"Come, all, let us move this stuff, and now." the Captain ordered.

Ten minutes later, they were in a defensive position along a well used trail. The weather was clear with a slight breeze from the southwest, which Albert hoped was blowing the fallout from the first bomb away from him. Less than twenty minutes later a lone partisan walked down the trail looking for booby-traps or mines. At times his eyes would scan the country-side, looking for ambushes or danger. This man was a very cautious man. Albert noticed the man was thin, of average height, and very alert. He was wearing, like Albert, a mixture of Russian and American clothing. His shirt and jacket were Russian, but he wore an American ball cap and a pair of jeans. His boots looked to be Russian, but due to the dense brush, it was hard to tell.

Five minutes later the main body of Americans moved into view and while they were carrying loads, none were a suitcase or big enough to be the bomb. Captain Kuklov let them pass and then waited until their drag man passed before he spoke. "We will stay where we are for now, because a second unit has been reported to be behind this one. I suspect they will be here in less than 30 minutes." He spoke in Russian, in a voice almost a whisper.

"They are coming!" Lieutenant Gagarin said almost 35 minutes later.

CHAPTER 15

I was tired, and fighting the straps of my pack. The heavy load I was carrying had the nylon straps digging into my shoulders and I knew at the next break I'd need to either place something under the straps or divide some of the unit gear I was packing. I knew beyond a doubt my pack was well over 70 pounds.

It was then Brewer squatted and raised his right hand in a fist. It was time to stop, because he'd spotted something.

From the woods off my left side, I heard a voice say, "Rapid!"

Brewer grinned and replied, "Deployment."

A tall man stood from the brush, not twenty feet from me, smiled and asked, "Want some coffee and hot grub?"

"You bet," I said, and then added, "I'm Quarterback."

"Well, you're right on time, sir. Come with me and we'll see your immediate needs are cared for and your supplies issued."

I followed, along with the rest of the group, the man back to his camp. He was just outside the swamp in a thicket of briers and brush, surrounded by oak trees. His unit, which had started with ten people, was down to five now, due to combat losses. While any unit with that few people left should return to base, they'd not, because of the importance of supplying us. While we were gathering goods and sipping on real coffee stolen from the Russians, I repacked my gear and removed a lot of junk. By now you'd figure I'd learned over the years exactly what I needed in the field, but I am a bit of a pack-rat.

I removed every single thing except what was mission essential, which meant rations, bullets, and munitions. Even my paperback book I'd found months ago and read at least six times was discarded. I did keep a Russian .22 pistol with a silencer and two magazines. I'd taken the pistol off a dead Russian Colonel years ago. All the rest I dumped. The unit gear was divided, so each of us carried some. Like most, I usually carried a change of clothing in the event I got soaked, and a light Russian jacket. I kept the jacket and my poncho, but threw away the extra clothes. I figured once I set the bomb, I'd have one hour to get the hell out of Dodge, and it was very likely I'd toss my pack to the side. I'd want speed and not munitions or explosives as I left Pearl. I figured anyone with me would likely do the same.

We spent the afternoon packing and repacking our fresh supplies, and of interest to all of us was the fact many of our items were made in China. My ammo, six grenades, and my rations were Chinese, and I had no idea what was inside of them.

"If you're wondering about the Chinese rations, the meal includes a compressed food packet, an energy bar, an egg roll with pork, a pickled mustard tuber, and a powdered beverage pack. Most of the rations contain high energy foods, such as instant rice or noodles that are self-heated and luncheon meat. You will find the entree pretty tasteless and mostly a rice or noodles dish, but the energy bar is pretty good." the team leader said with a grin.

Another man said, "They are a welcome change to Russian rations and while not as good as MREs, they'll keep you alive in a pinch. By mixing the three types of rations, a person can have a fairly decent meal, mainly because of the small bottle of hot sauce in the MREs."

"Any time change in the Chinese grenades?"

"Supposedly not, but I've discovered to take no chances, because some detonate early and some late, or not at all. I suspect they have a huge quality control problem with munitions."

"So pull the pin and pitch, right?"

"Pretty much, and I try to use Russian grenades to toss and Chinese for booby-traps."

"Got ya, and that's what I'll do," I said, and was beginning to think the Chinese helping us may not be that good of an idea.

"Any difficulty in reading the labels on the gear sent for our use?" I asked, and then took a sip of the wonderful hot coffee.

"There can be, but on most supplies they've sent, the contents are listed in both Chinese and English. I have no idea if that's because this gear was just sent to us, or if they do that all the time. But, the wording on the directions can be funny. It's obvious most of those translating from Chinese to English are not fluent in our tongue."

"We need a new medical kit. Do you have one?"

"Yep, and it's Chinese too. It's a field kit for a trained medic, similar to what an Emergency Medical Technician would pack. There's morphine and codeine in the bag for serious injuries. Over all, it's satisfactory." the leader replied, and then gave us a weak smile.

"Anything else we need to know?" Brewer asked as he met my eyes.

"Yes, you'll find 6 shoulder fired rockets, called a Queen Bee, in your gear. It is unguided, so make sure your aim is true, and it fires a 20 mm all-purpose high-explosive rocket. It comes equipped with a night vision sighting system, which I have found functions fairly well, and the rocket has a maximum range of about 800 meters."

"Do they work?" I asked.

"All have exploded so far and the optical sight, using night vision, has about a 500m range. It has a fire-control computer, a laser range-finder, and an LED display. You'll have no problems using it, and so far I like it. Well, better than the rations anyway." the team leader said, and then grinned.

"Okay folks, let's divide this gear and get on our way. Captain, I thank you for staying and waiting for us, when you had every right to leave. However, by staying you'll help make this mission a success."

He extended his hand and said, "Glad to help. Sergeant, get the troops ready to return home. Best of luck on your mission, sir, whatever it may be."

"Thank you." I replied, and was glad he was moving away from the area and had no idea of my actual mission. I felt some may not like the idea I was fixing to nuke one of the most heavily populated areas in the state.

Minutes after the small group left, I said, "We need to do the same. Brewer, booby-trap anything that's left behind. Alford on point and James, you bring up the rear. Let's move, and if we're lucky, you'll be shed of me in less than 24 hours."

We walked until dark, then moved into a grove of mixed trees. Supper would be cold rations and I suspected most of us would try the new Chinese rations. No sooner had we stopped than a couple of the men moved for the bushes to pee, while the rest of us removed a ration. I had no idea what the container said, but the sticker said it was a full meal for one. I opened it and was rather disappointed, because the servings were so small. I knew right then these meals would not please Americans at all.

I had some kind of noodles with meat, but the noodles were overcooked and had the consistency of the glue I ate in grade school. I did find the chemical warmer and heated my meal, which only made my glue hot. The mustard tuber I threw to the bushes, but the luncheon meat was fairly good. I also liked the egg rolls or whatever they were. I really liked the energy bar, but the rest was trash in my mind.

"This crap is plain nasty." Brewer said, and then pretended to gag.

"I have some sort of rice dish, but not sure what kind of meat is in the pouch." Carol said.

"Oh, it's likely dog or cat, knowing the Chinese." Alford said.

Carol's eyes grew large and I thought she was going to puke. She said, "That's plain nasty, Alford."

"Let's cut the chatter and keep our conversation mission oriented," I said, but it was good to hear them joking.

Since we were close to leaving the group, I had two guards at a time this evening. I fell asleep fairly early, tired from all the walking and the load I was carrying in my pack. If you ever want to sleep well any night, spend all that day carrying a 60 pound pack. You *will* sleep.

At some point, Tom touched my left ankle and said, "Company coming."

I slipped my NVGs on and moved to the trail, which was about 100 feet from our overnight camp. I instantly spotted a point man and a squad size unit behind him approaching us. The unit appeared to be partisans.

They were wearing NVGs too, but we were well hidden in the brush and wore face-paint too, so we'd be hard to spot. When the main group was in front of me, I said, "Rapid."

"Deployment." came the reply.

"Stop, right there. What is your mission?" I asked as I stood from the trees.

"We're hunting Russians, and we're to supply assistance to a special unit moving north. That's really all I know."

"Your name?"

"I'm Captain James Isbell, from Meridian, Mississippi." "Come with me, Captain, and we'll talk. I'm Colonel Quarter-back."

I led them to our camp and everyone was well hidden as they should have been. I smiled and said, "They're our troops, so come back to camp."

As folks filtered in, I noticed one of the new partisans seemed to recognize Tom Black. While I wasn't suspicious of either man, I did asked, "Do you know this man, Tom?"

"We attended high school together, is all, Colonel, and I thought he was dead, years back."

Lieutenant Colonel Pajari recognized Master Sergeant Sokoloff, but didn't dare say a word to the man. He knew his English was too poor and if he spoke he knew it would compromise the Master Sergeant's cover.

His acting Commander said, "That is enough small talk. You two can talk again one day back at camp. Sir, you're in danger even as you sleep here. We have spotted numerous Russian units moving around, and some are company size and larger."

"I am in charge here, and my troops need rest." I noticed the man looking around my camp, but thought nothing of it, because most military men like to know what is around them at all times. It's called situational awareness and just means to be aware of where you are and what is going on around you.

"I understand, sir. Do you have any immediate needs?"

"Uh, no, but if you get any Chinese rations, toss them." I said, more or less teasing.

"Chinese? Why Chinese?"

"I've been told they're assisting us in our war against the Russian Bear."

"Well, we need the help of some super power, because I'm about beat most of the time. Poor food, little rest, and missions all the time, well, it gets very old."

While it was nothing I could put my finger on, there was something about his mannerisms that I found different. While he seemed to be a Southerner in speech and behavior, he wasn't complete, but he may have lived out of the state for a long while.

"What now?" I asked. I wasn't about to tell him of my mission, mainly because he had no need to know. Just as the last group didn't know, this one wouldn't either.

"I'm looking for a group that is carrying a large suitcase. My orders are to assist that group in any way, sir."

"Well, it's not us, so good luck."

The man looked around again, turned to a man and said, "Get the men ready to move, Sergeant. It'll soon be light." Then looking at me he said, "Best of luck on your mission, sir."

I didn't catch Pajari and Sokoloff exchanging looks or see the Russian Master Sergeant wink. Ten minutes later, they were gone.

"There is something unusual about that group." Thompson said, "While they look like us, sound like us, and move like us, I'd bet all I own they are not Americans."

"Lea, get me Base on the radio."

Minutes later a Master Sergeant at base said, "No, sir, no one knows what you carry and no one knows about the containers, or your mission. Uh, I can't say more because our code may have been broken."

"Any units assigned with a team leader named Captain James Isbell, from Meridian, Mississippi?"

"Used to be one, but no more. Captain Isbell was killed about a month back on a routine mission when his team was ambushed."

"Are you sure?"

"Pretty sure, since I was standing right beside him when he was killed. No, there is no Captain James Isbell, from Meridian, Mississippi, currently on our roster. I suspect, sir, you were talking to Russians."

"Alert all partisan units to be on the lookout for this man and his unit. Quarterback, out."

"Tom, I want to talk to you now."

He neared, sat on a log and asked, "Yes, sir?"

"Where do you know the man from you recognized with the team that just left?"

"We attended high school together, but that doesn't mean he's not sided with the Russians. Many men and women work for them to keep their family alive, sir. I almost did, but discovered they'd both been killed by the bastards before they even contacted me. The next time I met with the Russian, I slit his throat, and joined the partisans."

"Who was held captive?"

"My parents, both of them."

"From what you know, could he be with the Russians?"

"I can't honestly answer that, sir. He was never a friend in school. I had some classes with him, but don't think I ever spoke to him. I thought him dead years ago, along with most of my high school class."

"Something is not right about that unit. The leader gave me the name of a dead Captain as his own and no one knows my mission, but yet he knew some of it, so I'm not sure that was a partisan unit at all. I strongly feel we just met a team of Russians."

"Their English was perfect," James said, "along with the Southern dialect."

"Some didn't speak at all, including the man Tom knew. I have notified other units to be on the lookout for them. I'm almost positive they're Russians. See, this is not the first time soldiers have dressed as the enemy and then tried to blend in. Hitler sent special English speaking units out during the Battle of the Bulge to screw up the Americans and they did, but only for a while. Soon they were rounded up and executed for being spies. Anyone dressed in their enemies uniform and is caught is automatically considered a spy. By military law, world law, they are to be executed."

"Oh, for goodness sake, Colonel, he speaks English, if he's the same man."

"I noticed his leader didn't allow you two to speak, now did he?"

Lowering his head, Tom replied, "No, and I found that strange, too."

"Alright, everyone up and ready to move. We'll move for a couple of hours and then call it a night. I won't stay here since someone knows our position. I want James on drag and Tom on point."

The next morning it was raining, but not hard, only it couldn't be called a drizzle either. The wind was light, temperature was a comfortable 75 degrees, or so I'd guess. It's bad enough to be wet; it's worse if it's cold too. Lea contacted base, gave them our information and paled when she got finished speaking to them.

"Is something wrong?" I asked.

"Yes, the position we were at last night when we met the other team was hit hard by Russian attack helicopters just after midnight. And, the unit that met us, the one with the man that knew Tom, was ambushed near dawn this morning, with all killed but two. They were taken out by a partisan unit, because the leader started talking in Russian as they moved along the trail right into the ambush. Between what we'd radioed in already and the Russian language, the partisan leader figured they were the bad guys."

"Good, I guess this will be a good day after all, rain or no rain." I grinned as I moved to the bushes to relieve myself.

CHAPTER 16

Albert was scared, and injured to boot, but not seriously wounded. What concerned him most was he was dressed as a partisan, had an injured man with him, and was likely to be killed on sight by Russians or partisans. He was still in shock, but he'd had enough sense to bandage Lieutenant Gagarin's side. He didn't have a radio; it fell when Private Trusov was killed, and he was still angry that Captain Kuklov had spoken in Russian. He suspected the man had spoken for his benefit, but his use of the Russian language had resulted in the deaths of 10 men.

"What now, sir?" Gagarin asked.

"We keep moving north and try to reach Jackson or Edwards."

"If we are caught, we will be executed, sir."

"I am fully aware of that, and if our own troops catch us, we will likely be shot as well."

"Should we keep moving or hide?"

"Moving, north."

"Yes, sir. How is your hand?"

"Just a scratch. Has your side quit bleeding?"

"I think so, and it is just the furrow of a bullet. I thought I was a dead man during the ambush."

"Quiet, and walk. We do not want to be seen, heard, or smelled, if it can be prevented."

"Trusov was on the radio talking to base and I am sure they heard part of the battle."

Stopping, Pajari said, "We must be quiet, Lieutenant, and that is an order. If Headquarters heard the battle they may look for us, so if I hear a helicopter, I will try to signal them. Now, unless I decide otherwise, no talking. Do you understand me, and nod if you understand."

The Lieutenant nodded, so the Colonel started walking again. *Here we are in the middle of our enemies and this fool wants to chat like a blackbird. Fools, that is all Moscow sends me*, he thought as he walked down the muddy trail. He'd still not learned to consider himself an officer. A number of times he'd almost called the Lieutenant sir.

I wonder if Sokoloff is in solid with the Americans. I can report him alive, if I get back in one piece, but he may be back before I am, if the two of us ever get back, Albert thought as he glanced at the sky and saw dark clouds.

At one point, the Colonel stopped and pointed out a trip wire to the Lieutenant. They stepped over it, but Albert wasn't comfortable doing that. Often toe-poppers were placed on the other side, just in case a man stepped over the wire.

They'd gotten rid of their packs in their run for safety, so they had very gear little with them. They both carried Russian weapons and they had ammo, but no food, maps or sleeping bags. In some ways not having the weight was a blessing, but by mid-afternoon, both were hungry. They were north of the swamp, in an area covered with trees, with trails leading in all directions. Albert kept taking the trail leading north.

Near dark, they were crossing a wide open field when a Black Shark helicopter flew over them, banked and returned for another look. When the bird was close, both Russians on the ground began to jump up and down, waving their arms.

"Base, this Black Shark, Attack 1."

"Go, Attack 1."

"I have two men on the ground dressed as partisans waving at me."

"Uh, wait one."

A minute or so passed and then, "Attack 1, do not engage the target. We have a rescue helicopter on the way. Remain on station to support the recovery of the two men. Copy?"

"Copy, I will remain on station."

Suddenly tracers zipped through the air, just missing Albert but striking Lieutenant Gagarin in the legs. It was followed by an explosion as a rocket struck nearby.

"Base, this is Attack 1, the two men on the ground are taking fire from the trees."

"Keep them safe, Attack 1, so take out the source."

"Roger, will roll in on the trees." the Black Shark said, began a gentle circle, and then lined up the front of his Gatling guns on the suspected tree line. As he moved, just feet above the trees, he squeezed the trigger and smiled as he sat in his vibrating chair, as the trees were torn to shreds. On his second pass, he used two missiles.

Gagarin, on the ground, looked up at Albert and asked, "Did the helicopter shoot me?"

"No, ground fire hit you, and the helicopter cleared that problem for us. I suspect there will be a rescue helicopter here soon. It looks like base knew to look for survivors."

"I hurt." the Lieutenant said.

The Colonel pulled a needle with morphine, injected Gagarin and then started dressing the man's new injuries, bullet holes through both thighs. He wrapped him up and by the time he was finished, the Lieutenant was almost asleep.

"How are you, Gagarin?"

"I am feeling no pain."

"Good. You just lay there, and we are fine."

Two partisans ran for their position, scared out of the woods by the helicopter. Albert raised and fired his Bison, hitting the man on the left in the chest and the man on the right in the head. Blood, bones and gore flew out behind both, before they screamed and fell to the grasses.

Twenty minutes later a rescue helicopter and a MiG-31 arrived. Then the jet and Black Shark circled the field as the rescue helicopter landed. Two armed crewmen ran to them, asked Albert who they were in Russian, and then as a safety precaution, cuffed both men's hands behind their backs.

As they lifted up, the helicopter pilot transmitted, "We are taking ground fire from the trees to our west." Pajari heard a series of *pings* and *klinks* as they took off and one of the door gunners stopped firing and reached for the first aid kit on the wall. His flight suit had blood on the upper left side and it was growing in size. He'd taken a round high in his shoulder, but it looked like it missed the bone. Once they were high enough, the other gunner dressed his wound better. They were then flown to the base hospital. Albert was sitting on a red nylon seat, while Gagarin was on a stretcher rack behind the pilots.

Albert was unhurt and immediately cleared by General Matveev, who came to see him. The General also cleared the Lieutenant and both were given a physical exam. Lieutenant Gagarin was admitted for treatment of three wounds, but Colonel Pajari was released back to his unit as fit for duty. He quickly informed the General of Master Sergeant Sokoloff's position on the partisan team and neither could figure out how that could have happened. The General frowned when informed the Russian team was ambushed when Captain Kuklov spoke Russian at the wrong time.

"Damn me, Kuklov knew to never speak Russian in the field. He must have done it for your benefit."

"Well, General, he almost got me killed. Ten men; men who were fluent in American Southern English are gone because of his error in judgment, sir."

"It is a shame. Are you certain there were no survivors except the two of you?"

"Certain as you can get, because I saw the mangled bodies. They were ripped to pieces, sir."

"Well," the General said, "I do hope your trip with the team at least opened your eyes to the potential damage groups like this can do."

"Yes, sir, it did. But, as I can speak from experience, all it takes is one mistake, just one, and you are a dead man."

After his visit with the General, the Lieutenant Colonel went to the officer's mess and had steak and eggs, washing it down with almost a pot of strong black coffee. Then after the meal, he had a cup of hot tea to relax. He was dressed in Russian field clothing now, without rank, which didn't matter to him, and needed a hot shower and some sleep.

As he was getting ready to leave, the club manager approached and ask, "May I see your identification please?"

"I do not have it with me, nor my wallet, nor my usual uniform. If you will be patient, Lieutenant, I will return to my quarters, get my wallet and pay you for this meal. My name is Lieutenant Colonel Albert Pajari, and I am the head of the Partisan Research and Termination branch. Call General Matveev and he will verify I have been on a top secret mission, something that you likely know nothing about."

"And, what is that last sentence to mean?"

Glaring at the man, Albert said, "And, what is that last sentence to mean, *sir?*"

"*Sir.*" the Lieutenant said, and then smiled.

"I have told you to call the General's office, and Lieutenants usually do what Colonels tell them to do."

"I have no idea if you are even an officer, but be assured I will make the call."

Shortly the Lieutenant returned, snapped to attention and said, "The General confirmed you are who you claim to be, sir. Consider your meal on the house, by order of Major General Matveev, sir."

Albert grinned and left for his quarters.

Once in his room, he poured a glass of vodka, and turned on the television. As he sipped his drink, he watched a documentary about Siberia, and hoped he was never assigned there. He'd heard of the brutal gulags there, so he feared being jailed in Siberia, like many Russians. There were a lot of Army officers serving time at one gulag or another in Siberia, and all it would take is one angry General.

His phone rang, and he picked it up. "Lieutenant Colonel Pajari speaking."

"This is Master Sergeant Yan "Yanka" Travkin, and I am your new Sergeant. How are you, Paj?"

"I will be damned, Yanka, how are you? The last time I saw you was my first tour here and it looked like you would lose a leg. I take it they saved the leg?"

"Oh, they used some nuts and screws and fixed me up like new! What is this I hear of you being the big officer now?"

"It is a long story, but I would be happier as a Master Sergeant."

"Well, why do I not come by your quarters, sir, and we can discuss my assignment? I just got in and personnel sent me to you. Sorry about the 'sir', but a Captain knows I am speaking with my new Commander."

"Come on over, Yanka. We will share some drinks like the old days."

"I will be sure to bring a copy of my orders, sir, and I will be right over, if I can get a ride. Oh, the Captain here says he will have his driver drop me off."

Twenty minutes later, the two men embraced at the door, and Albert said, "Oh, Yanka, I never expected to see you again, much less to see you standing on your own legs! I thought that mine blast ruined your leg, and I had heard they took it off."

"Oh, they wanted to remove it, but I fought them and won. It is ugly as hell, mostly scar tissue, but it works, and I can run with the best of them. I brought a bottle of top shelf vodka, too. So, tell me all about how you, a Sergeant the last time I saw you, are now a Lieutenant Colonel?"

"As my dear old mother used to say, 'God works in mysterious ways'; well, so does the Russian army." So, Albert told his story, but it didn't take him long.

"I know there was more to it than that, because they do not just give enlisted men an officers rank without something heroic taking place. I will hear all about it tomorrow from the enlisted men. Now, sir, we cannot get too drunk tonight, but let us sit on the sofa and update me on all you have been doing." Yanka said as he poured vodka in both glasses. He then handed one to Albert.

Two hours later, Albert was alone and realized once he retired, he would miss the comradeship he shared with all Russian soldiers. It was a fraternity of men and women who offered their lives to defend mother Russia. They were as brave as the Vikings or the American Indians. They were true professional warriors. He showered with the thoughts still in his mind and woke the next morning still thinking about it.

His first day on the job was all briefings and gathering information. He made sure Master Sergeant Sokoloff was listed as alive and his wife was notified of the change. He just hoped he'd not have to tell her otherwise in a week or so. He also made sure the Master Sergeant's pay was updated to include the various incentives for his risk. Unlike the American army of old, the Russians were paid for handling classified information, for risks associated with their jobs, and other small things that added up. At times, a Junior Sergeant stationed in America on jump status, handling classified information, exposed to enemy fire at times, and acting in a Sergeant's position, might make as much as a Lieutenant in Moscow. All the small things added up.

After work, Yanka invited his Commander into his office and shut the door. He pulled out a bottle and they both knocked back a double vodka.

It was then a siren went off and both men sat the glasses on the Sergeant's desk and made their way to the door. Looking out, five aircraft were seen approaching the base at a high rate of speed.

"Must be some of our jets diverting here for some reason." Yanka said.

"No, no, no, those aircraft are not Russian! Oh, my God, they are Red Chinese! Those are Xian JH-7 fighter-bombers! Run to your assigned position, *now!*" Albert screamed.

The JH-7's nosed down and made a run on the runway, missiles destroying some aircraft that were parked too close together. Albert saw a fuel truck explode, then the mechanics in the vacinity were splashed with burning fuel, which resulted in some stumbling around near other aircraft, in flames. In one pass, the Russian flightline was afire. He had no idea how many Russians died, but it must have been hundreds. He ran to his office, grabbed his camera and began snapping images of the Chinese aircraft. They made two more passes and in some of the images, he got tail numbers and one pilot passed so low in a banking flight, he got a photo of the man's head and face.

No anti-aircraft guns were in place and while some Black Sharks and MiGs attempted to take off, they never cleared the runway before they went down in flames. Requests in the past for any surface to air defense had been refused, with Moscow stating the Americans had no aircraft. He ran to the command post and heard Headquarters Jackson say over the radio that they did not believe the Chinese were attacking Edwards.

As the bullets flew and rockets exploded, the General screamed over the radio, "Do you not hear the combat noises behind me, you damned fool? We are under attack by the Red Chinese! I want this whole state on 100% alert and *now!*"

Oh, no, not the Chinese! Albert thought, *There are millions of them!*

He turned, looked out the door to see a few shoulder-fired missiles being handed out, but it was too little and way too late. The airborne defenses on the aircraft resulted in not a single aircraft being downed, but the Russians made a noble effort. There came a loud explosion and the earth shuddered. Albert suspected it was the ammunition dump going up, or at least part of it.

Ten minutes later the aircraft left, with most of the base burning. He was absolutely stunned as he walked around with Major General Matveev.

"S . . . sir," Albert said, "I have photos of the attack, aircraft tail numbers, Chinese markings, the works. I suggest we file a formal protest to Moscow and send the images by special carrier."

Matveev met his eyes and said, "You, Albert, have saved my ass again. Get the images developed, and now. I want color images of the damage done too, to accompany the protest, when we leave."

"We, sir?"

"Yes, of course, we. Since this is your idea, I think you are the best man to present this to Moscow and the rest of the world. I will write up the formal protest, but I want you to brief where you were, how the attack took place, and how our heroic troops had no anti-aircraft guns, but still resisted much better than could be expected. Show your images, brief the brass and let us see if Moscow is afraid of 2 billion Chinese. I hope we do not go to war over this, because I fear it is a war we cannot win. Their manpower alone is staggering."

"Uh, when do we, ummm, leave, sir?"

"At midnight, and in the aircraft being sent by Moscow to fly us home. I want you to go with me, present your information, and then return. Who knows, there might even be a promotion in it for you, but I do not have that kind off authority as a one star General. I have promoted you as far as I can alone, but I will make a suggestion, of course."

"Sir, promotions mean little to me, really."

"Nonsense, every man and woman likes to be promoted and to receive medals."

"Yes, sir, but I had only dreamed to be a Master Sergeant."

"Then you have gone far, Albert. See to our film, get packed, and let us prepare to leave. My driver will be at your quarters at 2300 hours."

"Yes, sir." Albert said, and then moved toward the base photo lab thinking, I do not want to go to Moscow and put on a dog and pony show. I know it will help my career, the Gene*ral will see to that, but I dread this. I should have remained on the farm. I damned sure do not want a war with the Chinese; good God, there are millions of them!*

CHAPTER 17

Master Sergeant Sokoloff, a.k.a, "Tom Black," was tired. They'd moved fast and long over the last few days and while in excellent shape, he was paying for all the vodka and lazy moments he'd had at the base. Of course, everyone on his team was tired, so it wasn't just him. He was leaning back against a pine tree, a poncho over his head, and a small fire burning between his legs, heating his Russian rations. He was unable to eat the Chinese rations, and found the food had the consistency of paste or mud.

At 1800 hours, Sara Lea contacted base and once done, she sat there, on her log, in shock. Everyone knew something was wrong, so I asked, "What's going on, Lea?"

"The Chinese attacked Edwards over an hour ago, met almost no resistance, and caused heavy damage, with a mountain of casualties for the Russians."

"The Chinese? Are you sure?" I asked, not believing the Chinese wanted to get that involved in our fight.

"The loss of life is estimated to be extremely high, with no Red Chinese losses. All base would tell me is the attacking aircraft were out of Texas. The only reason I was told, or so base said, is we can expect an increase in Russian activity. If taken prisoner, we can expect to be questioned about the Chinese."

Then, wondering how my mission could have been effected by this, I asked, "Any change in my mission?"

"Our mission was not brought up, sir. We can assume it has not been changed by this attack but it may make things rougher for us."

"No," I said with a grin, "it may make our mission easier. None of the Russian facilities that I know of have any anti-aircraft weapons installed, not a one, and it will take manpower to install guns and missiles, fill sandbags and man the guns. They'll need those defenses installed and manned as quickly as possible. They'll have to pull combat troops to establish air defenses. I'm sure the Chinese attack cost them a fortune in troops and aircraft, but I wonder why the Chinese waited until now to enter this war."

"They're getting something from this mess, you can be sure of it." Tom Black said.

"Yep, and Asians are good traders, so they'll get the best end of the deal." Brewer said, and then added, "But, I do love the idea of their aircraft hitting the Russians."

"Enough talk," I said and then added, "keep the noise down. Tomorrow, less than four miles from here, Carol and I will leave all of you. When we leave, I will take one man."

"Who will go with you?" Top asked.

"Tom Black will come with us." I said, and watched Top raise his eyebrows in shock. While Tom was one of us, there was still some matters of trust with the man. I simply thought it would be better to have him with me than worry about what he might do with the main group. All the evidence I had proved he was one of us, but that small voice in my head warned me he was dangerous.

"Tom, you heard the man, so go through your gear and any excess items should be given to me. You'll need to travel fast and hard for this mission."

"Sure, Top, but is someone going to tell me what our mission is?" he asked.

"No, not until we are in place." I said.

"What if something happens to you and Carol?" he asked.

"All I will tell you is it involves the suitcase. As for the rest, you have no need to know at this time. I want everyone to eat and then get some rest. We'll have the same guards as before. I want us up and moving at first light."

I moved to a huge oak tree, started heating up my rations, as I spoke to Carol in hushed tones. I told her my reason for bringing Tom and emphasized the need to watch him closely.

"After all he's done, you still don't trust him?" she asked, and I could see the disbelief in her eyes.

"Not completely, and my senses are highly tuned. Earlier in my life, I survived two combat tours, then a tour in a hostile environment, teaching our allies how to resist the enemy. I learned to listen to my senses, and there is a sense of survival, if you will, that warns a person when something is wrong or not right. That alarm goes off around Tom. Headquarters and the world may trust him, but I will not."

"Okay, but I need to give him one of these pills. These pills are in glass containers, so they must be bitten to work. Once you bite them, you are dead in a matter of a few short minutes. If accidentally swallowed, they will pass through your body harmlessly, as long as you have not broken the glass. Here." She handed me one of about six pills she had in her hand. She then stood and moved to Tom.

Little was said between the two and they were too far away for me to hear their whispers, but he took a pill. I knew the pill was designed to kill us to avoid giving out any information we had and to save us days of painful torture. I was positive anyone caught with a suitcase nuclear bomb would have the hell tortured out of them. I'd bite the pill for sure, if taken prisoner.

She returned to me, sat at my side, and I put my arm around her shoulders. She turned her head, met my eyes and said, "Colonel, I think I'm in love with you."

"Really? Well, Captain, I think I love you as well. However, we need to complete this mission before we can discuss anything about us."

"I disagree, because there is no guarantee we'll survive this mission. What we have to say needs to be said now, because tomorrow is not assured to anyone."

I pulled her in my arms, kissed her and whispered, "I love you."

The morning came too soon, and two hours before sunrise we were up and moving. I had Alford on point and Brewer bringing up the rear. We were wearing NVGs, which caste an eerie green tint to everything, but did allow us a great deal of freedom when moving at night. We'd been moving for a couple of hours, when Alford dropped to one knee and his fist was raised into the air. We all squatted.

Looking in front of my point man, I saw a Russian squad moving toward us, and they were wearing NVGs as well. I had everyone move into the brush that lined the trail and try to blend in. We didn't have the time to plant a mine or prepare an ambush; I hoped they'd pass us by, unnoticed.

As they passed, I grew nervous, expecting combat any second, but it didn't happen. As their drag man passed, I relaxed, but it was the wrong thing to do. Once the drag man had turned the bend in the trail, I heard an RG-6 grenade launcher fire two 40 mm rounds, which were slightly off target and exploded behind us, and then the small arms fire opened up.

I crawled to Top and asked, "Do you think you can hold them?"

"Sure, but why?"

"We're less than a mile from where I'm to leave you and I think during all this chaos, would be the perfect time for us to leave." I replied.

"Go, we'll handle this; good luck, sir." Top said and then winked at me.

I moved to Carol, but could not find Tom, so I took Alford instead. The three of us began to crawl away from the fire fight. When I looked back at my group, Thompson had his flamethrower in action and I heard screams from the Russians. I wondered why the grenade launcher hadn't coughed again, but Alford told me later he'd taken the man out as soon as possible with a head shot.

We moved straight back, then at a 90 degree direction to avoid any stray rounds, and while we didn't run, we moved at a fast clip. Less than a half a mile later, I heard what I suspected was grenade explosions, and then it grew still. I had no way of knowing we'd had James seriously injured, Lea and Brewer were both slightly wounded, with Tompson and Top the only two uninjured. Tom Black was now missing in action.

The Russians had broken contact after the loss of half their unit, and moved south. Top, wanting to complete his part of my mission, radioed base and informed them, "Game in progress." This was code to let them know I was moving toward Pearl, my intended target.

Now, I didn't want to rush to Pearl and take the risk of being caught. I had no urge to bite the glass pill, loved the woman with me, and fully trusted Alford. However, if I'd known Tom was missing my speed would have been greater. It's strange how some things we don't know can change our lives forever, sometimes in good ways, and at other times, in horrific ways.

Master Sergeant Sokoloff tracked the Russian unit, and while he fully intended to meet with them, he had to be cautious or they'd kill him on sight. As he moved, he decided to follow, but avoid contact, until they went into a night camp. He could call out then and hopefully they'd not be trigger happy. This group was good, covering their trail and moving in unexpected directions. If they were not Spetsnaz, they were well trained by the special forces group.

The Master Sergeant was not Spetsnaz, but had undergone a six month program in Russia to improve his Southern dialect, learn how to move without leaving much evidence of his passing, and how to kill silently. As he moved, he pulled the pill given to him by Captain Carol Logan and tossed it in the brush. He'd already been parachute qualified, but he'd been taught HAHO, high altitude high opening, and HALO, high altitude low opening, and he was scuba trained as well, so he was fully qualified for his missions. He was trained in the same areas as Spetsnaz, but his training was rushed and not as thorough.

I have earned my extra pay this month, he thought as he squatted to look at a track in the soil. With all his special training, being on a combat mission, and with the mission being classified Top Secret, he knew he'd bring in many rubles this coming month, if he survived this mission. It had been easy to leave the Americans, because he'd simply crawled off at a 90 degree angle and once far enough away, he remained motionless. They'd not looked for him long.

An hour before dark, he saw the Russian team move into the woods and knew they were establishing an overnight camp. He would wait until full dark and then call out to the team. As he waited, he wondered about Albert and if he'd survived his time with his unit. The *mosquitos* were getting bad now, so he applied a layer of insect repellent to his face and hands. *I must give these men names of our Commanders and tell them things only a Russian soldier would know after being stationed at Edwards*, he thought.

Once dark, he moved near the Russian team and said, "I am Master Sergeant Vlad Sokoloff, of the Russian army, and on a special mission. Can I come to your fire?"

"Stand."

"I am dressed as a partisan, because I speak English."

"Stand and remain still. I will send two men to bring you into our camp."

Sokoloff stood, two men approached him and placed his hands behind his back, handcuffing him. He was led to a very small fire, about the size of tea cup.

"Radioman, contact Edwards and let them know we have a man who claims he is Master Sergeant Sokoloff and he is on a special mission. Get me a description of the man, and some questions only he would know." the team leader said.

Each new man assigned to Edwards had filled out an authentication card to use to verify a person's identity if found in the bush or following an aircraft crash.

"Sir, a Master Sergeant Sokoloff was last seen with American partisans and is on a top secret mission. The description fits this man. I have his three authentication questions, too." the Radioman said.

"Ask him, then."

"What is your pet name for your wife?"

Sokoloff grinned, "Cat."

"What was your nickname in school?"

"Vee, because of the v in my first name, Vlad."

"How many children do you have?"

"I have three girls and four boys."

Smiling the radio operator said, "He's passed, sir, he's our Master Sergeant."

I moved north, once far enough away to do so safely, and moved down the trail quickly, not at a run, but a fast walk. I knew three people were easier to hide, made less noise, and were less likely to be seen moving, but if seen, we'd not be able to resist much if spotted by the Russians. It was as we moved I considered only moving by night and pulled my two people in close and told them of my plan.

"How far are we from your target, sir?" Alford asked.

"Not far as the crow flies, but we aren't crows. I expect to take two nights to arrive at where I need to be. We will move off to the right, sit back to back, then eat and sleep some. An hour before dusk we will move again. Now, moving at night is much more dangerous than daytime, but I don't expect us to encounter much in the way of Russians until we near Pearl. Pearl, Alford is our intended target."

The rest of the day passed quietly, with none of us speaking, and no one was heard moving on the trail. My biggest fear was a dog team, but the trail remained empty the remainder of the day. I suspected we were in a gray area, which neither side patrolled much, and where Russian teams were often inserted to start their missions. We were only a few miles from Pearl, so I didn't worry much about choppers flying overhead, because most partisans were a good twenty miles from us. I suspected most of the aircraft overhead would be from Jackson, since the Chinese had torn Edwards to hell and back. As a matter of fact, I'd not heard a single aircraft all day. There was also the likelihood that no Russian aircraft would fire on us this night, because if they were out of

Jackson, they may not have the locations of most of the Russian units in the field.

An hour before dusk, we were moving down the trail slowly, because this was a perfect time to be ambushed. At one point, on the edge of an open field, I spotted at least five heavy Russian tanks out in the open. I knew they were likely protected by a few companies of infantry, so we gave them a wide detour. The last thing I wanted was a fight with an armor unit.

A little after midnight, I heard, but did not see, a unit near the trail. Someone had snored and I heard it clearly, but try as hard as I could, I saw nothing. I stopped for a second, heard it again, and then moved on. I don't think they had a guard posted, but if they did, he either didn't see us or was asleep.

Near 0300 hours, while it was still dark, Alford raised his fist and moved to the brush. Carol and I did the same. I shivered as a company size unit of Russian infantry moved passed us. That was when I decided Alford needed to be at least a Sergeant, because he'd saved our bacon again. *I'll do something about his promotion once we return*, I thought, and seconds later he was beside us.

In the dim moonlight, I saw him holding up two fingers, and at that point I heard a laugh on the trail. I heard the sound of men moving, metal striking metal, and rustling of trouser legs as they moved. A short order in Russian followed and the laughter stopped instantly, along with the metal sounds. I squatted and watched another company file past us.

Near dawn, Alford found an abandoned house and I was tempted to stay there, since we had rain coming, but I didn't like the idea of being trapped in the place. Instead, we moved into the trees behind the house and once daylight, ate a fast breakfast. One of us would always stand guard, except for Carol, and that was because I didn't trust her to remain awake. This was her first experience in the field and while she was doing fine, she was exhausted each morning when we stopped. I couldn't afford to take a chance with her and told her so. She agreed with me.

Near noon, right after I'd taken over watch, I heard noises near the old house. I watched as a Russian tank drove to the place, revved it's engines a few times and then with a company of infantry, the big monster drove through the house, causing it to collapse. The infantry had more or less surrounded the house, in the event the tank flushed any partisans. But, this time they found no one. I woke the other two and we watched the Russians move south, away from us.

"Damn," said Alford, "I wanted to sleep there this morning."

"I did as well," I replied, "but something told me not to enter the place. *Always* listen to your inner voice, *always*."

"Do you think they're looking for us?" Carol asked.

"No, not really. I think they are partisan hunting and a tank adds a lot of fear for most folks. If someone had been in the house, they'd have run out, right into the arms of the infanty. They would have been taken captive or shot on the spot, depending on the mission assigned to the Russians. Right now they want us, know we're moving north, but have no idea how many of us there are, where we're at, or much about us at all."

"What now?" Carol asked.

"You two go back to sleep. I wasn't comfortable with you two sleeping and a bunch of Russians at our back door. You can still get a few hours of sleep."

After they left for their sleeping bags, I sat thinking a whole lot about nothing. I thought of my first grade teacher, my parents; Willy Williams came to mind, and he was a hell of a good man. It was one of those times when thoughts just zipped through my head, but at least this time I wasn't trying to sleep. I had the bad habit of thinking after laying down to sleep. I'd sent Dolly back with Top and I actually missed her as much as if she was a person. I then gave thought to all my dogs; Newt, Skillet, Benji, and Dolly. I'd had other dogs too, but those four were my favorites. I'd lived in the country then, and my 'babies' were well cared for. I can honestly say they were all treated better than some kids I knew. I've always wondered why some folks had children, when they couldn't take care of a dog or cat. Soon, it was dark.

All was uneventful until around midnight when I heard a Russian Bison open up and heard bullets striking the leaves on the trees around me, then an explosion of a grenade sounded, followed by screams. Then a second grenade and more screams.

I had Carol remain with me and we waited. We were all three wearing NVGs, but I had no idea what had happened. Minutes later, Alford came to us and said, "Group of Russians eating. One saw me and they opened fire. My grenade put 'em all down, but I don't think I killed them all. Let's take a detour and swing wide the rest of the night."

"Go." was my only reply.

The remainder of the night was quiet and I'd seen deer, a fox, and a 'possum as we moved. Simple things like seeing those animals made me remember the old days, before the fall. Times were different then, much different, and most Americans had no idea of the condition of our country. Our President downplayed everything, wouldn't stand up against our enemies, and he was so bad, folks began thinking he was favoring our enemies over us, his own countrymen. I'd not voted for him, not either time, and suspected from the start he was no good.

He was too smooth, and reminded me of a hungry used car dealer. I found out later he could barely say his name without a teleprompter. He'd doubled our deficit, and ruined race relations. Racial tensions were the highest during his Presidency than any time in our nation's history. Our nation's credit rating dropped, our deficit was in the trillions of dollars, he lied about many things and then later when confronted with his lies, lied again. But for the average citizen, all was well, at least on the outside.

I can remember taking my first wife on drives at night, on gravel country back roads, so we could see wild game in the headlights of my truck. We'd often see deer and other animals. It was then I felt my heart strings break and the tears flowed.

CHAPTER 18

Master Sergeant Sokoloff pulled the team leader, Captain Stepan Smagin, aside and told him of the partisan mission to plant a nuke near Jackson. He met his eyes and said, "Are you positive of this action?"

"I assure you, Captain, it is true. I lived and traveled with them a long time. I even saw one of the missing suitcase bombs."

"We will report what you have told me today to Headquarters, but in code."

"At all costs, sir, they must be stopped."

"That, Sergeant, is up to our superiors, not us. We will follow orders."

"Yes, sir, but stress to them I know what the partisans look like, as well as the general direction they are moving."

"I will do that; now let us get back to camp, eat breakfast, and get ready to move."

Once in camp, Smagin and his radioman moved away from the group to send a coded message to Base. Twenty minutes later they returned and the Captain said, "Master Sergeant, your request to follow has been refused. We are to continue south and attempt to take out partisans."

"Yes, sir." Sokoloff replied, but he was greatly disappointed.

The morning was rough because it turned to rain, and mud was causing problems. They were moving slower than usual, mainly because of booby-traps in the area. Near noon, their man on point suddenly stopped and began to scream. When they neared, he'd stepped on a trap the Russians called a teeter-totter trap. The board, balanced on a fulcrum, was flipped all the way up, and 6 sharp rough-metal stakes were embedded in the chest of the point man. The two barbed stakes were seen protruding from his back.

The medic was called to the front and he gave the injured man a lethal shot of morphine, because he was beyond help. Minutes later the soldier died quietly, the strong drug taking his pain away.

It was then a Chinese helicopter must have spotted the men, because the 30 mm cannon began to fire. Men dropped as limbs and heads were removed and bodies blown in half. As Sokoloff dropped to the weeds he found it strange to be under attack by a Chinese Z-10 attack helicopter in America. The cannon threw dirt high, almost ten feet high, as it continued to grind the men into fine chunks of meat.

The Chinese bird then slowly came down low to see the damage they'd done to the Russians. After circling a few times, with a man in the front seat taking photos, the helicopter rose into the sky and continued north.

Uninjured, but deeply stunned, Master Sergeant Sokoloff moved among his comrades and found all dead, and one man missing, the radio operator.

"Is it safe now, Master Sergeant?" a voiced asked from the brush.

"Come to me, and what is your name?"

"I am Private Goreva Luklov, Sergeant, and I am the radioman."

"Call base now and report we have experienced an attack by a Chinese Z-10 attack helicopter. Report you and I as the only survivors. Tell them we are continuing our mission."

"Continuing our mission? How can that be, with just the two of us?"

"Do as I instructed, Private, and do it now."

As soon as the Private finished, the Master Sergeant took the radio and removed the batteries. He handed them to the man and said, "Save these to use later. Right now, you and I need to be moving north."

"North? Our original mission was south."

"Sit on the log with me, Private, and let me tell you a quick story about an American football game, which may have a terrible ending for all Russians."

Ten minutes later the man blinked a few times and said, "That is like something out of a book to me. How do we stop them and not get our asses vaporized in the process?"

"I have no idea, but they must be stopped before the device is armed."

"And how is it armed, Master Sergeant?"

"When they insert a key, a panel will pop up, with a keyboard on the panel, but only with numbers. By typing in the proper code, the bomb is then armed. So, they must have both the key and code for a detonation."

"What kind of damage would a bomb like that cause in, oh, maybe if placed between Jackson and the airport?"

"Total devastation to both the airport and the city. I mean they would both be flattened, and then there is the fallout to consider, which could end up killing millions, including most Russians, depending on the winds."

"They must be stopped, because the one bomb that we exploded is already making some of my friends ill."

"Okay, on your feet, because we will travel fast and long this day. All I know about them is they said something about Pearl, but I know of no such town on our maps."

"It is a small village, closer to the airport than the big city of Jackson, I think. I once pulled guard duty at an abandoned fire station there." the Private said they walked north.

"How far from the highway is this town?"

"In some parts of town, you can walk to it quickly. It is not far at all."

"Okay, enough talk as we move; we will talk again later this evening."

The remainder of the day was slow and wet. But, near dark, the Master Sergeant picked up the tracks of three people, all moving north. While the Private wanted to stop and rest, as long as he could see the footprints Sokoloff wanted to continue following. It was near midnight, in a light drizzle, that he moved into the trees.

They used one poncho to make a shelter and the other as a ground cloth. They moved under the shelter and ate cold Russian rations for supper. As soon as they finished eating, the Private fell asleep, so the Sergeant let him. After three hours, he woke the man, slept for a couple of hours himself, and woke up feeling terrible; his eyes felt like they had sand in them, and his body was sore. He and the Private broke camp and moved north.

The Master Sergeant was the man walking in front, because he didn't trust the Private. More than once he had to stop and warn the man behind him of booby-traps or mines. Seemed the closer he got to Pearl, the more mines he discovered. He was able to clearly see the tracks of the partisans, so he continued to follow. Often he could see where the partisans had stepped over a trip wire or walked around a planted mine.

Master Sergeant Sokoloff was worried all day about the Chinese helicopter, and had never seen one before in the field. He'd seen one once at an air show in Moscow, but he was glad he'd never been under it's guns before. The cannons had torn his team to hell and back. The attack worried him, and in many ways. Did this mean the Chinese were now supplying and supporting the partisans? Just the thought of war with the Chinese scared him, because they had more people than any nation on earth and that meant an unlimited number of potential soldiers in their country.

At noon, they walked into the trees and ate a quick ration. As they ate, they spoke in low tones.

"Do you think base will be angry when they cannot reach us?"

"Not, really," Sokoloff replied, "because all radios have trouble at times, right?"

Smiling the Private said, "Sure they do. If we save the Russian army, do you think we will get a medal and promotion?"

"I am sure we will, but this is being done to save lives, not for our own personal reward."

"I know, but I would love to return home to my family and wife a war hero. It will help me get a good job too, once my two years of service are over."

"How much more time do you have to serve?"

"Four months, and I can return to my farm. I dislike the army, but mainly because I have no rank. When everyone outranks you, the army is not a good place."

Giving a light chuckle, he said, "Well, as a senior enlisted man, I can assure you, we all answer to someone."

"I hear you, Master Sergeant, but you do not spend all night guarding empty 55 gallon metal drums, have to shoot civilian hostages, or spend a day burning shit that has been mixed with gas and oil. The stink is never washed out of the clothing, and I cannot eat for two days after."

"I have done my share, Private, but in different countries and different conflicts."

"I know you have, only I had never considered that before. To me, it is like you have always been a Master Sergeant."

"There is nothing you do that I have not done years before. The army will never change and twenty or fifty years from now, someone will be complaining about burning human dung on a hillside in another country. Now, get your radio on, and let us move."

It was near mid-afternoon, when the Private motioned the Sergeant into the brush. Since both men were wearing camouflage clothing and face paint, they'd be hard to spot. As they lay in the grasses, a team of partisans moved south. Sokoloff suspected they were a special Russian team, like Albert had been assigned to, because all he heard spoken was two words in English.

He started to make his presence known, but suspected Headquarters would tell him to return to base and not follow the Americans with the bomb, so he remained quiet. Soon after their drag man passed, they were back on the trail moving north.

They'd been walking a good hour, with the private in front, when the man disappeared in a narrow wall of flames and sound. The blast was so loud, it left the Master Sergeant's ears ringing. He moved to the fallen man to find him awake, scared, and trembling with pain. Both legs and one arm was missing, and he had a huge stomach wound, as well. Knowing what needed to be done, he pulled a syringe of morphine from the Private's first aid kit. He then injected a fatal amount into the Private and held his head in his lap as the young man died.

"W . . . will I die . . . a hero, Master . . . Sergeant?"

"A big hero, my comrade. You will get sleepy in a minute so get some sleep. Do you hurt now?"

"No, my pain is gone, and I grow sleepy."

"Sleep, and I will wake you later."

"Tell my wife I love her." He began to quiver and shake. Finally he stopped moving, gave a loud sigh, and a rattling was heard deep in his body. Private Goreva was dead.

Damn this war and it's killing of innocent Russian boys! he thought. The Master Sergeant saw the radio was destroyed, so he started moving north, angry at the whole world.

Most of the gear carried by the Private had been damaged, except for most of his rations, which the Master Sergeant now packed.

Near dusk he moved into a thick grove of pine trees and heated a meal. Once the meal was eaten, he moved back on the trail and moved north.

Three hours later, as he was making a camp, he was discovered by a group of Russians dressed as partisans and gave his real name to them, knowing he had nothing to fear. He used the call sign Quarterback and contacted the partisan base. The Russian radio worked perfectly.

Twenty minutes later, he was cleared and authenticated by the partisan base as Tom Black. He'd reported all of his team was dead, including the Colonel and Captain Logan, and requested permission to continue the mission. He told them he had the key, but no code or didn't know where the bomb was to be placed. His message was sent in code, code taken from a dead radioman the day before.

Approximately fifteen minutes later, his activation code for the suitcase bomb arrived and with three words, "Pearl High School."

He smiled at how easy it had been to get the code. All he needed to do now was kill an American Colonel and a female Captain, and then take the suitcase bomb to the airport.

"Master Sergeant, my team has been assigned to you and your mission. You will lead the team, even though I am a Captain. The mission must come first. I have no idea what this is about, but Russian Headquarters gave you the highest level of approval to complete this mission."

"First, I must have rest. I have been traveling alone and under a great deal of stress. I will tell this group only one thing. My mission is more important than any or all of our lives and if we must die to complete it, then we have saved millions of lives."

The whole team had heard of the stolen suitcase bombs and, of course, of the bomb the Russians had detonated. They all realized, right then, the Americans were attempting to detonate their very own nuclear device, to avenge the death of their people killed by the Russian bomb. Most shivered and a few said, "Shit."

"Let me sleep for four hours, then wake me and we will start on our journey once more."

"Eat first, and then you will sleep better." the medic said.

"You are right, of course, so let me eat." The Master Sergeant opened a Russian ration.

Thirty minutes later, he was asleep, as half the team slept while the other half guarded. From now on they'd take no chances.

The next morning was cold and wet, with a light drizzling rain, which folks in Mississippi are familiar with. They were soon tracking the three Americans in front of them. The tracks were easy to follow. They were able to move faster by stepping in the tracks of those they followed, so their speed almost doubled, until noon when a helicopter flew overhead. Suspecting all aircraft over them were Russians, they waved back. The aircraft circled and then started to return.

As the aircraft was turning, the Master Sergeant said, "Chinese, and those are Z-10 attack helicopters, so wave at them."

"Chinese?" the Captain asked.

"Wave, they are on the side of the partisans. Wave, damn it, *all* of you."

The chopper approached close enough the pilot and co-pilot were seen in their tandem seats. Sokoloff had heard the pilot was in the last seat and the weapons system operator was in the front, but he really didn't know. They waved, the Chinese waved, and then they gained altitude and flew away.

The Captain asked, "Did any of you see that 30 mm cannon on the nose of that thing? I imagine it would really tear a man apart." He spoke in English.

"The last group I was with were dressed as Russians and out of ten, eight were torn to pieces and blown apart." Sokoloff stated in a flat voice.

"What happen to the other man?"

"He later detonated a mine and died in my arms. He was a hero, too; one to make all our comrades proud."

"Enough talking," the Captain said, "we need to spend more time watching the trail than talking. Miller, you take point. Lee, you take drag."

Miller was doing like they'd been doing all morning, moving fast by stepping in the tracks in the mud made by the three they followed, but he soon learned it was not always safe. As he moved, his foot pulled a thin 2 pound fishing line about two feet; as he stood there looking at the line in the mud, a grenade exploded. The blast knocked him on his ass in the grass beside the trail as shrapnel struck his head, face and chest—he began to scream.

The medic moved toward him, stepped on a toe-popper and took most of a 12 gauge shotgun shell in his groin and lower belly. He fell to the mud screaming in pain. The Captain, knowing both men needed a helicopter to survive, pulled his .22 pistol with a silencer, moved to the medic's side, and shot both of the severely injured men in the head. Headquarters would not send an aircraft for them, not on a top secret mission. They were expendable, just like all of them were.

"Go around the dead men." the Captain said, as he removed the medic's first aid pouch, and then he added, "Mike, take point."

Near noon, they started running into more and more Russian patrols out looking for partisans and it was becoming increasingly difficult to remain unseen. Finally, out of frustration, they contacted Edwards and asked them to recall most of the units within five miles of Pearl. Of course, it would take time for them to return to base, so Sokoloff decided they'd spend the day where they were. He figured most of the units would be back at base by dusk.

Albert was wearing his dress uniform, complete with his rank and medals, when the General's driver arrived. The enlisted man placed his bag in the trunk of the staff car, opened the door for the Lieutenant Colonel, and then crawled in behind the steering wheel. He had a bottle of vodka chilling in the back seat between the two officers.

Since it was evening and the night belonged to the partisans, they joined a convoy of about a dozen vehicles of various sizes going to Jackson. Two motorcycles rode in front and two at the rear of the convoy. Their speed would be low and constant, about 80KPH, or close to 50MPH, all the way to Jackson. If a vehicle broke down, a repair team would work on it, as they were guarded by a team of soldiers. The convoy, however, would continue to move, so the vehicle being repaired would be on it's own.

Off in the distance, a flight of three Black Shark attack helicopters flew circles in the air, and would escort the convoy once they began moving. A helicopter escort was rare, but was in place to protect the General and his passenger.

Right at the appointed time, the front motorcycle started moving and eventually so did the General's car. He was in the safest spot of a convoy, in the center, with fuel trucks or other large vehicles behind him. His car flew no flags and had no special markings to identify it as a special target.

They soon roared out the gate and onto the highway toward Jackson. It was then the attack choppers began to move. Their infrared systems were turned on, they tuned in the convoy's radio frequency, and did a radio check. Once satisfied, they began to weave over the line of vehicles, searching for hot spots along the road.

In the General's car, Matveev opened the vodka and poured a drink for himself and Albert. Albert was uncomfortable traveling by car, because he knew the partisans often ambushed convoys.

The General's glass tapped his as the man said, "May your mission in Moscow be a great success."

"To success, sir."

It was then the radio came alive, "Convoy leader, this is Eagle 1. Be advised we are picking up hot images about two miles further down the road."

The General's radioman was in the front seat with the driver. "Copy, Eagle 1, what is your estimate of the number of images?"

"Unable to get an accurate count, because some IR images are blended together, which means they are side-by-side. Uh, my guess is well over a hundred."

"What do I tell him, sir?" the radioman asked the General.

"Instruct him to hit the targets hard, with all three Black Sharks, and we will speed through as they are fighting them."

The Black Shark leader was informed and then said, "Copy, Convoy Leader, but be advised there will be considerable risk to you and the convoy. I will start my first run when you are within 200 feet of the first images. Do you copy?"

"Copy, Eagle 1, good hunting. Convoy Leader out."

Albert felt his stomach come alive with a small animal chewing on him and wished he had a gun. It was then the radioman handed both the Lieutenant Colonel and General a Bison along with an ammo belt with pouches containing magazines. Russian pistols were handed out as well, but only with a half-dozen magazines.

"Uh, Convoy Leader, we are beginning to line up for our first pass. We will pass one behind the other. Good luck to all."

"Copy, Eagle 1, and let us get the show started."

CHAPTER 19

I dried my eyes and realized the past was over and couldn't be changed. Here I was, a big bad partisan, crying over the deaths of both of my wives, the collapse of my country, and the fact Liberals denied the country was in trouble all the way to the gallows. First, the army turned against the President, mounted a military coup, and took over. I remembered watching the President, the First Lady, and all his cabinet members hanged or shot on national television. The trial had been short, less than 30 minutes, and they'd all been found guilty of corruption, murdering witnesses to their acts, and pocketing money from the tax payers.

The President and First Lady were both found guilty of treason by allowing millions of refugees into our nation that were totally dedicated to killing us, and some were even on the international terrorist watch list. The illegal aliens were all allowed to stay and given citizenship by the government. Each of these new "citizens" were provided with a free place to live, provided free food, given good jobs and given $200,000, of which they paid no taxes. What irritated the general public was they also received free medical and dental insurance, while our veterans died from the lack of treatment or mistreatment that often led to death. Soon after these "refugees" arrived, the bombings and murders started.

Then evidence was presented that confirmed our President was dedicated to the same goals as our enemies and had made millions of dollars in donations to terrorist groups over his 8 years in office. The First Lady had been active in laundering the funds, physically making some small cash deliveries, and even providing some wanted terrorists safety by allowing them to come to the United States on Air Force One, the President's aircraft.

I remember watching their executions on the television, and neither died bravely. She was crying and was a broken woman when they placed her on a trap door and placed a black bag over her head. Then the noose was placed around her neck, with the knot slightly behind her left ear. She looked drugged, which I think was the case.

The President was not much stronger than her and kept screaming, "You cannot do this to me, because I am the President of the United States! I demand you release me, now! I have changed America for the better!"

He was soon gagged, dragged to a trap door, and his feet and hers were tied securely. Another rope, attached to ballast weight was tied to their feet, so they'd die quickly, with broken necks. Then the Chief of Staff, an Army four star General read the charges, the decision reached by the all military board, and then the death sentence—signed by all members of the Joint Chiefs of Staff.

The General moved back near the railing and a preacher moved to the First Lady, he asked "Do you know our Lord, Jesus Christ?"

The First Lady screamed, "Go to hell, because there is no God!"

When he neared the President, he asked, "Shall we pray?"

The President gave an insane laugh and said, "All my life, everyone has assumed I am a Christian, when in fact, I am a Muslim. I have *always* been a Muslim. I have no use for your false God, preacher, so leave me alone."

When the preacher stepped back, the General nodded.

An army E-9 pulled the trap door releases and both prisoners quickly fell to their deaths. They were probably both in hell before they realized they were dead. The weight attached to the President's legs must have been too heavy because when he reached the end of the rope, his head popped off and rolled across the floor, as his torso fell to the ground, spurting blood from his neck. The television station had gone to a commercial then.

I brought back to the present as I scanned the countryside with my NVGs and spotted movement heading north. It was a

Russian team, so I woke Carol and Alford, and we crawled deeper into the brush. Over the next two hours, I counted 5 Russian teams moving north. My goal, if I could, was to avoid the Russians, plant my bomb and get the hell out of there. I had no desire to die in the resulting explosion either, so I'd have to move quickly. The timer would be set for one hour and once programed, I'd be making tracks.

Then, hearing a low rumble of thunder off in the distance, I glanced up to see rain coming and it looked to be rough weather, with dark almost black clouds. I felt a light breeze as trees and brush began to sway. The rain fell gently at first, so I moved to the trail and we began moving north. As we moved I was always looking for trees we could stand under in case it hailed.

There suddenly came a blinding flash of light, followed by a sharp *crack*, and a tree off our right burst into flames. It was close enough to us I felt the energy of the lightning bolt as it struck. The lightning strike scared the hell out of me, and I'm not a man easily frightened. I felt the hairs on my arms and at the nape of my neck stand up, and it took all I had to keep from running.

I did keep moving and once within a half mile of the school, I went into hiding in deep brush, hoping to stay out of sight. A year back I'd run into cannibals near the school and the year before that the Russian Army had troops living in the classrooms of the high school. I wasn't sure what I'd find there now. I decided to look it over during the daytime.

We'd been having trouble with our radio, so Alford changed the batteries and checked for loose connections on the inside. Once done, he tried to transmit.

"Base, this is Quarterback, over."

No reply.

"Base, this is Quarterback, over."

Silence.

"Base, this is Quarterback, over."

"Go, uh, Quarterback."

"Radio has been out for a couple of days, since we left the main group. How do you read, over?"

"Have you five by five. Uh, wait one, Quarterback."

"Quarterback, this is Coach, over." I knew the coach was the General so I took the headset.

"Go, Coach." I said, and wondered what was going on.

"Your game is unusual with two quarterbacks in the game. Tom Black notified us that all of you were killed. He has a copy of the play book, so be advised."

"He may have thought we were dead. Much going on here, with the Russians moving in all directions but mainly north."

"The Chinese are our Cheerleaders now, and things have changed, but your mission has not."

"Glad to hear this, Coach. I will alter a few plays and perhaps move my team forward a few yards."

"Copy and understand. Call 'em as you see 'em, Quarterback."

"Roger, will do. Quarterback out." I said, and then handed the headset to Alford.

"Why would Tom report us as dead?" Carol asked.

"Good question, but I don't like the answers I'm getting in my mind. It's either one of two reasons. He really thinks we're dead or two, he is a Russian spy. I'm more inclined to think he believes us dead."

"Why?" Alford asked.

"I don't really know, unless he's been monitoring the radio fre- quency and has noticed we stopped sending messages a couple of days back. But even then, we have the suitcase bomb, so he'd have to find our bodies to activate the bomb."

"If he's a Russian, they won't have to find a thing." Carol said.

"Huh?" I asked, confused by her comment.

"The bomb is harmless unless the key is turned and the code punched in. You can be sure, if he's a Russian, he'll not want the bomb to explode. I suspect, right now, he's looking for us."

"We remain where we are the remainder of the night. Then tomorrow, during the day, I'll scout around the school. The last thing we need is to blow this mission, especially when we are so close. In the past, I've seen cannibals and Russian troops at the school. I've not been here in well over a year, so I need to look around in the daylight. If all goes well, we'll have this baby in the school by tomorrow night and be gone from here."

Neither spoke, but I could clearly read the doubt in their eyes. No, it wasn't doubt we'd be successful, but doubt if we were doing the proper thing. It is a real mind opening experience when you realize you have the power to kill hundreds of thousands of people instantly, and then cause the death of many more over the years from exposure to radiation. I couldn't guess when this area would be safe for people again, but I have a mission to complete and I'd do my best.

The night passed slowly, but a couple of hours before dawn while Alford was on guard, he woke me and we listened to a gun battle going on not too far away. I'd guess it was close to the Pearl High School, and that worried me. Leaving those two with the suitcase, I donned my NVGs and moved overland toward the school.

The way was rough, with tangled vines, thick trees, and fallen logs, and I saw more than one poisonous snake slither away as I moved forward. They were Copperhead snakes, and I avoided them when possible. The last thing I needed was a snakebite. I then heard two loud explosions, followed by screams. The small arms fire continued, but just as I reached the end of the trees and could see the clear grasses around the school, the fighting stopped.

I spotted a group of cannibals and they were leading 3 men to their fire, which was south of the school. Staying in the trees, I moved with them. Then, near a fire, I saw a mixture of men, women and children, jumping up and down over the capture of the men. When they led the prisoners near the fire, I spotted Tom Black and two Russians dressed as partisans. I knew they were Russians because they were yelling in Russian. Tom said not a word that I could hear. I suspected he'd been captured by the Russians, and they were taking him to a gulag.

I watched as the bodies of six or seven others were brought into camp; all were quartered, and then a human thigh was placed on a spit over the fire to roast. Most of them returned to their robes and blankets as the meat cooked. I saw the cooking was done by an old woman that must have been seventy years old or more.

Then I saw the bodies of cannibals who must have died in the firefight brought into camp and added to the other bodies. I always wondered if they ate their own dead, and now I had the answer.

I knew I had to rescue Tom, but I'd not help the Russians. Some would call me cold for this, but it was their invasion of my country that turned those folks into cannibals, so let them feed them.

It was still dark, so I moved to the rear of the shelter the three men were in. I used my skinning knife to slice it down the back. It was then a cannibal warrior approached in the dark. I was fairly sure he didn't see me, so I waited, knife in hand. Just as he started to move away from me, I jumped him, with my left arm tightly around his throat. I suspected he was a guard, and sooner or later he'd find Tom gone or see the cut material. My long 9 inch blade slid into his back like butter, three times, and each time I yanked the knife from side-to-side, hard. He jerked and danced in my arms, so I reached up and cut his throat. I held him securely as blood, emitting a strong copper smell, spurted from his neck injury. Minutes later he was still. I felt no pulse, so I dropped him to the dirt.

The three prisoners were tied and gagged. I cut the bonds on Tom and then helped him from the shelter. We then melted into the predawn grayness.

Back with the others, the rain started again and I looked up and around, not wanting another lightning strike if avoidable. I saw no trees very much higher than the others. While I'd been gone, they'd used ponchos to make a simple lean-to shelter against the rain. We moved under the shelter and I asked Tom, "What happened, and how'd you end up with the Russians?"

"When I didn't hear from you after a couple of days, I assumed you'd been killed."

"How's that possible? The last I knew, you were missing in action."

"I was captured within an hour of separating from Top and the rest. At that time, I was with a group of Russians disguised as partisans. I could hear the radio and what was being said, and not once did I hear you or your people mentioned. Then two days ago, I was with them when they were attacked by a Chinese helicopter. I waited until the aircraft left, used the radio to contact Base and got the code. I was looking for you to get the key when I was taken prisoner again."

"You're a very lucky man," Alford said, "because in about a week you'd have been on the supper menu."

Tom blinked rapidly a few times and said, "Then, well, you saw who killed the Russians and took me prisoner, cannibals. You have no idea just how scared I was."

"I've never been their guest," I said, "but you're not the first person I've saved from them, and probably this same group."

I wonder if the school building is not being used." I said aloud.

"Just before they ambushed us, I saw the building and there were no lights on inside, but I'm sure no Russian troops are close to these animals." Tom said, and then slowly shook his head.

"We have a choice, but not much of one. We can use almost all our munitions to clear the area of cannibals, or we can try to sneak around them tonight and get into the school. I think we'd better save what munitions we have for the return trip. Any suggestions or ideas?"

"Sneak around them. They'll be so busy feasting on the bodies, they'll not see us." Alford said.

"I'm inclined to kill them," Tom said, "But the nuke will do that, and wipe out the whole group."

I looked at Carol and she said, "Sneak around them, if possible. I can think of nothing more sickening or frightening than being a prisoner of cannibals. That is one group of people that needs killing."

I gave a dry laugh and nodded.

"What now?" Tom asked.

"Well, here," I said and handed him a Russian pistol with four magazines. "Alford, you need to hand him a grenade and you do the same, Carol. I have an extra knife I'll give him, because he left those animals out the back door, with no weapons."

"Hell," Alford said, "just to get away is a good enough deal in my eyes."

"Oh, yes; just the thought of those nasty people touching me makes me shiver." Carol said.

"Did they smell?" Alford asked, curious now.

"They had a sour smell, like unwashed bodies, and the camp smelled too."

"The camp," I said, "smelled like burnt pork."

"Gag me; horrible." Carol said, and then gave a visible shudder.

"Quiet, we have no idea who may be near," I said and then

Top had moved almost a fourth of the way back to base, when he had a sudden feeling that things were not going well for Quarterback. The retired E-9 knew the commanding General of all the partisan troops in Mississippi, because they'd served together in the middle-east. Top had been an E-6 then, and the General was a senior Captain at the time. The officer had gone on to retire from the army as a Full Bull, 0-6. He contacted him by radio during their noon rest and food break.

"Base, this is Top Cat."

"Go, Top Cat." came a quick response.

"I need to speak with Base Actual."

"Uh, give me five."

"Copy, it's my dime." Top joked, but suspected the attempt at humor wasn't understood or appreciated.

Three or four minutes later a voice said, "Top Cat, this is Base Actual."

"Sir, I have reason to believe Quarterback is in trouble. I'm concerned about Tom Black, and suspect his knowledge may compromise our mission. I cannot prove anything, but I suspect Black is a two-timer, sir."

Silence.

"Actual, this is Top Cat, did you copy, over?"

"Uh, copy, Top, but wait one."

"Will do." Top looked at his troops and shook his head. Covering the mic, he said, "It's just like using a phone in the old days, everyone puts me on hold."

Three minutes later, "Top Cat, Actual."

"Go Actual."

"Top, right after your team moved out for your current mission, we began fingerprinting all of our partisan troops. This was done to improve our security by being able to confirm people found on their own, as well as identification of bodies found, and finally, to provide a list of who actually served with the partisans during this war. We feel each man and woman should be listed."

"Uh, copy Actual, but how is that related to my mission, over?"

"Our fingerprints for the dead that were taken in the field, where Tom Black was at, tells me the real Black is tango uniform, repeat, Black is tango uniform. His current position is a Sierra Poppa Yankee, and needs to be terminated."

So Black, as I know him, is a spy; interesting, because his command of the English language is better than mine, Top thought, but replied, "Sir, no can do without transportation closer to the game. Even without mines or ambushes, we could never run there in time to help."

"Copy and understand. Look for fried rice in approximately two hours."

Fried rice? Has the old man lost his damned mind? Top thought. He then said, "Say again, Actual."

"You're to have fried rice, and it will be delivered by `bsyrwar ap551so asv nwoNNos asaf OPEPP1llee`. That is in code, my friend. Once decoded, if you have questions, contact me and only me. Over."

"Copy Actual, and thank you for the rice."

He heard the General give a light chuckle just before he said, "Base Actual, out."

Brewer looked dumbfounded but he opened his code book and started decoding the message.

Thompson asked "What was all the phonetic stuff? I got lost."

"The General said, Tom Black, the real Black is tango uniform, or teats up—dead. His current position is a Sierra Poppa Yankee, or in simpler words, a SPY, and needs to be terminated, killed with extreme prejudice."

"They must have compared fingerprints of all the dead men and Black's body was there, but torn to pieces." James said.

Top replied, "I have no idea if the real Tom Black was killed earlier, blown to bits, or is still wandering around in the woods lost. All we can bet on is the current Tom Black is not the real one. This one is to die."

"I've decoded the message but it's as bad as before I decoded it." Brewer looked totally confused.

"Well, read the damned thing to me." Top said.

"You will be picked up by a Communist Chinese helicopter and moved to within one mile of the football field. Your chopper will have others along to provide security and complete your team. Your new call sign is Dog 17."

"That's it? Now, where in the hell did the old man get a Chinese helicopter?"

Grinning, Lea said, "Prolly from the Chinese." She then smiled.

"There has been some communications on the radio of Chinese airstrikes and such, but I never expected a ride from them. I think this stresses just how important this mission is."

"But why are the Chinese involved?" Lea asked.

"The Russians and Chinese have a love-hate relationship, and with more hate than love. I suspect they just want to see the Great Russian Bear lose this war. I do see a problem if we have to speak to a Chinese chopper crew."

"Not me," Lea said, "because I speak fluent Chinese. Give me a number two and number five." she then laughed.

"I'm glad everyone thinks this is funny, because here in a bit, we'll be going for a ride with those people. Lets get to a clearing and prepare for the chopper."

CHAPTER 20

Thinking as hard as he might, Sokoloff could think of no way to save his two Russian mates currently held by the cannibals. It was likely if he failed his mission, they'd never feel the detonation of the bomb anyway. If he was successful, it was still unlikely he could rescue them alone. But the man-eaters had plenty of human flesh, so if he could prevent the bomb from exploding, he might be able to somehow send Russian troops to rescue the men before the animals ran out of meat. He was sure they would eat the fresh meat first and save the live men for later.

They'd moved deeper in the woods and it was mid-afternoon when I got a radio call from the General. Most of it was in code, which I handed to Carol to decode, and I had Tom watching the road.

"Your other man," the General said, "is a *Benedict Arnold*. Keep your six clear and after reading the message, contact me if you have questions."

"Copy, and Quarterback out."

Five minutes later, after Carol decoded the message, I knew as much as Top did and all about Tom Black, too. I wasn't overly shocked to learn he was a spy, but in some ways I had to respect his skills and dedication to his service. The General had stated very clearly in the message I was to kill this Tom Black, so kill him I would do. Top was not to meet me for another two to three hours and I was to wait for him before I moved.

I glanced at Carol, kissed her on the tip of her nose and said, "We can eat or sleep, because we have a few hours."

Kissing me back, but deeply, she broke the kiss and said, "I think we have another choice too, if you're interested."

The road on both sides of the highway had dirt and rocks thrown up ten feet in the air, as the Black Shark helicopters ran the length of the convoy, shooting at glowing images on their screens with a 30 mm cannon. Single red glows were seen running, but the aircraft concentrated on the groups of red and turned the grass median between the roads cerise with blood. A troop deuce and a half truck went up in flames as a hand launched RPG struck the cab, killing the occupants instantly. Albert watched as the troop carrier left the road, tilted steeply to the left side and then fell over, exploding. Machine-gun rounds struck the General's car, but it was equipped with armor plating where needed. And Albert prayed none struck the glass or they'd all be killed.

When the helicopters banked and lined up for another pass, a Russian shoulder launched rocket zoomed into space, causing a Black Shark to explode in air. Albert watched in horror as a twisting mass of rolling and burning metal struck the highway behind him. It missed the convoy, but not by much. A huge fireball exploded into the air.

The remaining two helicopters launched missiles at the red glowing lights on their infrared monitors, and then came back around to use machine-guns on their external racks to fire into the trees.

"Uh, Convoy Leader, this is Eagle 1."

"Go, Eagle."

"I have two fast burners that will light up the median, as well as the woods south of the highway, with napalm. Shortly after that we will return to base to rearm and refuel. By then, another group of Black Sharks from Jackson will be on station to escort you the remainder of your trip. They will go to the airport with you."

"Any idea of the number of partisans killed?"

"Uh, a conservative guess is close to 100, but it is more probable it was double that figure."

"Copy, between 100 and 200 killed."

"Here come your jets, Convoy Leader. Good luck on your trip."

"Copy, Convoy Leader out."

Both sides of the highway suddenly exploded with high flames as the napalm canisters struck the ground. In an instant, all the partisan wounded were visited by death from above.

My God, thought Albert, *what a horrible way to die.*

"More Vodka, Colonel?" the General asked.

"N . . . no, I am fine, sir. I cannot believe there were that many partisans waiting to ambush this convoy. It is almost as if they knew you were part of it."

"Come, Colonel, I am sure they knew I was in this car. Very few things are planned or discussed on the base that the partisans do not learn about. It is very likely some of the men and women employed on the base are in the resistance and they are spying on us all the time."

As they drove, the radioman said, "Sir, we lost one heavy troop carrier with 20 troops and one motorcycle rider. The man on the motorcycle was decapitated when his motorcycle drove under a thin wire. The troop carrier was struck by what looked like an RPG and exploded. Of course, none of the bodies will be picked up until after daylight in the morning, sir."

"Contact both Edwards and Jackson. Let both of them know what has happened. Tell Edwards I said the dead Black Shark pilot is to be posthumously promoted and decorated."

"Yes, sir."

In Moscow, Albert was a nervous wreck. He'd gone over and over his presentation so many times he had dreamed of it the night before. He was dressed in his finest and looking sharp, but hoped the Generals didn't turn on him as they had most officers from occupied America. He'd heard some real horror stories about the morning briefings with the Generals.

He was kept in a side room, because much of what they discussed was classified and he had no need to know. But finally the door opened and a tin soldier wearing the rank of Captain said, "It is time for your presentation, Colonel."

"This is Lieutenant Colonel Albert Pajari, gentlemen. He will brief us on his firsthand account of the Chinese involvement in America." General Matveev said and then sat down.

When the first slide popped up on the screen, it had Colonel Pajari's name, rank, unit and date on the slide. It was classified Top Secret. It showed in vivid color the destruction done to Edwards Air Base.

"Gentlemen, three days ago I personally took these photos with my own camera. Any expert can confirm they have not been doctored or manipulated in any way." He pushed the button for the next slide.

"This is a Red Chinese Xian JH-7, fighter-bomber, and we were attacked by a squadron of them, without warning, and with no anti-aircraft defenses in place. In the next slide, you will be able to clearly see the pilot's Asian face, and he is wearing a clear visor, so look at his eyes, and notice the smile on his lips. His name is below the canopy window, but I did not make note of his name."

On and on he briefed the Generals, until his allotted hour was complete. General Matveev, walked up on the stage and said, "This officer has done a great service for the Motherland. I think his presentation, which proves the Peoples Army of China is active in occupied America, and his prior work under me, demonstrates his rank is too low. I am now asking that Lieutenant Colonel Pajari be promoted to the rank of Full Colonel. Each of you has read or had the opportunity to read his resume and I think he is most deserving."

There were a number of loud claps and finally General Faddey, the senior General, stood and walked to the front of the room. He smiled and said, "Finally we have a man in America who knows his job. Pajari, you are, as of this minute, a Full

Colonel and the new base Commander at Edwards. I will add this too; if you continue doing the job you are now, you will leave Edwards as a newly promoted General. This meeting is adjourned, and the new Colonel is buying drinks at the officers club. We will not keep this man long, because as a surprise to him, we have brought his wife here to join him at the club, so keep it clean around her. Dismissed, and Master Sergeant, do not call the room to attention."

At the club, his wife was surprised to see her husband dressed as an officer and with Generals all around him. *He is so thin, and lost so much weight in America. Maybe he has come home to retire with me back on the farm. I do not like it here, Moscow is so big and confusing to me. Oh, Albert, you look so bad, my dear husband. Please, bring him to me,* she thought from a table up front. A dozen red roses and a bottle of champagne were on the table, which looked out of place with her simple dress of cotton and her headscarf.

A man wearing a military uniform with more medals than she could count led Albert to her and said, "Your husband, ma'am, Full Colonel Albert Pajari."

The General then walked away.

"Albert, are you in trouble in some way?" she asked as she stood.

"Hug me my dear, please." As they hugged she began to cry and he asked, "What is the matter? I thought you would be happy to see me again."

"Have you done something illegal? I went to the bank to withdraw enough rubles to buy some things and you had way too much money in the account. Then it happened again this month, but this time there was even more money. Please, stay an honest man, Albert."

"I have been made an officer and my pay is larger, is all. Save what you can, so it can be used after I retire. I am now a Colonel."

"Is that higher than a Senior Sergeant?"

"Yes, it is much higher. Now come, my dear, and let us dance."

"Dance? In Moscow? I am a peasant woman."

"You are the wife of a Colonel, the Commander of a base in America. So, hold your head up high, my love, your husband is an officer." Albert said as he led her onto the dance floor.

Two morning later, Albert stepped off a dispatch jet at Jackson International Airport, and smiled. No one knew he was coming, and he walked into the main building hoping to get a fast ride to Edwards in a two seater Ka-52 "*Alligator*" which everyone on the ground simply called a Black Shark as well, although it was a two seat model.

He entered Base Operations and said, "I am Colonel Albert Pajari, the new Commander at Edwards, and wondered if I could get a flight in one of your Alligators to the base. I have already been to the base and was assigned there for well over 10 months, but this is a new assignment."

A Colonel in a flight suit said, "I am to go out in a few minutes and look some countryside over, primarily looking for partisans. I would be happy to drop you off at some point."

"Good."

"But, you need a flight suit, so come with me."

Thirty minutes later, Albert was wearing a flight suit and helmet as he sat in the side-by-side cockpit, and he was overwhelmed by all the gauges and switches. He wondered how one man could remember what the purpose was for each.

The Colonel climbed into his seat and said, "Do not touch anything, okay?"

"Oh, I will touch nothing, because I have no idea what any of this stuff does."

The engine came on, the communications in the cockpit came alive, and minutes later they were in the air.

"My call sign today is Bulldog and if you want, we can fly around a bit and I will show you how well this aircraft flies. It is capable of loops, rolls, and even funneling, where I can keep a target in sight, no matter my airspeed, altitude or elevation around it.

I have full infrared capability and at night, this baby is hard to beat."

"Your squadron and the Black Sharks have saved my ass many times." Albert said.

"Let us move south a bit and look for some partisan traffic, unless you need to get to Edwards right now."

"No, I am in no rush, and as the Commander, this ride will give me a better idea of your capabilities to support my troops on the ground."

"Tighten your seat-belt and chest harness, because I want to show you an example of a loop and roll. Hang on." the pilot said, and the aircraft responded instantly to his touch.

After doing one roll and one loop, the pilot looked at Albert and saw him smiling.

"Fun, huh?"

"Oh, yes." Albert said, fighting the urge to puke.

"Bulldog, this is Sioux 19 and I am under attack by an unknown number of partisans. Do you read me, over?"

"Uh, copy Sioux 19, what is your location?"

"I have no idea. I am only a Corporal, sir, and the team leaders are both dead. You have to hurry or we will all be dead."

"Wait one." Bulldog replied, turned a knob and said, "Base, this is Bulldog and I have an emergency request from one of our teams on the ground. Do you know of this?"

"Copy Bulldog, and the last position called in by the team was just before the ambush. They are approximately two miles south from you." The base gave Bulldog the map coordinates.

"Copy and out, base." Bulldog turned the knob again and said, "Sioux 19, are you still there?"

"Yes, sir, but I am scared to death. We are down to four of us out of ten and it is not looking good."

"Listen to me, son, and know I am coming to help you. Take a few deep breaths and when I overfly your position, I want you to say, overhead now. Can you do that for me?"

"Yes, sir, but hurry or the words will be spoken in English the next time you hear my radio."

"I have your general location in sight, so let me know when I fly over you."

Bulldog nudged Albert and pointed out a couple of partisans shooting at them. He then said, "We are pretty safe, even if they launch a missile at us, because we are well protected by the electronic counter measures system that is computer operated. It is all automatic."

"Uh, you are over me, now! I am about 20 feet to the left of when I said now. Is that good enough, sir?"

"Excellent, Private. Now, I want you and the survivors to put your heads down low. I am coming in hot with my 30 mm cannon."

"Copy, and thanks!"

Bulldog gently banked the aircraft, lined up the nose, then dropped to maybe 50 feet above the ground. Albert had a hard grip on the armrests and his eyes were glued to the nose of the helicopter. Then the 30 mm cannon opened up and he had a hard time thinking with the noise and vibration of the aircraft.

As they completed the pass, Sioux 19, said, "Right on the perfect spot, Bulldog. How about hitting west of me, in the tree line?"

"I will do that next with missiles. Get your heads down, here we go again." Bulldog said as the aircraft banked sharply.

"Uh, Bulldog, this is Knife 2, a MiG-31, carrying some napalm and machine-guns. Do you need some help with Sioux 19, over?"

"Roger that, Knife 2, are you near our location?"

"I am overhead now. When you make this pass, point out the location of the good guys."

Albert looked up, saw a single jet circling and then almost lost his breakfast when the Alligator dropped suddenly and started toward the trees. About a 100 meters from the dense woods, the helicopter pilot said, "Friendlies under me, 3...2...1...now!"

"I see them, Bulldog. After this pass, move to the east and let me go to work."

"Copy, Knife 2, and releasing my missiles now."

White smoke from the released missiles were seen moving for the trees, and when the helicopter was banked, Albert saw the explosions. They then moved east and circled to watch the MiG.

The jet approached the trees at an unbelievable speed to Albert, and just when the nose was even with the trees, two canisters were released that tumbled toward the ground. From the helicopter, they looked like two auxiliary fuel tanks, but when they struck the ground, a huge wave of flames rose above the trees and then fell to the ground below. He knew anyone in those trees was dead. If the fire didn't kill them, the flames would take all the oxygen, so they'd smother to death. It was the first time Albert had seen napalm from above, and it was impressive.

"Knife 2, this is Sioux 19, and what will you use on your next pass?"

"Gatling guns on an external pod. Where do you need me?"

"I need you to come in close. The enemy is moving in too close to us for safety. Can you put the rounds within 15 meters of us?"

"I will do that, but keep in mind, what you want me to do is extremely dangerous, Sioux 19."

"I have little choice, Knife, because all of us are wounded down here."

"Hunt a hole, because I will be coming in hot, fast, and mean."

"I understand. Thanks, Knife 2. This is Sioux 19, out."

"This is very dangerous, Colonel, and there is a good chance some friendlies will be killed or injured. The partisans often move in close to us and snuggle up."

"I have had to do exactly what that young Private is doing right now, before. It is scary, but it is the only way to kill those in close." Albert replied.

The MiG-31 banked as the pilot lined up the nose of the aircraft on his suspected targets. He then increased power to his engines and they reacted instantly to his throttle changes. He shot over the ground at a fast speed and then those on the ground heard what sounded like a huge zipper being unzipped in one quick fast pull.

"Knife 2, excellent job. Is it possible get you to do the opposite side for me now?"

"Roger that, Sioux 19, so stay low, here I come again."

The MiG was half way through the strafing run, when the Private screamed over the radio, "Break, break, break, you are hitting friendlies! Break, please, my God you are killing us down here!"

The machine-gun fire instantly stopped and the MiG pilot pulled back on the stick and moved toward the sun, twisting as he climbed.

"Sioux 19, this is Knife 2, what is your situation down there?"

"Uh, wait a few minutes, because I have a mess on my hands."

"Copy." the MiG pilot replied with a flat voice.

A good five minutes passed before the young Private said, "Knife 2, I have less hurt than I thought I did. Your bullets had dirt flying all over us and many of the screams I heard were of fear, not pain. I have one man struck in the leg, but the rest are still alive. I need for one of you to contact base and let them know we need to be picked up by helicopter."

"Okay, glad to hear all is well. I will contact base for you." Bulldog said, and then turning a knob, discussed the team on the ground with base.

He turned the knob again and said, "Base said negative on the pick up right now. There are things going on that need the aircraft, things of a higher priority."

"Bulldog, my batteries are getting weaker. Tell those sonsofbitches at Base, if I have to walk back, I intend to beat the shit out of all of them, starting with their Commander, over."

"Copy, Sioux 19, I will pass your message on to them. Uh, Knife 2, what is your fuel status?"

"I am good for maybe another 45 minutes."

Five minutes later, Bulldog said, "Base said if you can stay where you are for a little over an hour, a helicopter will pick you up. Now, Sioux 19, I have contacted my squadron and have another aircraft coming here to assist you. I suspect the partisans will leave to lick their wounds."

"Copy, Bulldog, and I owe you a bottle of vodka."

"Get a bottle, and you and your men enjoy it for me. Sioux 19, out."

"I will stand guard until your helicopter arrives, Bulldog." Knife 2 said as he waved his wings to say goodbye.

CHAPTER 21

Top was confused when base contacted him that the Chinese Chopper was enroute and their call sign was Tiger 24. He again had them confirm it was a Red Chinese aircraft and crew. Base warned them the English spoken by the crew was terrible, but they had a Chinese American at Headquarters who was speaking with them.

James pointed into the sky and said, "There is our taxi ride."

Lea spoke into the headset, "Tiger 24, this is Dog 17. Do you read me?"

"Lodger, I hear you."

"Do you need smoke?"

"Yes, prease."

Lea said, "Pop smoke, Brewer."

A minute later the voice on the Chinese chopper said, "I see smoke. I come down and you come to me fast."

"Okay," Top said, "Base said there are five Americans on this bird that will make up the rest of our team. Once this thing touches ground, follow me to the open side doors. I will be the last man on the aircraft."

Brewer was guiding the aircraft down as a crewmember had his head out the door feeding the aircraft Commander how much tailrotor clearance he had. The second the aircraft touched down, the partisans ran for the door. It was then three pock marks materialized on the skin of the bird, and the door gunners opened up with their machine-guns. The bullets from the Russians struck the helicopter and then *zinged* off into space as the team loaded.

Once on board the chopper, the team fastened their seatbelts, and glanced at the new members of their team. All of the replacements they knew, and some they'd worked with before. The pitch of the engine changed, and the aircraft began to move forward, nose slightly down as it seemed to slowly climb invisible stairs to avoid the ground fire. But in just a minute or two, all that was heard was the aircraft engine and wind blowing in the compartment from both removed doors. The gunners relaxed and smiled at the Americans.

These gunners can't be full grown, Top thought, *hell, they ain't either of 'em over five foot and two inches. But, they knew what they were doing back there on that hot Landing Zone (LZ).*

One of the gunners handed a headset with a microphone to Top, knowing as the last man in, he was the one in charge.

"I need to talk to base." Top said.

"Talk den."

"Uh, Base, this is Dog 17, over."

"Copy, Dog. How did the pickup go?"

"We took some ground fire as we left. What can be expected at the next LZ?"

"Unknown at this time, Dog. The Russians may think you are a Russian team."

"Any good NCO or officer with his head out of his ass, will know this is no Russian Chopper, base."

"The LZ condition is unknown at this time. Be advised they will fake a half-dozen insertions before you have to get out and walk, but be prepared for a hot LZ, over."

"Copy, base, I will be prepared for a hot LZ. This is Dog 17, out."

The rest of the flight they spent looking at the inside of the helicopter, watching the crew, and glad they had a ride and didn't have to walk. Top, listening to the crew talking, found the language difficult for him and he couldn't make heads or tails out of any of it.

Finally the aircraft Commander said, "We now land, but you no go. Stay wid us."

"I understand." Top replied to the Commander.

"Good."

Then Top screamed to be heard over the chopper engine, "They're starting the false insertions. Stay on the bird until I start to leave. Before we leave this chopper, we'll lock and load."

Heads nodded.

Fifteen minute later, after a number of false landings, the pilot said, "Next land, you reave us. You must go."

"We get off on the next landing?"

"Yes."

Top began checking his gear and watched his people doing the same thing. Then, he prepared his weapon and heard the others doing the same.

As the chopper descended slowly to the ground, Top expected to get small arms fire, but he heard nothing. Right when the skids struck the ground the pilot said, "Go now. Goodbye."

The team left the aircraft and moved away from the bird's nose, or the helicopter's 12 O'clock position. They moved approximately fifty meters and then spread out. They then went into a defensive circle to wait and see if they'd actually been inserted in a cold LZ.

An hour later, Top picked up the headset and said, "Quarterback, this is Dog17. Do you read me, Quarterback? Quarterback, this is Dog17, over."

We'd been having trouble with our radio and I suspected it was the batteries. The batteries in the unit were the last we had on hand. So, that meant we needed new batteries and the only place that might have some was on the trail where the cannibals had ambushed the Russians with Tom. They'd likely take everything but a radio. I hoped they'd just left it.

"Tom, did you see the radio in the camp of the man eaters?"

"No, I think they threw it aside. They'd have no use for one."

"Good, we need to find it and take any batteries we can locate. Our radio is almost completely dead."

"I don't look forward to doing that, not in the daylight." the Master Sergeant said, and then thought, *This will be the perfect time for me to kill him.*

"We need the radio, so you and I will go, but we'll leave these two here with the suitcase."

"Okay, I understand. I was more or less thinking out loud."

Grinning I said, "I understand and I don't like the idea much either, but the bomb needs set at some point this evening. Let's move."

I had Tom lead me to the ambush spot and then we began searching for the radio in the brush and leaves. It was only as I moved over the ground that he'd covered that I found it. Thrown near the radio I also discovered two spare batteries. I wondered why he'd not seen them, but knew from experience it's hard to spot things at times, so I said nothing to him. I didn't want him to know I knew he was a spy, until later. I stuck the spares in my pocket and carried the other one.

"Move back toward our camp." I whispered.

As I moved, I was walking faster than normal, knowing the area was not mined and wanting to speak with Base. Acting as if things were normal, I moved to lead us back to camp. About half-way back to the others, I felt a strong arm grasp my throat and felt a knife slide over my neck. Warm blood ran down my neck to my shirt and his grasp on my throat was so tight I passed out.

I came to minutes later but saw no sign of Tom, who I'd known attacked me. As he pushed me away, I'd seen his face clearly, and he was smiling. I felt my neck and realized I was lucky when I turned my head. He'd severed a muscle, but missed my *jugular vein.* I unbuttoned my shirt, pulled off my tee, and used it to bandage my neck. I was in bad pain, still bleeding too, but didn't dare use the morphine in my first aid kit. The drug would cloud my mind and make me sleepy. I took a codeine-based pain pill and began moving to my camp. Tom had taken my Bison and sidearm, but as I walked, I pulled my .22 pistol with a silencer from a side pocket on my pack. Partisans called the pistol a "Hush

Puppy," just as special forces had called the weapon during the Vietnam War. Mine was magazine fed and it would work for what I planned to do, which was to kill me a Russian spy sonofabitch.

When I neared camp, I heard Carol say in a loud voice, "Where is his body then?"

"I had to leave him because the cannibals were all over the place. I told him daytime wasn't a good time to try to get batteries."

"You said you had batteries," Alford said, "so where are they?"

"Look, I panicked and ran, okay? I must have left them there."

"You're a liar, Tom, and this whole story is bullshit. I insist you take us to the Colonel's body and now." Her Bison came up level and her finger slipped the safety off.

"What in the hell are you doing?" Tom asked.

"Pull your knife and do it now, Tom." Carol said.

"W . . . why?"

"Because I said to pull it, but do the job slowly or my finger might jerk. Alford, you cover him too."

"Where'd the blood on the blade come from?" Carol asked as he pulled his knife.

"From me," I said and then walked from the brush, with my small pistol in my hand.

"I thought you were dead." Tom said, his eyes large in surprise.

"You didn't cut me deep enough, although you tried to kill me."

"I did no such thing." Tom said, and then threw his knife at me, which stuck in my upper left shoulder. I fired just as the man started moving and knew I hit him, only I had no idea where. I heard Carol fire and Alford as well and knew of the three, Alford was by far the best shot.

"Damn it all, he got away!" Carol said as she moved to me.

"Alford, see if you can track him," I said, as I grew weak from the loss of blood.

Carol soon had me fixed up like new, almost. She'd cleaned me well with alcohol from my first aid kit, sewed me shut and then bandaged me. She was afraid of working on my neck wound, but did clean it well and wrapped it tightly. I was hurting, and badly too, when Alford returned and said, "I lost his ass in the trees."

"Is he injured?" Carol asked.

"Yep, and the blood is bright red, so he's on borrowed time."

"Get a battery in the radio and try to contact base. We must warn them that Tom Black is loose." I said as I handed the batteries to Carol.

"Base, this is Quarterback." I finally heard her say.

"Go, Quarterback."

"Sorry about the down time, but our radio was out of juice. Be advised that Tom Black is loose and free."

"Copy, Quarterback. There have been a lot of communications problems here. Is the first string quarterback still in the game?"

"Roger that, but he has some injuries."

"Football can be a dangerous sport at times. When does the game kick off?"

Carol gave me questioning look and I said, "2000 hours today."

"Roger, Quarterback, copy today at 2000 hours. Have you been contacted by Dog 17 yet?"

"Negative. We contacted you first. Is Dog 17 to play in the game?"

"He will play as needed. He may come in handy if you are forced to run during a broken play. You can throw to him short or a long bomb if needed. He's well qualified to do most plays."

"Who is Dog 17? Send in code." Carol said and a few minutes later, the conversation over, she decoded the message and said, "It's Top and a team of partisans. We are to be extracted at 2030 hours on the high school football field by two Chinese choppers."

"Are you sure about the Chinese choppers?"

"That's what it says when decoded."

"Hand me the radio, please." I said, and felt like passing out just from moving.

Alford brought it to me.

"Dog 17, this is Quarterback, over."

"Quarterback, this is Dog 17. How do you read me?"

"Five by five, Dog. We need to meet. Give me your position and I'll come to you. A small group like us will be harder to spot than a whole team."

"I agree." Top said, and read off his map coordinates to me.

"I've a wound, so we'll not be there soon, and Tom Black is loose in the trees. While he's been badly injured, he's still a threat. Beyond all doubt, he is a Russian spy, too. Kill the man on sight."

"Copy, and I have orders from Base to take him out. Come to me, Quarterback, and we'll go over the game plan."

"On our way. Quarterback, out." I said to Top and then said, "I can walk, but Carol, I need for you to guide me and make sure I don't pass out. Once with Top, the medic can pump some more blood in me. He has a complete field first aid kit, while all we have are individual kits. Uh, Alford, you bring the suitcase. Move north by east. Let's hurry this along if we can."

As we moved, I had my moments of weakness when I wanted to just sleep, then at other times I felt restless, and excited. I found out from Top's medic later, both are signs of blood loss. The distance was a little less than a mile and it took us an hour to cover it, all because of my injuries.

When we were close, I asked Carol to contact Top by radio. At that point I must have passed out. I awoke listening to Carol and Top arguing over something.

"W . . . what is going on?" I asked, feeling much better. Looking up, I saw an IV bag and following the line, it ended at my arm.

"We are discussing who will arm the bomb this evening." Carol said.

"If I'm able, I'll still do it. From the conversation, at least the part I heard, neither of you are crazy about the idea of wasting hundreds of thousands of people. I can do that and not bat an eye, because the Russians must learn. They must learn when they hurt us, we in turn will cripple them."

I saw both of them lower their heads.

"Any sign of Black?"

"Negative," Top said, "and it's as if he's disappeared."

"What time is it?" I asked needing to keep a close eye on the time.

"Six, and it will be dark soon." Carol replied and then asked, "Do you honestly think you'll be strong enough to complete your mission?"

"Top and his crew will provide security inside the building as you and I arm the nuke. We both know where the key is and know the code, so either of us can complete this job if something happens to the other."

"I . . . I hope nothing happens to, uh, either of us."

I smiled and said, "Just a little over three hours and we'll be back at base, okay? All is well right now and should remain that way, unless Black reaches the Russians. If that happens, well, we're all dead meat."

"What about the pain from your injuries?" Top asked.

"I'll have your medic stick both with a local anesthesia and I'll be good to go. Right now, I need a drink, a long drink, of water."

I'd not been given morphine by the medic, so I grunted getting up later to go pee. I felt good, overall, but at times the pain from both injuries hurt me. I needed to complete this mission, climb on the Chinese helicopter, and then have a medic kill my pain. Until that time, I'd suffer my pain as quietly as I could. I was surprised at how much better I felt with a couple units of blood in me.

At seven thirty, it was pitch dark as I called Base on the radio.

"Base, this is Quarterback and we're minutes away from game time."

"Copy, Quarterback."

"Any changes to my game plan?"

"Negative, the game goes as planned."

"Roger that, and I'll let you know when we score."

"Know all your fans are behind you, Quarterback."

"Copy, and Quarterback out."

"How are you feeling?" Top asked.

"Get your medic to give me two locals and I'll be fine. I'll carry the ball on this play."

"Johnson, you heard the Colonel, so fix 'em up."

Ten minutes later, most of my pain at an acceptable level, we moved toward the school with the three from my team in the middle. All of us wore NVGs and as a result we moved faster than expected. The school looked terrible now, falling apart in many places, but I remembered a time when the hallways rang with the laughter of young men and women. Here I was sneaking into the place to blow it and most of the surrounding towns off the map.

At the school grounds, I waited and said, "Top take three people and check the school. Try not to make much noise, because the cannibals are about a hundred meters from here."

Winking at me, he said, "I hear ya. Johnson, Mays and Cotton, you three come with me."

I held my breath as they crossed a wide open area of grass and then entered the school through a broken window. Now was the moment when I'd learn if Black had been able to report to the Russians or not. As the seconds turned into minutes, I wondered if everyone could hear my heartbeat pounding in my ears. I felt Carol's hand on mine and when I looked at her, she smiled.

Ten minutes later, Top returned and said, "Clean on the inside and I don't think anyone has been in there in years."

I glanced at my watch and the time was 2000 hours, so I had thirty minutes to place the bomb, arm it, move to the pickup spot and get away.

I met the eyes of Top, Alford and Carol, and said, "Top, I'm taking my three people in. I want half your team out here and the other half moving around the halls inside. When it's time to leave, we need to physically count each member. This is one mission no one wants to be left behind on. Let's move, folks."

CHAPTER 22

Entering the building was simple, and within minutes I had moved to the main office, where I felt the bomb should be placed. As originally planned, I took Carol and Alford with me. I placed the suitcase on an abandoned desk, opened it and removed the key from a chain around my neck. It was then I felt dizzy.

I'd inserted the key and heard a series of shots inside the school, which surprised me. I had Alford position himself by the door and cover us as we worked. I turned the key and a console popped up. Two bullets struck the desk while a third struck me in the thigh and down I went. I heard Alford firing slow and deliberate. I knew with each shot from his gun, someone died.

"Carol, enter the number to activate the bomb now!" I yelled at her.

There were five numbers to the code and before she could enter the last number, she fell beside me, a bloody gunshot wound to her chest. The shots were louder and closer now, just outside in the hallway, as I tried to reach up high enough to enter the last digit. With a blood covered finger, I was finally able to push the number 5, and then fell back to the floor with a smile.

Top and Alford entered the room with one of Top's men. Top looked at the bomb and said, "It's armed, so time to get the hell out of here. Thomas, you take her as I help the Colonel." He quickly removed his belt and used it on my leg to slow my bleeding down.

I saw a Russian grenade roll across the floor and watched as Alford scooped it up and tossed it back into the hallway, where it exploded. Top shattered a window and out we went, one at a time. I was getting weak again and worrying about Carol. I could see so little of her wound in the building, but now outside, I could see nothing.

We moved as quickly toward the pick up location as we could, but Carol and I both slowed them down. Once in place, Top counted our troops and said "All are accounted for or here. We left two dead back there."

"Give me the radio," I said.

"Here's the handset, sir," the radioman said, as he handed it to me.

"Base, this is Quarterback."

"Go, Quarterback."

"Touchdown. I repeat, Touchdown."

"Copy, Quarterback, and your ride home is five miles out. They will contact you as they near."

"Get the beer ready, but we have two KIA and two WIA, over."

"Roger that, and be advised there is a doctor on board. I re-peat, there is a doctor on board the aircraft."

"Quarterback out."

The medic was working on my thigh and I asked, "How's the woman?"

"Not good, sir, and she needs more than I have with me."

"Is she going to live?" I asked.

"Honestly, I don't know. I have the sucking chest wound cov-ered, but she's lost a lot of blood too, just like you. I just gave her my last two units of blood, so you're shit out luck, sir."

Here I was waiting for a ride home from the Chinese, have set a nuke bomb to blow, a woman I love may be dying, and his com-ment brought an insane laugh from me. A psychologist might say it was gallows humor or a laugh brought on by tension, but it didn't last long.

"Dog 17, Dog 17, this is Eagle 34, over."

"Copy Eagle 34, are you our ride home?"

"Affirmative, Dog 17. I am approaching from the east and will show you my running lights for a second, now."

"I have you visual Eagle, so come on down once you locate us."

"I have you on my infrared screen, if you are about a hundred meters from the woods, in the large field. I count 11 of you."

"Roger Eagle, you're looking at us."

"Taking fire! Ground fire on the right of the field." A machine-gun on the chopper opened up as a Z-10 attack helicopter flew past the landing zone, it's cannon pounding on the way by.

"Load quickly, my new American friends. This is not a good place to be."

A Russian squad suddenly broke from the trees; as one soldier attempted to fire a shoulder launched missile, the door-gunner took him out. Bullets knocked holes in the side of the aircraft as they struck, only to ping off in some wild direction. I looked around to see Russians starting to move toward us, a *lot* of Russians. A Z-10 passed and the Russians were gone, most killed or injured by a 30 mm cannon.

What I didn't see was Master Sergeant Sokoloff line up the cross hairs of his sniper rifle, take a deep breath and then, as he slowly released the air, he gently squeezed the trigger. While he knew he'd die now, he'd at least make me personally pay for the success of my mission.

I was the last man to climb on the second chopper and just as I stepped up, I felt a severe blow between my shoulders. I was knocked to the floor of the aircraft and could clearly see the rivets on the floor. The chopper began to rise and a Chinese doctor was looking me over. I was trying to figure out how I got to where I was when the rivets grew blurry, my vision slowly grew gray, and then gray turned black—then I knew no more.

The End — or is it?

See Book #6 coming this fall:

"*The Fall of America, Russian Revenge.*"

THE FALL OF AMERICA:
BOOKS 1-3

*Now available as audiobooks at iTunes,
or at Audible.com.*

About the Author

W.R. Benton was born on his grandfather's farm, delivered by his grandmother, near Vida, Missouri, down in the Ozark Mountains. He attended public schools in the local area and graduated from Rolla Senior High, Rolla, Missouri, in 1971. After graduation, he joined the United States Air Force and began a career that would span over 26 years. He has an Associate's Degree in Search and Rescue, Survival Operations, a Bachelors Degree in Occupational Safety and Health, and a Masters Degree in Clinical Psychology completed, except for his thesis. It was his safety training that improved his above average writing skills, because he learned to sequence mishaps in formal reports. His first western released was *"Silently Beats the Drum,"* and 34 more books have followed.

W. R. Benton is popular among readers who love hard, continuous action and adventure. As a young reader, he would often turn pages to find more excitement. So, when he turned to writing, he decided his readers should be entertained, made to think, and feel the emotions of his characters. Many readers say his work grasps them in the first paragraph and maintains their interest until the last paragraph, which is exactly what W. R. strives for when writing. Mister Benton lives in Mississippi, with his wife, dogs, and cats, on an imaginary ranch with thousands of make-believe cows and horses.

www.wrbenton.net

www.facebook.com/wrbenton01

"Simple Survival - A Family Outdoors Guide" is more than a book—it is an outdoor resource bible that every family should have a copy of. This is one of those books that you should have in your camping bag along with the tent and other equipment.

Gary L. Benton

However, reading it at home before you go off on some outdoor adventure would be a great help when potential situations happen.

Available at Amazon and other online bookstores

Impending Disasters - This helpful and comprehensive book covers most major disasters and how to stay safe if you decide to evacuate or stay. It has a section on prolonged survival, which will assist keeping you alive after the natural disaster has done its

damage. Many people die following natural disasters, from one mishap or another, but you can learn to survive.

Learn to deal with Tornadoes, ice storms, hurricane, flooding, blackouts, riots, and much more. Contains easy to understand information, and critical gear/equipment lists you will need.

Available at Amazon and other online bookstores

A struggle for ultimate control
The elites have always manipulated global politics, but now a select group will launch their ultimate bid for power, *The New World Order*. They envision one world bank, only one currency, and one leader to control it all! They promise having one government will end global conflict and bring a peaceful, comfortable life to all humanity.

But with this new government comes personal costs, to free will, to self-determination and to liberty and some will find those costs too high to bear.

Both are available at Amazon and other online bookstores

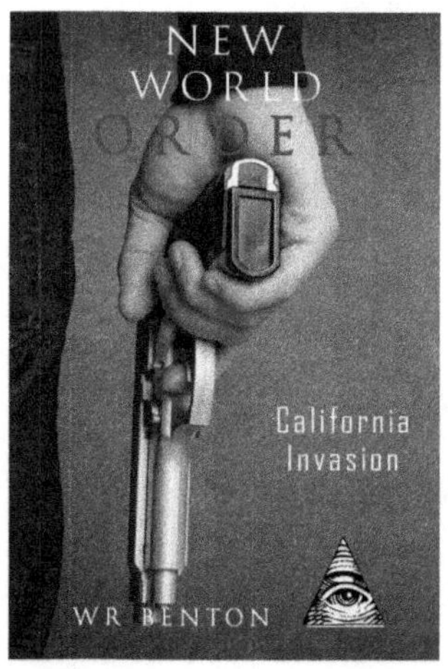

The New World Order moves forward with its twisted plans.
Facing bitter resistance, the New World Order clamps down on the American forces. It's a fight against global domination, with the freedom of the human race at stake.

In *Volume 2* of the *New World Order* series, the Order shows a new U.S. President what will happen if he doesn't do their bidding. These shadowy puppet-masters will sacrifice anyone, even elites at the upper circles of power and they prove that to the new President in vivid detail. Individual lives mean nothing when their objective is so close they can taste it.